Thea Harrison is the pen name for author Teddy Harrison. Thea has travelled extensively, having lived in England and explored Europe for several years. Now she resides in northern California. She wrote her first book, a romance, when she was nineteen and has had sixteen romances published under the name Amanda Carpenter.

Visit Thea Harrison online:

www.theaharrison.com
www.facebook.com/TheaHarrison
www.twitter.com/theaharrison

Praise for Thea Harrison:

'Once I started reading, I was mesmerised to the very last page. Thea Harrison is a master storyteller, and she transported me to a fascinating world I want to visit again and again. It's a fabulous, exciting read that paranormal romance readers will love'
No. 1 *New York Times* bestselling author Christine Feehan

'Harrison's spectacular ability to deliver stories that have memorable characters along with intricate plotting and high-stakes adventure reveal that she is a born storyteller. There's no doubt that Harrison will soon become a genre superstar'
Romantic Times

'*Dragon Bound* has it all: a smart heroine, a sexy alpha hero and a dark, compelling world. I'm hooked!'
J. R. Ward

By Thea Harrison

Elder Races series:

Dragon Bound
Storm's Heart
Serpent's Kiss
Oracle's Moon
Lord's Fall

Game of Shadows:

Rising Darknesss

Rising Darkness

THEA HARRISON

piatkus

PIATKUS

First published in the US in 2013 by The Berkley Publishing Group,
A division of Penguin Group (USA) Inc., New York
First published in Great Britain in 2013 by Piatkus

A CIP catalogue record for this book
is available from the British Library.

ISBN 978-0-7499-5897-8

Printed in Great Britain by Clays Ltd, St Ives plc

Papers used by Piatkus are from well-managed forests
and other responsible sources.

Piatkus
An imprint of
Little, Brown Book Group
100 Victoria Embankment
London EC4Y 0DY

An Hachette UK Company
www.hachette.co.uk

www.piatkus.co.uk

Rising Darkness

Chapter One

TERROR WAS THE color of crimson. It had a copper taste like arterial blood.

The criminal has escaped and left our world.

She stood beside her mate in a circle of seven. Their combined energies shone like a supernova. Dread darkened the group's colors. Their leader's grief and outrage was a smear of gray and black.

The change in her mate was that of a warrior rousing from sleep. She felt her own energy resonate to his, ringing like strained crystal.

We must find a way to stop him, or he will do untold damage.

All seven committed to the task and said good-bye to their home. They would never be able to return. With power and arcane fire, their leader prepared a potion from which they must drink in order to transform and travel to a strange world.

Her mate confronted his final moments with strength and courage. As his beautiful eyes closed, he promised, *I will see you soon.*

They had fit together with such perfection. They had been born at the same moment and had journeyed through life together, contrast and confluence, two interlocking pieces that sustained and balanced each other.

But no matter how connected they were in life, they each had to cross that midnight bridge on their own. Her energy bled ribbons of bright red as she faced the final moments of the only life she had known.

She tried to reply to him, but the poison had already disconnected her from her physical body. She sent him one last shining pulse of love and faith as darkness descended.

She had died such a long time ago.

Thousands of years ago.

Wait. What?

No.

Mary flung out a hand and cracked her knuckles against something hard. Pain shot up her arm.

She surged upright and wobbled where she sat. Shards of color surrounded her, like fractured pieces from the ruins of a stained-glass window. After several uncomprehending moments, she realized where she was. She was sprawled on her bed in a chaotic nest made up of her comforter, pillows, a pile of her clothes and scraps of material.

Her heart erupted into a conga drum medley then slowed to a more normal tempo. Her head, not so much. It pulsed with a steady throb of pain.

The bedside clock read 6:30 A.M. For Christ's sake. She'd only gotten home five hours ago. Her ER shift had been twenty-six hours long. It had involved a five-car accident and two gunshot victims, one of whom, a seventeen-year-old single mother, had died.

She thought of her dream and the criminal that the creatures had pursued. Sweat broke out as dread, mingled with a sense of unspeakable loss, ricocheted through her body with the intensity of a menopausal hot flash.

Some people played golf in their downtime, or went hiking or took aerobic classes. She dreamed of rainbow-pulsing creatures that drank poison Kool-Aid in some kind of bizarre suicide pact. Was that better or worse than dreaming of the gunshot victims?

She sucked air into constricted lungs. Maybe she shouldn't try to answer that question right now.

Something stuck to her face. Her fingers quested across her skin. She pulled a scrap of cloth from her cheek and stared at it. The cloth had a blue and green paisley design.

A blurred memory surfaced, like the smear of color atop an oil-slicked roadside puddle.

She had found the cloth a couple of days ago in a clearance bin at the fabric store, and she was planning to incorporate it into the pattern of her next quilt. Still wound up from her overlong work shift when she had gotten home, she had released some of her nervous energy by doing household chores. She had fallen asleep in the middle of folding laundry.

Adrenaline had destroyed any chance of her getting back to sleep. Dragging herself off the rumpled bed, she yanked at her wrinkled T-shirt and shorts. She attempted to finger-comb her hair, which crackled with electricity. The tangled curls coaxed fingers into blind alleys and dead ends. Her shoulder-length tawny strands hinted at a mixed-race ancestry and were so thick and wavy she had to keep them layered by necessity.

At present her hair seemed to have more energy than she did. She gave up trying to untangle the mess. It sprawled across her shoulders unconquered, a wild lion's mane.

She scooped up her house keys and sunglasses on the hall table, slipped on tennis shoes and grabbed a hooded sweatshirt. In less than a minute, she was outside in the early warm spring morning. Bright sunshine stabbed at her before she slipped on her sunglasses.

She lived in an ivory tower near a place she had privately nicknamed Witch Road. The ivory tower was a squat, crooked building in a wooded working-class neighborhood, located by the St. Joseph River in southeast Michigan. It was a shabby, unfashionable river dwelling, built almost a century ago, with a two-bedroom living area on the second floor over the garage that protected it from the river's periodic flooding. She had rented it since her divorce five years ago.

The ivory had become dingy over the years, the aluminum siding loose at one corner of the building. The outside concrete stairs leading up to her front door were narrow and crooked. The stairs were dangerous in an ice storm. Once while she was at work a heavy rain had turned to sleet, and she had been forced to crawl up the icy steps in order to get inside.

Still, the interior was warm with old pine paneling and scarred but beautiful hardwood floors, and it had a brick and flagstone fireplace. The first time she had stepped inside, something seemed to flow over her, embracing her in an invisible hug. She fancied it was the spirit of the place, welcoming her. Despite its condition and the many ways in which it was inconvenient, she had known she would live there. Sometimes she wondered if she would die there.

For all its shabbiness the ivory tower embodied an ordinary yet powerful magic. In the view from the second-story picture window, there was no sign of the street below or the neighboring houses that dotted the dead-end road. The scene gave the generous illusion she was in a cabin in the woods, far away from anyone else. She could stare out the window for hours at the evergreens, oaks and sycamores, watching flurries of white snow swirling in a snowstorm, or the moving shadows in the trees as daylight changed and faded.

Witch Road was a nearby street in the same neighborhood, part of a loop she had mapped for a daily two-mile run. The route cut close by the nearby river and had gradually pulled her under its spell as she jogged it repeatedly through the change of seasons.

Small houses were overpowered by tall, thick deciduous trees whose bones were uncovered with the death of every year, from the ones with straight willowy lines to those that had a more arthritic beauty, their gnarled joints and twisted limbs that shot in unexpected directions, ending in thousands of spidery-thin fingers grasping at air.

The underbrush was secretive and tangled. Thick vines and fallen limbs discouraged trespass from outsiders. The trees met overhead to rustle and whisper in the ebb and flow of restless, windy days, enclosing the narrow asphalt road with a leafy green canopy in the summertime.

She was too tired for her normal run. She walked the route instead.

The leafy canopy was fast returning with the warmer weather. On the other side of the green-edged lattice of tree limbs, fluffy cumulous clouds traveled across the sky at such speed, they seemed to be running from some unseen menace. The trees shifted and rustled. Leaves and twigs, the detritus from the death of the forest last autumn and winter, danced in circles that followed her down the street.

The swirling circles whispered to each other in small voices.

She's not the one, stupid.

Yes, she is! She smells like blood. He'll feed us well for this.

Mary paused and turned to look behind her. What a thing to fantasize.

She was imagining that, wasn't she?

Other than the murmurous trees and the distant report of a car door slamming, the day was silent, while the wind tumbled sticks and leaves around like a child playing at jacks. A shadow covered the dancing debris, smearing it with darkness.

How could a tree cast that kind of shadow when the sun was not yet high in the sky? She glanced upward. Or perhaps it was a shadow thrown by a cloud.

Malice brushed the edge of her mind, and the tiny hairs at the nape of her neck rose. Or perhaps the darkness was something else, with an unfriendly agenda.

She shook her head at her own overactive imagination, turned back around and resumed walking again.

You saw! She looked at us. Does that mean she heard us?

Normal people don't hear us. We must tell!

She jerked to a halt and broke out in a fresh sweat.

I didn't just make that up.

I'm hearing voices.

I'm. Hearing. Voices.

An internal quake rattled her bones. She turned backward in a circle, staring around her with dry eyes. There was no one else close by. Down the street a couple of children exploded out of the front door of a house, their school bags slung over thin shoulders.

A few yards away twigs and pine needles tumbled in a dark pagan dance.

Everything else had stopped. There was no wind, no lick of breeze against her skin. Even the trees overhead had gone silent, waiting.

There was nothing around that would cause that wrong, impossible turbulence of air.

Her teeth clenched. She stamped her foot at the dancing sticks and leaves, and hissed, “Stop it!”

The small voices burst into chatter.

Yes, she heard us. She did.

We must go!

As abruptly as they had started, the voices stopped. The leaves and twigs dropped to the ground.

Nothing else disturbed the stillness, just a few cars pulling out of driveways as people headed to work under the watchfulness of the looming forest, as some of the trees only tolerated the humans who had moved into their territory—

Where had that thought come from? Why would she think such a thing?

Panic clawed her. She was used to dreaming strange dreams. She’d done it her entire life. Hearing voices though, and seeing what she saw—seeing what she thought she just saw—that was psychosis.

She clamped down on the panic. No. She was just too tired and not fully awake yet. She was still half-caught in a dream state where Dalí’s clock melted and Escher’s stairways led on an endless loop to nowhere.

Coffee would shake off this crazy fugue. She turned around and headed back in the direction of her house, working to a lope as she rounded the corner.

Her ex-husband, Justin, stood on her deck at the bottom of the concrete stairs. His dark hair shone with glints of copper in the early morning sun, his narrow, clever face bisected by dark Ray-Ban sunglasses. He was dressed for the office in a functional yet elegant suit, the jacket unbuttoned in the unseasonal warmth of the spring morning.

When she caught sight of him, she groaned under her breath and slowed to a stop. Justin caught sight of her before she could pivot and jog away.

Oh, great. Just what she needed, on top of everything else.

Well, the sooner she talked to him, the sooner he would go away again. Resigned, she walked forward to meet him.

Chapter Two

MICHAEL HAD BEEN in a rage for as long as he could remember, long before he understood the reasons for it.

As a small boy, over thirty years ago, he had been prone to screaming fits and spells of inconsolable sobbing that had lasted hours. Once it had lasted days. In his memory of that time, his parents were vague, ineffectual shadows, pantomiming concern and alarm. That one time had involved doctors, along with a hypodermic needle.

He hadn't liked shots. Five adults had been needed to hold him pinned down. After that he had gone through a period of medication and therapy. The medicine taught him a valuable lesson. It made him feel odd and fuzzy. He realized he would have to curb his behavior if he wanted to be free of it, so he learned how to be cunning.

He colored a lot of pictures and studied the therapist as much as she studied him. As soon as he figured her out, he told her everything she wanted to hear. Eventually the sessions stopped, and so did the medication.

Still, he remained a stormy, headstrong, brilliant child. Despite all of their early literacy efforts, his parents could not interest him in reading until he saw an evening news segment on the First Persian Gulf War. Rapt, he watched unblinking until the news program was over, and then he demanded that his father read every article in the newspaper on the subject. Within a few years, his reading comprehension approached the college level.

School was pastel. It didn't make much of an impression on him. The other children were pastel too. He didn't have friends. He had followers. By observation and raw gut instinct he knew what the teachers thought of him, that they were both intrigued by him and also worried about his future.

He didn't care. They were pastel. Nothing external was ever quite as real as what shouted inside of him.

He was well on his way to developing into an adult sociopath. His dreams of release from pastel rules were as yet unformed but increasingly dangerous. He had already been in several fights with other children, and he had discovered that he liked violence.

And he was good at it.

One day when he was eight, an old woman appeared at the fence of his schoolyard playground.

Michael was as aware of her presence as he was aware of everything else around him, but he ignored her while he organized his group of followers for a strenuous bout of playground mischief.

Then the most extraordinary thing happened.

Boy, the old woman said.

That was all. But she said it *INSIDE HIS HEAD*.

He turned to stare at her.

The old bat looked exceedingly pastel. She looked like just a nondescript woman with a cheerful apple-dumpling face who had paused to watch children run and play during a school break.

His eyes narrowing, he walked toward her, school, stranger-danger, followers and mischief, all else forgotten. Several of the other kids called his name, and some kind of missile thumped him on the shoulder. He ignored everything else and stopped about fifteen yards away from the six-foot chain-link fence. All the while, the old woman watched him with bright, black raisin eyes.

"How did you do that?" he asked.

Shrieking children ran between them, playing a game of tag, but she still heard him in spite of the noise. Her face crinkled into a friendly smile. *It's a secret*, she said. *I know a lot of secrets*.

His breath left him. He stared at her in wonder. She might be old and wrinkled, but she was definitely not pastel. He took another quick, impetuous step toward her. "Teach me!"

Her smile wrinkles deepened although she never stopped watching him. Those bright eyes of hers were alight with amusement and something sharper. *I might*, she said, her mental voice casual. *Or I might not. It all depends*.

Never before in his short, pampered life had he been stared at as if he had been weighed and found wanting, but that was how the old woman stared at him now. He scowled, not liking the sensation. "It depends on what?"

On whether or not you know any manners, young man, she told him. *And whether or not you're still salvageable*.

He had never seen eyes as old as hers. He was too young and ignorant to understand how deadly they were. All he knew was that this strange conversation was more real than anything else that he could remember.

He ran to the fence, clutched metal links in both hands and looked up at her. "I'm sorry," he said. The unaccustomed words stuck in his throat, but he forced them out anyway. "I'm sorry I was rude. Please, would you teach me how you did that?"

Her face softened and she touched his clenched fists with gnarled fingers as she spoke aloud for the first time. "Well said. And I might teach you, but it still depends on one more thing."

He shook his head in confusion. It was so odd. From a distance she had seemed so small, barely taller than he was. Now that he was right up next to her she seemed to tower over him.

"Anything," he promised. He had been so young.

She bent forward and locked gazes with him. He realized that he had been wrong about her eyes too. They weren't like friendly little raisins. They were hot and full of burning power like black suns.

"You must keep it a secret," she whispered. "Or I will have to kill you."

Terror thrilled him. Never, in reality or his wildest imagination, had an adult spoken to him like that. And she might even mean it.

(Whereas the man he had grown into knew very well that she had.)

He pushed against the fence. "I promise. I won't tell anyone."

"Ever," said the old woman.

He nodded. "Ever."

She raised her eyebrows. "Cross your heart and hope to die."

Those words. She meant them. Wow, this was so cool. He held her gaze and grinned. He crossed his heart and hoped to die.

The old woman smiled her approval. "Atta boy."

She told him to be quiet and wait, and he did, though it was one of the hardest things he'd ever done.

He was rewarded for his patience two weeks later. Walking home from school, he saw a U-Haul van parked in front of a small house located a couple of doors down from where he lived.

Curious, he wandered over to watch half a dozen men unloading furniture, appliances and boxes. There were no toys, no bikes, nothing weird or spooky, just ordinary furniture. Pastel. He had started to turn away when he heard a thin, elderly female voice from within the house call out to the men.

A sharp, delicious shiver, like the flat of a cold blade, ran over his skin.

He hadn't heard that voice for very long, but he would recognize it anywhere.

He knocked on her door. She gave him a cookie. To the

hired movers they looked like a pleasant, ordinary old woman making friends with a well-mannered, curious neighborhood boy.

A week later the old woman met his parents. Soon after that he was taking piano lessons from her on Tuesdays and Thursdays. His family didn't own a piano, so he also went over to her house on Mondays, Wednesdays and Fridays so he could practice on hers.

His parents were amazed and delighted at the strength of his artistic dedication. It seemed to be just the key they needed to settle him down. When his mentor invited him for summer vacations, they agreed with a poorly concealed relief.

In the meantime, Michael grew from a troubled little boy with messy, uncontrollable emotions into something quiet, controlled and infinitely more deadly.

He learned who he was.

More importantly, he learned why he was the way he was.

"You lost the other half of yourself," his mentor told him. "It happened a very long time ago. So long ago, in fact, that I am surprised there is any sanity left in you at all. You must remember who you are. You must remember everything you can, and rediscover your skills and your purpose. I can help you do that."

As he learned meditation and discipline, he grew to understand what his mentor meant. He felt that raging part of him like a beast that was too lightly restrained. He harnessed that energy as he grew older, turning all of his focus onto it, and scarlet threads of memory began to unfurl into the past.

Past before his birth in this lifetime.

Past into distant history, so very long ago.

And he began to remember what he had lost. *Who* he had lost.

The other half of himself.

An unshakable determination settled into him. If she still existed in any way, he would find her again.

He would find her.

Chapter Three

EARLY ON THAT bright spring morning, Mary continued with obvious reluctance toward her ex-husband as he stood in front of her house.

"Oh that's flattering of you," Justin said with a grin. "Good thing my ego is so preened and shiny. Good morning, and screw you too."

"You show up uninvited, you get what you get," she said. Her voice sounded rough. She cleared her throat. "For pity's sake, man. It's not even seven o'clock yet. I never talked to you this early when we lived together."

"Then why don't you answer your phone?" he said in exasperated reply. "If you'd pick up, I wouldn't have to stop by unannounced."

She squinted at him then jogged up the stairs to unlock her front door, while he followed her at a slower pace. "Because it didn't ring."

"Is it even in the house?" he retorted as he came up behind her. He peered past her at the riotous mess inside. "How can you tell? The hood of your car is cold but you weren't answering when I knocked. I was going to let myself in to make sure you were all right."

She sighed. "Don't make me regret giving you that key."

"You'll have to arm wrestle me to get it back, and you know I cheat." Once they had both stepped inside, he looked at her again more closely. Something in his face changed, the humor dying away. "Are you okay? You look really pale."

"I'm fine." She removed her sunglasses and rubbed at her face. She could still feel creases on her cheek from the cloth she had slept on. The pounding in her head had grown worse. She turned to walk to her kitchen and said over her shoulder, "I need coffee. Do you want a cup?"

"Yeah." Justin followed her. "Look, do me a favor. Make an appointment to see your doctor, okay?"

"What? No. I said I'm fine." Mary stopped in the middle of her kitchen and looked around in confusion. She knew exactly where she was, but everything still seemed alien, incomprehensible.

She didn't belong here. Panic clutched at her again, like a drowning victim trying to pull her underwater. She flung it off, shaking herself hard like a wet dog as she headed for the coffeepot.

"I don't think you're as fine as you say you are." Justin frowned at her.

She waved a hand as if to brush away his words. "I had a day from hell yesterday. My shift was twenty-six hours long. We had a multiple car accident and a couple of gunshot victims."

He shook his head. "That's rough. What happened?"

"The accident was a pileup on I-94. No fatalities, thank God. The shooting was a different story. Some girl found out her BabyDaddy had another BabyMama. She borrowed her brother's nine-millimeter and emptied the clip into the pair while they sat outside at the local Dairy Queen." She glanced at Justin, her expression grim. "Now she's in jail facing murder charges. BabyMama Two is dead and BabyDaddy is in ICU. He may or may not make it, and all the babies have been taken by Child Protective Services, which, when you think about it, might be the best thing that's happened in their little lives."

Justin's voice turned hushed. "I heard about that on the news."

She yanked open a cupboard, pulled out the coffee and a filter. She said over her shoulder, "To top it all off, I got maybe four hours' sleep, so of course I look like shit. It's no big deal."

He sighed. "Look, I don't have time to argue with you. I've got twenty minutes to get to work—so just promise me you'll go get a checkup and shut up already."

She filled the coffeepot with water, poured it into the reservoir and switched on the machine then slammed the pot onto the burner. "Seriously, Justin," she snapped. "Do I come over uninvited to your house and tell you and Tony what to do?"

"Honey, I'm sorry," he said in quick contrition. She startled as he put a gentle hand on her shoulder. "It's just—hell, even I know you're never supposed to talk to a woman about her weight, but you've lost weight you couldn't afford to lose. You were always a little bit of a thing, the original five-foot-two-and-eyes-of-blue gal."

She gave him a grim smile as the pungent aroma of coffee filled the kitchen. "Don't start inflicting Dean Martin songs on me again at this time in the morning, or I swear I won't be responsible for my actions." She pointed at him. "And that's what I'll tell the police when they arrive with the body bag."

He didn't smile back. Instead his handsome features took on a mulish expression. "I'm being serious here. You're not looking good, Mary. You're all bones and nerves. If you won't have a rational conversation about it, I'll have to make an appointment for you myself to go see Tony."

"The hell you will." Her smile turned to a glare.

He pulled out his cell phone, turned his back and ignored her. After a few moments he started to speak on the phone. He moved down the short hall to the living room.

Mary felt the urge to scream. Instead she blew air between her teeth, like steam escaping from a pressure cooker. She poured herself a cup of coffee and took it to the table. As she shifted a stack of magazines and mail off of a chair, she discovered the cordless phone.

She clicked it on and listened. No dial tone. The battery had gone dead. She had a cell phone, but she used it for work, and Justin didn't have the number. She hung up the phone to recharge it and sat to put her elbows on the table, resting her forehead on the heels of her hands as she hunched over her coffee.

Her mind arrowed back to her dream. She was dreaming with more frequency and they were getting more vivid. This time the bodies of the seven creatures in the circle were translucent. Ribbons of colored light had streamed from them, flowing and moving in the air as if the creatures were some kind of alien anemone. The poison had tasted bittersweet and smelled like cloves.

She had dreamed in color several times but she had never before dreamed a smell or a taste. Was that development somehow connected to her hearing voices and seeing impossible things?

Panic tried to grab hold of her again. She flinched away from it. No, don't go there right now. Pulling her hands down, she stretched them out in front of her and stared at her fingers. Slender and dexterous, they were an advantage in the OR, but at that moment, they looked strange, as if they belonged to someone else.

Justin walked back into the kitchen with a brisk stride. He poured himself some coffee then came over to pat her on the back as he gulped hot liquid. "Tony moved some things around. He can see you this afternoon at three. And," he added, "I don't trust you to go on your own so I'm leaving the office early to take you myself."

"I was such a needy rabbit when I married you," she said. "But hey, pre-med plus law school equals the American Dream, right? Thank God those days are gone." Thank God she had stopped trying to create a lifestyle for herself that looked normal on the outside.

"What are you talking about, doctor girl?" Justin said. "What needy rabbit? You're the original Marlboro

Man. Except for the cigarettes, the ten-gallon hat and the penis."

She slanted an eyebrow at him.

"Well okay, you're quite a bit not like the Marlboro Man." He grinned. "But you've got this brooding, silent hero thing going on, with a hint of something tragic in your past, except I know your past and it's as ordinary as dirt. It's very sexy. I'd always wanted to marry a doctor—and if you'd only had that penis . . ."

"Therapy has made you too cocky," she said.

"Which Tony appreciates," he told her.

She rolled her eyes. "Get out. Go to work."

He sobered. "I'll be back this afternoon at two thirty to pick you up. Be ready or I'll do the he-man thing and throw you over my shoulder."

"Quit being so damn patronizing. I'm not going." Her mug was empty. She stood and headed for the coffeepot.

"Whatever," Justin said, eyeing her. "I guess Tony isn't going to care if you haven't shaved your legs."

"For God's sake!" she exploded, turning on him. He scowled at her, looking as mutinous and adorable as a two-year-old. She tried to rein in her impatience. "Look, I appreciate your concern. It's sweet of you."

"Sweet." He snorted.

Her expression hardened. "I'm warning you, I'm not putting up with your stubbornness and interference, and I am not going to go see Tony, of all people."

"But why not?"

"Because he's your partner and I socialize with him, dimwit!"

"Well, you kind of don't, you know," he pointed out. "You haven't been over to visit with us in forever. When I try to set you up on a date, you won't go. As far as I can tell, you don't socialize at all. That's the problem with brooding, silent Marlboro Man types. They're not much for talking."

Mary closed her eyes. It would do no good to ignore him. He cheerfully refused to acknowledge any silent messages that didn't suit him.

She snapped, "Today is my first day off in a very long time, and I don't want to spend it in a doctor's waiting room." She paused. "Besides, there's nothing wrong with me."

The lie reverberated in her throbbing head. She was cracked down the middle to her foundation. Whatever her mysterious internal ailment was, it was getting worse. If she didn't figure out what was wrong she was going to break into pieces, deep inside where nobody could see but where the most vital part of her lived.

He ran a hand through his hair and glanced at his watch, looking hassled. "I don't have time to argue with you."

"Good," she retorted. A belated curiosity struck. "Why did you come over this morning anyway?"

"Oh. Yeah. I wanted to know if you could dog-sit Baxter again. I needed to know, and you weren't answering your phone." He hesitated, and she listened to nuances shift in the silence. "Tony and I got invited away for the weekend, but we don't have to go either."

"I didn't answer my phone because the battery is dead. It didn't ring." She repeated it with as much patience as she could muster. Then she remembered what she was doing and poured a second cup of coffee for herself. She held it to her nose, closed her eyes and let the steam warm her chilled skin.

He was right. Somehow between her work and preoccupation, Justin, Tony and that dog had become her entire social circle, and she hadn't been to see them in months.

She would have to add another item to her to-do list. Fix toilet. Fix lamp. Fix self.

Out loud she said, "Of course I'll watch Baxter for you. I love that dog."

"Thanks, I appreciate it." He glanced at his watch again. "I've got a deposition and I really have to run. But I'm coming back, and we're going to duke this out later. I'll see you at two thirty."

She felt the bones in her body compress with the urge to smack him over the head. She gritted her teeth instead. The quicker she stopped arguing with him, the quicker he would be out the door. "Hurry or you'll be late for work."

"Oh hell." He bent forward, kissed the air by her cheek and dashed out of the house.

Mary moved to the large living room window to watch with narrowed eyes as he drove away. She tapped a fingernail against the glass. "You can come," she whispered to his retreating car. "But I'm not going to be around when you get here."

SHE FOLDED HER laundry, put it away and straightened her bed. There was another load of colorful cloth scraps waiting in the laundry room. After she put the scraps in the washing machine, she tidied the living room.

Since she lived alone and the two-bedroom house was more than big enough to suit her modest needs, she used the living room as one of her workrooms. She had four quilts in varying stages of completion. The most colorful piece, by far, was the patchwork crazy quilt. She fingered the cloth, but the quilt wasn't speaking to her. It seemed a lifeless fact, separate from her existence, as though some stranger had left it in her house.

She moved down the hall to the second bedroom, which she had turned into a studio. There she spent two hours trying to capture on canvas something of the elusive imagery from her dream.

Those creatures had shone from within. The colors that had shifted within their bodies and flowed outward in whorls of light were too delicate and strange for her to capture on paper. The colors seemed indicative of emotion or personality, as if the creatures had senses so different from humans, they could actually see the pheromones their bodies released.

She had been plagued with strange dreams for as long as she could remember. The one she had labeled the sacred poison dream was only one of several that recurred on a regular basis. Sometimes the details of the sacred poison dream were vague or just different, but several details remained constant. There were seven people or creatures, of whom three pairs were mates, and an escaped criminal. They always drank poison, and she always felt terror and a sense of appalling loss when she awakened.

She shook her head and frowned. Some people believed each person had a soul mate, but she didn't. The concept was too convenient, too romantic, without real substance. Since she didn't believe in it, she could never understand why that was a major recurring theme in her dreams.

People met other like-minded people because they shared things in common and engaged in similar activities. Birds of a feather really did flock together. Either that, or they met by accident.

At least she could be grateful that, no matter how violent or overwhelming the sense of loss might feel in the aftermath of the sacred poison dream, it held her in its grip for only a brief time before fading away. No one could endure that kind of raw anguish for long, at least not that Mary had witnessed. People seemed to suffer intense grief in waves.

When she had been a child, the dreams had not been as intense or vivid, but they had always been unsettling. They had gained in color, detail and emotion as she had grown older.

As a med student at Notre Dame University, in an attempt to put whatever demons existed inside her mind to rest, she'd taken advantage of the counseling offered through the university. For over a year, she and her counselor had explored her childhood and the possible symbolism involved in the dream imagery.

Justin was right. She had lived an entirely normal childhood. She had fallen out of trees, tripped and misspoke in school plays, made cupcakes for bake sales and had sleepovers with friends. She remembered her childhood with detailed clarity. Other than the death of her parents when she was fourteen, there was simply nothing for her to be haunted about. Even then she had gone to live with a loving aunt who had been attentive to the needs of a grief-stricken child.

She wasn't interested in sex, although for a while she wanted to be. The concept, while intriguing, was less than compelling in execution. Instead of finding intimacy to be emotionally and physically rewarding, she felt clinical, detached and rather repulsed by the act, and she loathed casual dating.

At first she had been relieved that Justin hadn't seemed to be very interested either in physical intimacy. During their marriage, their sexual relationship had been perfunctory at best. When he had finally faced the truth about himself and admitted that he was gay, she had made an almost seamless adjustment into the role of supportive friend. Their split-up had been a relief for the both of them.

She had tried for a brief time to blame her tendency to isolate on the early loss of her parents, but she couldn't convince herself for long. There was a reason why she didn't have a social life, and it wasn't just because she had a hectic job with irregular hours.

She just knew she had this desperate need for . . . something . . . but she couldn't figure out what it was. She only knew that other people couldn't give it to her. She had to find a way to heal herself, to fill her own needs. Maybe then she could make a meaningful connection outside of herself.

When she realized that the therapy didn't seem to be leading anywhere, she had terminated the sessions. Then she got accepted into med school, and she and Justin divorced. Now she lived in her ivory tower. As far as she could tell the attempt at counseling had been a complete failure.

The painting she was trying to work on was a failure as well. No matter how she tried she couldn't replicate the impression from her dream.

She lifted the canvas from the easel and set it against one wall to dry. Then she took up sketchpad and pencils, hoping that the change in medium might help her convey some of the delicacy that she could see so clearly with her mind's eye.

As she worked, an old memory shook itself out of a dark recess in her mind. She paused to let it solidify.

She had always drawn as a child. As soon as her fingers were big enough to clutch a crayon she would draw, over and over again, people in cages.

It became an elaborate secret project over the years. The

people acquired names and personalities. They had rooms in their prisons. She would draw crude beds, chairs, bookcases, kitchens, all behind bars. They were her people, and she would never let them go.

Over time, she had stopped with that obsession but she had never spoken of it to anyone, and she'd always destroyed the pictures with a hot sense of shame. What kind of monster was she to daydream about caged people?

Seven. Her breathing hitched. She had always drawn seven people.

How could she have forgotten that?

She sketched, her movements slow as she struggled past the adult's acquired finesse to approximate something of the child's crudity as she worked to recapture the details from years ago. A simple triangle of an ankle-length dress, the long sleeves, the curl of hair . . . she hesitated at the hem of the dress and her forehead wrinkled. If she remembered right, she had never drawn hands or feet.

Her college counselor would have had a field day with *that* imagery. She shut the sketchbook with a sharp slap.

Chapter Four

THE DAY WAS filled with blades.

The thin spring sunlight knifed through budding leaves on trees. Sharp yellow light and green shadows surrounded the old woman as she tore slender shoots of weeds from the garden bed by her front door. She regarded the dark and light that dappled her gnarled hands, savoring the fugitive promise in the sunlit warmth even as a frigid wind blew off the lake and tore through her battered jacket with invisible talons.

Breathing deep, she lifted her face and sat back on her heels. The serrated wind held a hint of moisture from the vast, restless body of nearby water, the trace of perfume from early wildflowers, the scent of pine and damp loam, and news.

She cocked her head. Using senses and skills alien to the elderly human female she appeared to be, she attuned to the patterns of energy swirling around her. Then she started down the path in the woods toward the small bay where Lake Michigan lapped at a pebbled shore.

She stood waiting at the pier when a battered, sturdy motorboat chugged into view and coasted to a gentle stop. The boat carried two dark-haired occupants who bore a clear family resemblance to each other, their indigenous ancestry revealed in the strong, broad angles of their faces.

A handsome, slim boy-man sat at the motor's helm. A much older man hunched on the floor of the boat, his dark, graying hair pulled into an unruly ponytail. He leaned against the young man's legs, wrapped in blankets against the slicing wind.

The old woman studied the pair, her wrinkled face impassive. A miasma of intense grief hung over the pair. She had never seen the boy before. Usually the older man piloted the boat, his eyes squinting against the smoke of a cigarette that hung perpetually from one corner of his mouth.

Now the older man huddled under his blankets, his normal rich copper skin a pallid gray. His lips were a cyanotic shade of blue.

"Jerry," she said in greeting.

"Grandmother," the older man whispered. It was a title of respect, not ancestry.

Aside from Michael, Jerry and Jerry's son Nicholas, no one else knew how to find her home. Clearly Jerry should be in a hospital, but instead he had risked his life to come here, so the news he had brought was urgent and important enough to warrant such a sacrifice.

She jerked her chin toward his companion. "He one of your boys?"

"Grandson," Jerry gasped. "Name's Jamie. Figured it was past time I showed him how to get here."

She studied Jamie. He wore his hair long and pulled back in a ponytail, and leather and silver bracelets on each wrist. His hair gleamed black like a raven's wing, and he had the same rich copper skin as his grandfather, along with the same strong, proud features, only his were molded with a sensuality that Jerry's did not have. Those large, dark eyes and full, shaped lips must have come from his mother. He was older than he appeared at first glance, perhaps twenty-two or twenty-three. Tall and rangy, his body had yet to finish filling out the promise of power in those wide shoulders.

Jerry had to have had good reasons to teach Jamie the way to her home. That meant he trusted his grandson. It also meant he would have given the boy other sacred teachings as well, old, secret ways that were passed down to only a select few. Jerry was grooming Jamie to take his place when he died. But just because he trusted his grandson, that didn't mean that she would without questioning. Jamie would have to pass her own scrutiny before she would let him leave this place with the knowledge of how to return.

As she considered the boy, he held a bundle out to her, the whites of his wide eyes gleaming. His grandfather Jerry's skin carried an unhealthy pallor, but the boy's face was whitened underneath the copper hue, and smudged with tears. The package he offered was wrapped in a length of protective red cotton cloth and tied with undyed twine.

The old woman looked at it for a long moment. She knew what was wrapped inside. The packet was a traditional petition to a native elder for help. It would hold tobacco, and white sage, and whatever cash they could afford to scrape together. If she took it, she undertook a sacred obligation.

She did not take it. Instead, she asked the boy, "Can you carry him up the path to the cabin?"

Jamie nodded. His outstretched hand, and mouth, visibly shook.

She steeled herself against the heartbreak in that mute entreaty. "Then help him up." She looked at her old friend Jerry, who was an elder himself in a nearby Ojibwa community. "You know I can't make you any promises, but of course I'll do what I can."

He nodded. "Thank you."

She pulled herself up the path's incline toward her cabin as the boy gathered his grandfather up in his arms and followed. Behind her, Jerry gave Jamie hoarse-voiced instructions. "After you get me up to the house, you'll give thanks for our safe trip, down by the boat. Do it proper. Offer tobacco."

The boy's voice was deeper than she expected and raw with emotion. "Yes, sir."

She had held off asking for as long as she could. When she could no longer wait, she asked without turning, "Who died?"

Stricken silence fell. In the end it was the boy who answered. His voice choked with tears, he said, "My uncle Nicholas."

Oh no. No.

The news bowed her at the waist. She had known before the boy had said it. She hadn't wanted to. She had hoped otherwise until it was said.

Jerry's hoarse whisper: "Put me down. Go to her."

She put up one age-bruised gnarled hand. "No," she said. "Leave me be."

More silence. After a moment she could straighten and stand upright. She continued up the path. They followed.

Inside, the boy laid his grandfather on the couch in front of the empty fireplace and helped him out of a worn flannel-lined jean jacket. At her order, the boy set a fire to warm the room. She grunted as she sat down on the sturdy cedar coffee table in front of Jerry. Their gazes met, grim and grieving at the implications unfolding from their loss.

"You don't talk," she told him, sticking a crooked forefinger under his nose. As firelight began to dance in the room, she said over her shoulder to the boy, "Tell me what happened."

The boy came to kneel on the floor beside his grandfather's head. He stroked Jerry's hair, his head bowed as he told her what they knew.

They didn't know much at this early stage, but they knew enough.

Nicholas Crow, a former Green Beret and the head of the Secret Security detail assigned to guard the President of the United States, had been killed in an apparent robbery late last night while off-duty outside a restaurant. He had been stabbed multiple times, and his throat cut. Given his abilities and his position, Nicholas's murder would get an aggressive investigation conducted at the highest level, while White House security had rocketed to red alert. The President had chosen to remove to Camp David for the week. None of it had been in the news.

"He was the only one we had among our people who was even close to being in the right position," Jerry whispered. "My fine brave boy. There is no one else."

"I told you, hush," she said. Her own voice was clogged with tears she did not have time to shed.

She didn't ally with very many humans anymore, and Nicholas had been one of the most important human allies she had ever had. She and Jerry had personally seen to his training, since he was a young boy. Losing him now was a terrible blow, not only for the sake of the strong, bright man Nicholas had been, but also for what it said about their enemy's knowledge and intentions.

Setting that aside for the moment, she rested a hand on Jerry's chest and concentrated. Grief and stress, along with too many years of heavy smoking, meant that his heart was in serious trouble.

A cold, quiet part of her mind assessed the damage. She had a limited capacity for healing. Over the years, she had done what she could to boost Jerry's heart, but time and aging had taken an inevitable toll.

She could do it again. She could heal him. It was, just barely, within her ability. But it would take a prodigious amount of energy that she didn't dare expend on him. Not right now. She could not afford it.

Her friendship with Jerry had spanned decades. He knew secrets few other humans had ever been entrusted with, and still her answer must be no.

She withdrew her hand. She told both him and the boy, "I have a tincture that will help this."

She told them the truth, such as it was. The tincture would ease his symptoms and make him more comfortable, but it wouldn't heal him. If she sent them away at this point, Jerry would most likely die before the boy could get him to a hospital. Airlifting him was out of the question. She could not allow the authorities to know of this place.

The relief that lightened both their faces was a scourge.

She pushed heavily to her feet and said to the boy, "Come with me. I'll tell you how to dose him as I mix it up. Then you'll put him in the corner bedroom. When you've seen him settled and comfortable, you can bring in firewood. We'll need to keep the cabin warm. That will be your job."

"Yes, Grandmother," the boy whispered, his eyes lowered.

She went to her worktable. The boy followed. She prepared the tincture and gave the instructions to his downbent head. She got heartily sick of looking at the part in his glossy black hair, until her patience broke. She demanded, "Are you paying attention?"

He lifted his head. He was trembling all over. His widened eyes shone with grief and awe, and an exalted terror. "I'm so honored to listen to anything you wish to say, PtesanWi."

PtesanWi. White Buffalo Calf Woman.

Her scourge deepened at the obvious worship in his eyes. She snapped, "Don't call me that."

"But Grandpa said you are the ancient one who gave the *chanunpa*, the sacred pipe, to the People," he whispered. His trembling increased. "You're our savior. You taught us the sacred rituals, and how we can connect and speak to Spirit—"

She had always taken the long view. A very long time ago, so long ago, the time was shrouded in human legend, she had taught the First Nations how to see and connect with the spirit realm in the hope of giving them some protection from her old enemy, the Deceiver. But mostly she had taught them in the hope that they might prove useful to her one day in this interminable war.

Now, so many centuries later, she reaped a bloody harvest from all that she had sown. She did not deserve this boy's reverence. She deserved to be shot.

"Overwrought fool," she said. She grabbed his hand and slapped the small brown bottle of tincture into it. "You don't know what you're talking about. Go tend your grandfather. If you know what's good for you, you'll keep your mouth shut. If you must call me anything at all, you call me Astra. Nothing more. Do you hear?"

"Yes Grandmother," the boy breathed, clutching the medicine. The worship in his eyes did not dim, not by as much as a single watt. "Thank you, Grandmother."

Thus she watched as another noble child threw himself into her service, much as his dead uncle had. And she knew she would use this child too, if she had to, even if it killed him.

The cabin was stifling. She went outside to let the wind slice at her.

A day of blades.

An invisible presence gusted into the clearing. It said, *Grandmother.*

She closed her eyes, sighed and braced herself.

What word do you bring me? She asked the question as the presence had spoken, silently, in a way that no ordinary human would be capable of hearing.

Invisible fingers plucked at her jacket, her slacks, and touched wispy tendrils of her hair. *I've been many places today and seen many things.*

The children of air had a mercurial curiosity for all manner of things. Existing half in the physical realm and half in the psychic realm, some were creatures of light, while others were darker and more predatory. Because their energies were often slight and subtle, they could be easily overlooked. If one took enough patience with them, they made excellent, if somewhat erratic, spies.

They also had a tendency to flightiness. She reached for calm and exhaled gentleness and affection. The gust of breeze that curled around her warmed with pleasure.

She said, *It has been a good day for you, hasn't it? What about those things for which you searched?*

The breeze seemed to hesitate in its constant swirling.

She injected a stern note in the gentleness. *I need to know what you discovered, child. There is no protection for either of us in pretending they do not exist.*

The wind spirit pulled back.

Pain, it admitted at last. *Pain, dreams and confusion. The dark ones hunt. They spill blood for sport as they look for the one who was lost. They are laughing and confident. They are sure they will find her soon.*

She knew of the dreams and confusion. The strength in them haunted her rest, but her lips thinned at the news of the dark hunt and the spilling of blood. She put one hand on a nearby tree and leaned on it. The tree poured its upright greening strength into her, a lavish and generous gift.

Thank you, she said to the tree. She stroked the bark.

Grandmother, the tree replied.

She straightened. So it began again, with a blood hunt, and with a good man's murder, and his father, a faithful friend, condemned to a slow, painful death. She had had years to prepare, yet she still felt grief and a sharp upsurge of fear and dread.

Her distress agitated the wind spirit. It curled upon itself in jerky slashing movements. She held out a hand and projected calm. *Did you find the lost one?*

No, Grandmother, the spirit replied. *But neither have they, yet.*

She hadn't expected any other reply. Still she tasted disappointment. *What of the warrior?*

He hunts as well, the spirit whispered as it curled around her again. *He sends you his greeting, and a warning to be prepared.*

Yes. She drew her jacket closer around her and forced herself to ask, *And do you have any news of the Deceiver?*

Where the dark ones are, he is always nearby, the spirit answered. *But I dared not look too closely for his location.*

You were wise. Like her, the Deceiver did not overlook subtle changes in spirit energies. One whiff of the spirit's presence, one hint of its mission, and he would rip apart its delicate essence with a careless thought. *Thank you, child.*

Grandmother.

She sent the spirit on its way and limped the rest of the short way to the bench by the cabin's door.

She had been born once into this world, ages and ages

ago, and she refused to give up her memories and pass into the oblivion that was death. She was too afraid to let go, to allow herself to forget. Now this body she wore had been sustained far beyond what a normal human lifespan should be, and it felt heavy and worn to the bone with carrying her for so long.

The green living things around her, the strength of the land itself, had sustained her for countless years. The strength was abundant and given to her freely, but she wondered now if it could possibly be enough.

"I'm tired," she whispered.

She sank onto the bench and put her wrinkled face into her hands. A fox slipped out of the forest's edge and came to curl around her ankles. She reached down and stroked one large, anxious ear.

And so the nightmare began again. They sought, all of them, to push through a veil. They did not know what was on the other side, only that they must fight each other and push, even to the end of their existence if they must.

She was so tired and afraid. She did not know if she had the strength for another week of living, let alone another battle.

Even though the sun shone she huddled into herself.

May God forgive her.

She doubted that anybody else would.

Chapter Five

MARY'S OLD HOUSE was near the south side of the river. The community hospital where she worked was on the north side.

The city of St. Joseph lay at the mouth of the St. Joseph River. Benton Harbor was just on the other side of the river. Together they were locally known as the Twin Cities, but their only congruence was geographical. They were far from identical.

St. Joe had a predominately white population with a median household income that held its own with other parts of the Midwest. It had all the usual amenities and attractions of a smaller lakeside city. In a location that was easily accessible from much of northern Indiana, the city was also close enough for those in Chicago who were affluent enough to own weekend homes and determined enough to make the commute.

Minutes away, just north across a bridge, Benton Harbor had a predominantly black population, with a median household income that was well under twenty thousand.

Mary had to commute daily across the divide to get to work, but she did not have to make that trip today. After shutting the door on her painting studio, she took another cup of coffee to the bathroom and showered. As the coffee sat on the sink and cooled to a drinkable temperature, she stood under jetting hot water and let the heat soak away the tension that had built up in her shoulders and neck. Then she soaped her hair and body, feeling the protrusions and angles of bone under the fluid shift of skin.

Did she really look all bones and nerves? Her appetite had dropped off sharply over the last month or two. Drying quickly, she wrapped her hair in the towel and rubbed fog off the mirror over the sink.

Like her hair, her skin also hinted at a mixed-race heritage in her family's past. Her natural complexion was a rich shade of honey. Large blue cat eyes looked back at her from a face that had always been thin but had now turned sharp. Cheekbones, nose and jaw were pronounced. Only her lips had retained their original fullness.

She glared as she watched those lips shape silent words.

What's the matter with you?

As she considered her reflection, she thought about changing her mind and going with Justin to see Tony. As soon as the thought occurred, she rejected it. She didn't need another doctor to tell her what she already knew. Whatever her problems were, they weren't physical in origin.

She went into her bedroom, which was as cluttered as the rest of the cottage, and she dragged on a pair of jeans and a light cotton sweater. After braiding her damp hair off her face, she slipped on tennis shoes and grabbed her jacket and purse. She paused to tape a note to her front door.

Gone in search of cigarettes and a penis. Bring Baxter by any time on Friday. M. Man.

Then she read what she wrote and sighed. It wasn't funny. She didn't seem to have any real humor in her today, and she needed to stop trying to fake it.

She left the note anyway, climbed into her Toyota Camry and backed out of her driveway. Just before she pulled onto the street, she slammed on the brakes and sat chewing her lip in indecision.

Justin was going to be pissed. Well, piss on him for trying to control her behavior. He'd wait around a while then go away and try to argue with her later. She scowled, double-checked the street and pulled out.

The day had brightened into a beautiful May afternoon with puffy cumulous clouds swimming in an azure sky. The wind was still chilly but the sun was shining, so the interior of the car soon grew hot. She rolled her window down part-way, and a breeze gusted in to ruffle her jacket and hair. Since she was broke, she drove to a nearby bank and used an ATM to withdraw a hundred dollars.

Conscious of the haunted, bony face that had looked out at her from the bathroom mirror, she stopped at the nearest drive-thru and ordered a large chocolate shake and a bottle of water. She threw the bottle of water in the passenger seat and jabbed a straw into the lid of her shake. Sucking hard on the straw, she turned on impulse onto Highway 31 and took it south.

She wasn't aware until much later how such simple desires and decisions were the first steps along a path of action that helped to save her life.

THREE QUARTERS OF a chocolate shake and half of a U2 album later, Mary crossed the southern state border into Indiana. After she had graduated, married Justin and moved to St. Joseph, she had rarely made the journey to either the Notre Dame University campus or its neighboring city of South Bend. As a result she had grown unfamiliar with the exits off the 31 Bypass. She took a guess and picked the wrong exit.

She realized her mistake as she drove into South Bend itself. She would have to travel back north and east through the city to get to the Notre Dame campus. The route would take longer, but she had the afternoon to kill anyway. With a shrug she committed herself to the city streets, driving at an unhurried pace through an unfamiliar part of town.

While she waited at a red light she noticed a wooden sign

in front of a charming ramshackle Victorian house: PSYCHIC CONSULTATIONS. TAROT READINGS. WALK-INS WELCOME. The sign looked hand-painted. The ghost of beautiful detail lurked in the curvature of the lettering, which matched the house's deep pink gingerbread trim. Now the sign was old and battered.

The spring wind, still erratic, blew sharp and hard into her open window. It tugged an unruly lock of hair loose from her braid. Reaching up, she tucked the lock behind her ear.

A little voice whispered, *Stop and see.*

Her tongue came between her teeth as she considered. She'd never had a tarot reading before. Aside from any amusement factor, if science didn't have an acceptable cure for her, what might superstition offer?

By the time the stoplight had changed she had made up her mind. She pulled into the small parking lot beside the house, walked up the narrow sidewalk to the front door, checked the hours posted and stepped inside to the sound of a tinkle from an old-fashioned bell.

The breeze gusted in with her, and she had to struggle to shut the door behind her. Then she turned and took in a shabby, spacious foyer and a large open front room decorated with an eclectic mix of modern and antique furniture. To her left a massive staircase curved up to a second floor. A dusty but otherwise magnificent antique chandelier hung from the high ceiling. She gawked at it.

At her entrance a woman rose from the couch in the front room and set aside a book. The woman smiled and walked toward Mary, who blinked and readjusted her expectations. She had expected something that was either exotic or tacky, or an unfortunate combination of both, but this woman was plump, comfortable-looking and middle-aged.

"Good afternoon," the woman said, offering a freckled hand that sparkled with QVC bling.

Mary shook the other woman's hand, with an instinctive liking for her direct friendly gaze. "Hi, I just saw your sign and decided to stop," Mary said. "I was wondering if you had time for a consultation or a tarot reading or whatever it is you do, but of course I understand if you don't since I don't have an appointment. Really, this was just an impulse thing—"

Stupid, she meant to say. Off-the-wall, loose-cannon, embarrassing, about-to-do-something-you'll-regret stupid.

Before she could talk herself out the door, the woman interrupted with a cheerful smile. "I certainly do have time. Business is slow today. This is the first nice afternoon we've had in weeks and everybody's gone outside. My name's Gretchen."

Gretchen the psychic. A hiccup of laughter exploded in Mary's nose.

She clapped a hand over her mouth and turned it into a barking cough. What the hell's the matter with you, she thought. Be a grown-up.

She managed to say, "I'm Mary."

"Please come in and have a seat. Make yourself comfortable." Gretchen gestured to the living room area.

Mary chose an overstuffed armchair. The soft-cushioned chair tried to swallow her. Good thing it didn't have teeth or it could have done some major damage. Nervousness kept her perched on the edge of the seat. She noted Gretchen's quick glance at her erect posture, and she tried to relax.

She explained, "I've never done this before. I don't know why I'm nervous."

Gretchen grinned and shrugged. "Blind date jitters. I think it's a typical reaction. We don't know each other, and you have no idea how this is going to go. Would you like a drink? I've got Diet Coke, or I could make tea or coffee."

Mary forced herself to smile back. The muscles in her face felt stiff, the smile false, and she rubbed the back of her neck. Apparently she had left her social skills in the hall closet along with her winter coat. Her headache wouldn't budge no matter how she ODed on caffeine, but never call her a quitter. "A Diet Coke would be nice, thank you."

"My pleasure. I'll be right back."

The older woman was as good as her word. She left Mary

just enough time to shrug out of her jacket before returning with two cans of Diet Coke and glasses filled with ice. Gretchen didn't want to lose her unexpected fee. Mary's smile turned wry. She accepted the drink with a murmured thanks.

"So," Gretchen said. "You have never done this before." Mary shook her head, pouring soda into her glass. "Well, perhaps you can tell me what you're looking for and we can figure out where to go from there."

"I'm . . . not sure." Mary sipped at her fizzy drink. She bet she knew what was coming in this next part. This was where Gretchen pumped her for information then regurgitated it back for money. She suggested, "Why don't you tell me what your, er, specialty is. Perhaps we should try that. Is it tarot readings?"

The older woman frowned. Strong sunshine fell through the window on the back of her head and on one round shoulder, throwing most of Gretchen's face into shadow. The unforgiving light showed a thin strip of gray- and mouse-colored hair at the roots of a vivacious butterscotch rinse from L'Oréal. "Actually, I tend to pick the medium from instinct depending on the client and what questions he or she might have."

This was supposed to be for entertainment purposes only, but they hadn't reached the entertaining part yet. Mary looked at the front door, already half regretting her impulse to stop. She was a fool.

"Usually," Gretchen continued in a quiet voice, "people come in with some kind of question on their minds, even if they're skeptics and it's just a frivolous question. Do you have a question, or are you one of those rare people that doesn't?"

Keeping her gaze fixed on the front door, Mary asked, "What do you think dreams are?"

A pause. Then Gretchen said, "I believe dreams are our minds freed from the definitions placed upon us by our physical bodies."

Mary's gaze turned to the other woman. She leaned forward. "What do you mean?"

She heard a rustle of clothing as the other woman shifted.

"I mean that when we dream, we are able to use our minds while being free of our bodies. We could dream of something we imagine, dream to relieve stress, or we could dream of our past. We could dream of our past lives and we could dream of our futures, or of other worlds, other realities. We can travel and speak to people we know who are alive, or to those who are dead. Or maybe we can speak to people who were never alive in any sense that you and I understand that word. Maybe we can even sometimes speak to those creatures that aren't people."

The other woman fell silent, and Mary laughed. "That covers a lot of ground."

Gretchen smiled. "Yes. That's what the dream world allows us to do."

"You believe we can dream of the future."

"Absolutely."

"How can that be when it hasn't happened yet?"

"Well I'm no genius scientist, but I do think we perceive reality through the limitations of our human senses and brains. Our actual reality is a lot bigger than we are. In our dreams we aren't subject to a linear existence, which is how we experience time in our physical bodies. Why not dream of the future, or of the past? All times are now."

Mary looked into her dark bubbling drink and struggled with that concept. She had never been all that good at understanding quantum physics either. She muttered, "Sometimes I have dreams that come true."

"Do you? I do too," said the other woman. "I always wished I could turn it into something useful, but usually for me it's nothing more than my hairdresser getting sick, or my cat running away. Once I did dream what my tax return was going to be. This was before all the fancy software programs that calculate what your return will be before you file. In my dream, my return was more than I thought it would be, so I kept rereading the check in disbelief. Turns out I was correct, right down to the penny, but of course you can't gamble on things like that, in case you're wrong and you just had a dream of imagination or wishful thinking."

Mary stared and then chuckled. She had made one of the hardest confessions she'd ever made to another person, but it was clear Gretchen was not very impressed. "How mystical and yet pragmatic."

"I think you just described my cultural heritage," said Gretchen with a twinkle. "I am part German and part Yugoslavian."

Mary was still processing what Gretchen had said earlier. She said, "You mentioned past lives, so you believe in reincarnation."

"Yes, I do," Gretchen replied, sipping her drink. "At least I believe that some form of it exists. A more Greek version of reincarnation is to 'transmigrate,' or to pass from one body at death, drink forgetfulness from the river Lethe and then pass into another body. Or something like that, anyway. My memory is a bit fuzzy on the details."

Mary had heard of the river Lethe, but she had never heard of transmigration before. "You said something about spirits."

"Yes, I believe in spirits. We are spirits inhabiting bodies, and everything alive has a spirit. And there are spirits who have never had a body that we could conceive of, or understand, like, for instance, the Wakean."

"The Wakean?"

"The Wakean are the American Indian thunder beings. I always smile when a good thunderstorm rolls in, and I hear them crashing around up in the sky."

Mary watched the older woman in fascination. Gretchen sat not fifteen feet away but lived in an entirely different world from hers. She said in a doubtful voice, "What it all boils down to is that you think your dreams can either be real or not."

"Oh no," Gretchen said. "I believe every dream is real. I just think it takes a dexterous and sophisticated mind to determine to which level of reality a dream belongs. That's the difficult part."

Mary sighed. Disappointment crept in. After this whole conversation, she didn't have much more than what she had walked in with, aside from an odd thought or two that carried a bit of Gretchen's QVC sparkle. She had been ridiculous to hope for more. "Well, thank you for your time. How much do I owe you?"

"That's it?" Gretchen asked. "Are you sure you don't want something else?"

"No, I think that's it for today. You've given me a lot to think about," she said, keeping her tone polite. She drew out her checkbook. "How much do you charge?"

"Nothing." Gretchen smiled as she looked up and began to protest. "No, I'm serious, please forget it. I wasn't busy, I enjoyed the visit and you didn't ask hardly anything of me. I wouldn't feel right taking your money. If you want to change your mind and come back sometime, though, I'll sock you with a bill then."

No matter what Mary said, the older woman wouldn't be moved. After a few minutes she gave up. Gretchen saw her to the front door and pressed a card into her hand. "Call me," she said.

Mary smiled at her. "Thank you."

Gretchen gripped her hand. "You have blood on your hands."

Ice slithered down Mary's spine. "Excuse me?"

"You have blood on your hands. A lot of it. And I don't know why the color red is so important to you, but it is. I didn't want to say it earlier, because you were nervous enough, and I didn't want to frighten you." Gretchen looked at her searchingly. "Yesterday the blood was all down your front. Are you an EMT?"

"I'm a doctor," she whispered. "I work in an ER."

"Someone died yesterday."

"Yes." Her lips felt numb.

"I thought I felt someone hovering around you. Maybe even a couple of someones. I'm sure she's grateful for everything you tried to do for her." Gretchen smiled and squeezed her hand. "You're a good healer. A lot of people are thankful for what you do."

The conga drums were back, playing an encore in

Mary's chest. Boy howdy. No more caffeine for her today. And this conversation had turned far too *Ghost Whisperer* for her. She swallowed, pulled her hand away and forced herself to say, "Thank you."

After she walked to her car, she stood for a few moments, looking around and breathing hard. Okay, that last bit rattled her. Why was she so upset? She was a fool. For entertainment purposes only, remember? How could she have allowed herself to hope for something else—from a psychic consultant, of all people? She was tired, that's all. She was strung out from feeling this pressure building up inside of her, and if she didn't work hard to avoid it, she was going to . . .

What was she going to do? Explode? Crash?

Her mind felt frozen, her thoughts running thick and sluggish, and yet inexorable, like mud in a landslide. What was BabyMama Two's name? The girl was scheduled for an autopsy today. That shouldn't be the only thing you remember about a person.

Pain filled Mary's chest. A thin keen came from the back of her throat as a feverish heat flashed through her body. She pressed a hand to her sternum.

It was an actual, physical pain. It felt like someone who was shattered with grief, like someone who was so far beyond the end of her rope she didn't know where the end was, like someone who was at the mercy of a convulsing sob.

Sweating, taking short, shallow breaths, she blew out through her mouth until the tight band around her lungs had loosened and she could draw in a deep gulp of air. The wind burst against her cheeks with a frantic urgency.

Is this what a psychotic break felt like? Her thoughts turned to Justin again. She knew that if she called him, he would reschedule the appointment with Tony. If she asked him, he would even come to pick her up. He would be angry and worried, and he would pull more strings, and she could continue down the rational path of Western medicine in the hope of discovering what sanity felt like.

With jerky, graceless movements, she unlocked her car and climbed into the driver's seat, rolling her window down as far as it would go. After resting for about fifteen minutes she felt calmer, and her body had cooled. Starting the car, she drove with care through downtown South Bend and turned north onto Eddy Street.

Ten minutes later she pulled onto the Notre Dame campus and drove past spacious green lawns. The white domes of the sporting facilities, the jutting silhouette of the library, the glimpse of the golden dome in the distance, all the familiar landmarks soothed her. After some confusion, she managed to locate the small visitor's parking lot on the northeast edge of the main campus.

As she walked through the grounds, she let the sights and sounds of normal university life wash over her, drifting through the memories of her time as a student. It hadn't been that long ago, but she still felt completely disconnected from the younger woman she had been.

As a college student, she had been more carefree, although she hadn't realized it at the time. Her dreams had been nothing more than a cipher to be figured out with time, therapy and conviction. Then they wouldn't trouble her anymore. She pulled her face into a wry twist. Where had all her stamina gone?

Eventually she reached a familiar incline, and she walked through a grove of trees to reach the Notre Dame Grotto, located by a small picturesque lake.

Built over a hundred years ago, the Notre Dame Grotto was an exact replica of the Grotto of Massabielle near Lourdes in France, only the Grotto at the university had been built a fraction of the original's size.

The shrine was dedicated to Mary, Mother of God. As she approached the entrance to the man-made cave, Mary glanced up at the statue of the Virgin Mary, which was located in an overhead niche.

Mary, Queen of Heaven. This month—May—was Mary's month, she remembered, as she wandered over to the glowing candles. A couple stood nearby, talking together in quiet voices. They nodded at her and smiled as they walked out, leaving her alone in the Grotto.

She was grateful for the solitude but wary as to how long

it would last. The Grotto was a popular place. She stood for a while looking at the lit candles, letting herself drift into thoughtlessness. Occasionally the restless wind gusted in and caused the candles to flicker, but no one came to disturb her solitude.

Finally she roused herself to do what she came to do.

Hail Mary, Mother of God. . . . she said mentally and smiled. This is Mary Katherine Byrne, praying to you for the first time in what seems like forever. I haven't said the rosary since I was a child. I don't remember how it all goes. I do have a good Irish Catholic name, though, and my parents saw me baptized and at least halfway raised. But then they died, and my aunt didn't care for praying. Do you forgive such things? Do they even cross your awareness?

She found an unlit candle and a taper, and she lit the candle with care. Strangely, though the breeze still gusted around her head and shoulders, the candles had stopped flickering. The tiny flames stood pure and straight.

Queen of Heaven, she thought as she watched her candle. Do you watch over your namesakes? Or are you only concerned with matters that involve your Son?

I NEED HELP!

The mental outcry burst out of her with such force, she staggered. Heat flooded her again. She felt as though her clothes might burst into flame.

Gasping, she tore off her jacket. The breeze had come back to circle her in a whirlwind. She flung out a hand to catch her balance and knocked over candles. The back of her hand felt seared.

What had Gretchen said?

Gretchen had said . . . had said . . .

We could dream of our past lives and we could dream of our futures, other worlds and other realities. We can travel in our dreams and speak to people we know who are alive, or those who are dead. . . .

And that was important, it was a message, it was something she needed to hear, but that wasn't *IT*. That wasn't what she needed to remember.

Gretchen had said . . .

Mary said aloud, her hoarse voice an experiment of air and vibration, "My dreams are real."

As she said it, the intolerable internal pressure that had been building up over the last month, over her entire life, burst. Something tore and she didn't know what it was, whether it had been inside her or around her.

Something tore away.

The breeze that had turned into a whirlwind now became a maelstrom, and her mind was filled with howling.

Her sight glazed with light. The world tilted, and she fell. She curled into a fetal position to protect herself from the storm, wrapping her arms around her head. She lost track of time. She might have lain forever on cold stone, an effigy, and all her life had been a dream.

A countless, ageless time later she attempted a breath, then another. Her arms loosened from around her head and her body uncurled. She patted the ground with a trembling hand. It seemed solid enough.

In slow degrees she struggled to her knees, wrapping her arms around herself for she had cooled again and was starting to shiver. Her head still rang from the aftermath of a gigantic noise, and she felt blank with shock. She had no idea how to categorize what she had just experienced.

A woman bent over her. Mary started and shrank back, staring up into dark, lustrous eyes. "I'm sorry," she stammered. "I seem to have, I don't know, fainted, I guess. . . ."

Child, the woman said, reaching out one hand.

"Thank you." Automatically she reached back. Somehow she found herself on her feet. Those incredible, compassionate eyes. Mary couldn't stop staring at them. They were filled with such beauty, dark and yet lit as if starlight shone in them.

Her world lurched again. It wasn't starlight in those eyes but candlelight.

The light wasn't from a reflection in the woman's gaze

BUT FROM THE CANDLES THAT SHONE BEHIND HER.

Mary sucked air, and everything she thought she knew about the world crashed into ruins.

Child, the woman said. *You called, and I came.*

The words were there and Mary clearly heard them, even though no sound had been made. She pressed fingers against her mouth, and without thinking, she answered in the same way. *Holy crap. I mean, Holy Mother. Th-thank you.*

Ephemeral fingers seemed to brush her cheek. Tears spilled down Mary's face as a brief, desperately needed wave of calm washed over her. *Brave traveler*, the woman said. *You cannot go home again.*

Mary scrubbed at her eyes with a fist, greedy for every moment she saw the woman. *I don't understand. Why can't I go home?*

You must work hard to remember. The lines of the cave and floor were visible through the woman's body. *Remember who you are, and take great care. You are in danger. You have a powerful enemy, and you must not try to go home. You must work hard to find me.*

Mary shook her head as her eyes blurred again. Blinking furiously, she said in that mental voice, *I'm sorry. I still don't understand. How do I find you?*

You must travel north.

The last few words came at her as if from across a massive divide. Then her vision came clear and for a moment all thought, all movement, was suspended.

The woman was gone, the maelstrom silent and quiet as if it had never existed. The sun shone outside on a bright serene spring afternoon.

Mary stood alone in the Grotto.

Chapter Six

AS MICHAEL LEARNED meditation, the first memory that he recovered was the strongest, and also the strangest to him.

It wasn't strange because it was of that first, alien life. That ancient memory was patchy and indistinct, and it came to him much later.

No, the first memory he uncovered was strange because he was happy in it.

Happy.

What a bizarre concept, happiness. As soon as he connected to the emotion in the memory, he realized he had never felt happiness, not in this lifetime or in many others.

In this lifetime, he had never given much thought to happiness before, but when he had, the concept had seemed pastel, an insipid, shallow thing that others claimed to either desire or feel.

Happiness led to other pastel emotions like contentment. It also seemed to be connected to things he had no interest in, things like steady jobs, marriage, children and community. Or it was connected to myths that people believed. Wealth would make them happy, or popularity would, or social standing.

But when the memory surfaced, and Michael touched the actual experience of *happiness*, even though it was only a shadow of the real thing, the feeling was so passionate, so golden and complete it shone a light on all the rest of his life. By comparison every other emotion he had felt was fractured, dirty and gray.

The details of that former life came to him piecemeal.

He had been a Norman lord under William the Conqueror. After the Battle of Hastings, he had been given a castle in York to live in and defend on behalf of the king, and *she* had been there. The other half of himself.

They fit together. Such simple words and yet so profound. They fit. Interlocking pieces, contrast and confluence.

And remembering that was, completely and utterly, the most devastating thing he had ever experienced.

Over the years, he returned to that past life again and again in meditation, painstakingly recovering shards of lost treasure.

The look in her eyes when she smiled at him. She was luminous. (If only he could see the details of her face more clearly, even though he knew that what she looked like did not matter in the slightest.)

How they talked late at night, discussing everything from the latest harvest to their great enemy. (For the danger was with them always, a thundercloud of war that shrouded their entire existence.)

Flashes of a mysterious and powerful intimacy. Her arms around his neck, his face in her perfumed hair. Their bodies entwined, and his spirit expansive and vibrant. (Not this thin, sharp sword that he had become.)

Laughter. Her laughter, and his. (He never laughed anymore. He had not laughed in so long, he had forgotten that he had forgotten how.)

The person he had been in this former life: this was who he was supposed to be. He took the memory and made it the cornerstone of his soul, and he built everything else around it, until he became a fortress.

* * *

IN THE GRAY light of predawn, Michael pulled his car into the small parking lot at the bottom of a lookout point. He took advantage of the early solitude and remote location to give his body some much needed rest, dozing for an hour or so behind the wheel.

Then something made him open his eyes, turn his head.

The shimmer of a transparent figure stood by his car. It was a strong quiet, steady presence. Recognition kicked him in the teeth. He straightened, staring.

The figure was that of a tall man. In that faint shimmer he caught a glimpse of short black hair, distinguished aquiline features, copper skin.

The figure was a ghost.

Michael, it said. *I have fallen.*

Heaviness plummeted onto his shoulders. Maybe it was grief. He didn't know. It was certainly disappointment. They had not been friends, not quite. More like comrades-in-arms. Michael had met him when he had traveled north to spend summers with his mentor. Each year the boys would meet again, having grown taller and stronger, and they would assess each other as possible adversaries all over again. For a brief time, many years ago, they had been sparring partners, until Michael grew too dangerous to train with other children.

Michael slowly opened his car door and stepped out. He was the same height and stood shoulder to shoulder with the tall ghost. He said, *Damn, Nicholas. I'm sorry.*

There was a faint gleam in the dark, intelligent eyes that regarded him with a grave expression, without self-pity. *I will not leave*, Nicholas told him. *I will do what I can to protect him.*

Michael nodded. Most humans passed on to wherever it was they went after death, but a few who were especially passionate were able to turn away from that journey.

The ghost lifted his hand in good-bye, already fading as he turned to walk away.

Semper fidelis. Always faithful. Nicholas had loved his country and his President, and his continued devotion would help, but it wouldn't be enough.

Which was why Nicholas had been killed, of course.

MICHAEL CLIMBED UP to the lookout point and sat on a short bluff above the western shore of Lake Michigan. The lake sparkled silver and blue, while green pines dotted the broken rocks of the coast. The bluff was north of Racine, Wisconsin, south of Milwaukee, and right in the middle of nowhere.

Even though the sun shone, the weather was unseasonably cold for late May. In some parts of the Midwest, rivers were flooding and people had been forced to evacuate their homes. This close to the Lake, especially with the fading of daylight, the wind felt as though it could peel flesh from the bone.

He didn't notice. He was deep in meditation.

He had soaked up all the teaching Astra had to offer him with the ravenous appetite of the starving. Somehow he had managed to keep alive during the process, although looking back he knew he had been close to death several times. Most importantly, he had discovered the history and reason for his rage. He had grown into the kind of man who controlled himself with complete discipline and who used his anger as sustenance and weapon.

Now and always, he hunted.

Eyes closed, breathing deep, he had entered into the mental state the Buddhists refer to as utter mindfulness. He was quite aware of his surroundings but unaffected by them. With the hard-won patience he had learned over years, he called in all his messengers and companions. He asked each of them the same questions. He did this as a process of elimination, always aware that the enemy searched with as much eagerness and relentlessness, and with much more cruelty than he.

Voices sounded behind him. Teenagers scrambled up the path to the bluff, their raucous laughter and off-color jokes whooping through the quiet, windswept area. He ignored them, letting their voices flow through him like sand flowing through a glass.

One of them, a female, said, "Mm-mm, will you look at that."

A boy laughed. "What, a freaking weirdo on a freaking park bench? Dime a dozen, babe."

"You got no imagination. That there's a juicy piece of USDA prime beef. Look at them muscles. I could love me some of that. Think his organs have been injected with growth hormones?"

"Girl, you a ho."

Another called out in a high voice, "You guys. Look at the sky."

Various exclamations followed. "That's like something from a horror flick. Hitchcock, right? Or was it Scorsese?"

"How do they get the birds to do that? Are we on TV?"

"What kind of birds are they?" the girl asked.

"Hawks, I think. Hundreds of them. Maybe a thousand? I've never seen so many circling around."

"They look like a tornado. That's not right. It's not natural."

Michael continued to speak to his people. *Brothers, we keep hunting south.*

Still along the Lake? one of them asked, tilting in his flight so the sun shone on proud red-tail feathers.

Always along the Lake, he answered. He and his old teacher had narrowed the search down to the shores of Lake Michigan. That was still a massive amount of territory to cover, and they were fast running out of time.

Then:

I NEED HELP!

The cry ripped across the psychic realm. Unprepared, wide open, Michael reeled from the shock. He heard the babble of teenagers as though through the roar of rushing water. Hands hooked under his arms to help him to his feet. He shook them off, focusing all the considerable force of his attention on that internal, ephemeral place.

There she was.

She was coming awake. She had ripped through the veil herself, and energy blazed from her like she was a psychic version of Chernobyl. Anyone with the capacity to see the psychic realm could see her. She was completely unprotected, and he was too far away.

His heart kicked.

He twisted, lunged down the path to his car, roared at the sky.

A whirling tower of a thousand hawks screamed in reply and hurtled southeast.

Chapter Seven

MARY NEVER REMEMBERED how she got from the Grotto back to her car. She simply became aware again of her surroundings when she was sitting behind the wheel, her head lying back on the rest. The sun had angled lower on the western horizon. The reflection of it caught in her rearview mirror, a great orange-red blaze that blinded her so that she had to squint and turn her face away.

She was covered in sweat as though she had raced the entire distance back. For all she knew, she had done just that. Taking a deep, shuddering breath, she pulled the sleeve of her sweater over one fist and scrubbed at her face. Then she rolled down all four windows to let in the cold fresh air.

She shied away from thinking about what had just happened. It was too much. She couldn't wrap her brain around it. All she knew was that she felt different. She felt eerie, light and hollow like a bird's bone. The horrific pressure that had been building up inside of her, as though someone had been piling rocks one by one on her chest, had disappeared as if it had never been.

The world looked different as well. Everything around her seemed in constant motion, rippling as if a transparent

Van Gogh painting had been draped across reality. She didn't know how to interpret what she was seeing, but the trees along the line of horizon seemed to have a glow about them, a shimmer like a desert mirage. She sensed whispers again around the edges of her mind.

Van Gogh had cut off his own ear. Had he heard whispers too? Had he been trying to make it stop?

Without her permission, her mind slipped back to what had happened in the Grotto. What had the Lady said?

You're in danger.

"Riiight," she croaked, just to hear the sound of her own voice. It seemed to shock the silence in the car. "Let's review. I'm fucking nuts. Any questions?"

What had they said in psych class? Just because you're paranoid doesn't mean anything. You're just paranoid. She continued speaking out loud, as she needed to hear the sound of her own voice. "I guess I've had that psychotic break now. I'm suffering from delusions—and now I'm talking to myself. Gretchen should have warned me that I had a seventy-two-hour psychiatric detention in my near future."

There went her medical license and career. Whoopsie.

All of a sudden she was ravenous, as though her lack of appetite over the last couple of months had finally caught up with her. Images of different dishes flooded her mind and made her mouth water. She craved normality as much as food, and she desperately wanted to be surrounded with noise, humanity and banality. Her fingers trembled as she started the car. She had to find somewhere to eat. She was too shaky to drive the hour or so trip home without it.

Those incredible eyes, starred with candlelight. *You can't go home*, the Lady had said. *You must try to find me*.

What the hell did that mean? And why was she looking for meaning in something that was so clearly insane? She shuddered and told herself to stop. She would eat first, get steadier, dig through her purse for her car keys and her sanity, and then think about what had happened. Where should she go for dinner?

Unsure about what the dining options were after several

years' absence, she drove north to Cleveland Road, cut east and turned south on Grape Road in the neighboring town of Mishawaka.

The area had once been farmland but had, due to urban sprawl, become the main shopping and dining area for the region. Over time, as many of the businesses had moved to the Grape Road district, Mishawaka had received welcome additions to its tax revenue stream, but as a result the downtown area of South Bend was riddled with urban decay.

She caught sight of a T.G.I. Friday's, and on impulse she pulled into the parking lot. The restaurant was everything she had hoped to find: cheerful, noisy and banal. She parked, stripped off her jacket and left it in the car. Climbing out and locking the doors, she went inside and stopped at the hostess desk. Overloud music, flickering imagery from high-mounted flat-screens, the red- and white-striped decor and the babble of various conversations crashed over her head.

The wavy Van Gogh effect was everywhere in the restaurant. Reflections of light were sharp on the polished wood and edges of glass. For a moment everything seemed to shift, as if it were breathing. She stood disoriented and somewhat sick, as a young waitress in jeans hurried toward her.

"Hi, how many?" the waitress asked in a bright voice.

The girl was very Van Gogh, radiating near-invisible ripples like steam rising from a pot of boiling water. Trying to make it stop, Mary blinked several times as she looked around. Even though the day had faded into early evening, the tables were crowded. A high proportion of the patrons were families with young children. Everyone was haloed with the same kind of rippling effect.

She shifted from foot to foot. Maybe coming here was a mistake. She would hate to cut off her ear in public.

She became aware of the waitress's fixed, patient smile and consulted her watch. It was already almost five o'clock. Where the hell had the time gone?

"I'm alone," she said. "I can eat at the bar."

"Okay! Here's a menu. Just go have a seat, and someone will be with you in a minute."

She took the menu and went to the bar, where the music was somewhat lower. Unfortunately, it still competed with the noise from the flat-screen mounted high in one corner. The local news would be starting soon, so she chose a seat nearest the television, although she still wasn't sure she would be able to stay. The overload of input made her head throb worse than ever. The light, hollow sensation from earlier had intensified until she felt as if she was only loosely connected to her flesh.

The bartender worked in an area ringed by the bar. He came up to her, a young, blond male with an appreciative, blinding Donny Osmond smile.

"How're you doing today?" he asked. He wiped the area in front of her.

Mary cleared her throat and tried not to look at his mouth. "It's so noisy in here."

His smile turned crooked. "Yeah, I've gone deaf since I started working here. I can ask the manager to turn it down, but I can't promise anything. It's out of my control."

"Thanks."

"Can I get you something to drink?"

"Coke, please." She opened the menu and the items blurred in front of her. "I'm starving, so anything sounds good. What's quick?"

"The burgers come up pretty fast."

She ordered a burger with everything, fries and a salad, and sucked down the Coke he placed in front of her. He brought her the salad and refilled her drink as she tore into the food. "You weren't kidding about being hungry."

The high fructose corn syrup from the Coke and the first few bites of food helped to anchor her back in her body. Conscious of the bartender's speculative expression, she swallowed and told him a version of the truth. "I've been too busy to eat right these last few weeks, and all of a sudden it caught up with me."

"Oh yeah? I do that when I'm studying for finals. I live on caffeine and cigarettes. Afterward I sleep for three days."

"Where do you go to school, Notre Dame?" she asked.

He laughed. "Naw, can't afford that. I'm going to IUSB. I'm majoring in business administration."

The South Bend area was filled with higher education schools. Notre Dame University was the most famous of the schools, but there were also Indiana University at South Bend, St. Mary's College, Holy Cross, Bethel, Ivy Tech and others. The wide choice, together with a relatively low cost of housing, made the area a good place to pursue a higher education.

When her aunt had died, the inheritance Mary had received had been relatively modest. She had been able to afford the prestige of a Notre Dame degree but little else, so she'd had to share an apartment with three other young women to cover housing costs.

The bartender leaned against his side of the bar and talked about school while she polished off her salad. She kept one shoulder hunched against the intrusion of his admiring presence, as her gaze returned again and again to his moving mouth. Those strong, bleached teeth would make quite a bite impression.

She had treated a bite victim last week. It had been a human bite, not animal. Each tooth mark had made a distinct puncture. Dots of blood had welled from the tiny wounds. After dressing it, she had given the victim a tetanus shot and a round of antibiotics. Nasty things, human bites.

Her burger and fries seemed to take forever to arrive. At last the bartender took away her empty salad plate, brought her the burger platter and moved down the bar to serve someone else. She tore into her burger with the same single-mindedness she had shown for the salad, chewing while she sprinkled catsup on her French fries.

Then she caught sight of the bite she had taken out of the burger. The beef patty oozed pinkish juice. She looked at the bright red sprinkled across the fries, and the food in her mouth transformed into a rock as her ravenous hunger fled as abruptly as it had appeared. She fought to swallow, gagged and gulped more Coke to shift the clump down her throat.

The early evening news caught her attention and she

looked up. The bar area was noisier than she thought it would be, and the TV's volume was turned low. The channel was set on a news show that was more sensational than she preferred, so she didn't think she was missing much.

She glanced up a couple of times as she struggled to eat a few more bites. She was unable to hear the news anchor's voice-over, so she had no warning. From one glance to the next, the scene changed. When she looked up, she found herself staring at a broadcast being filmed live from her neighborhood in St. Joe.

They were filming her house.

It was on fire. Flames poured out of the windows.

The HDTV swam in her vision. She coughed food.

"Hey," said the bartender. He moved back toward her. "Are you all right?"

She waved her hand toward the television and wheezed, "Turn it up. That's my house."

"What?" He glanced up. "You're shitting me. Hold on."

He searched for the remote while Mary stared at the scene of trucks, firefighters and flames that shot out of every window of her ivory tower. The bartender found the remote and punched the volume up in time to catch the end of the news segment.

". . . A neighbor called it in just after three o'clock this afternoon. No one knows yet if the owner was inside. Officials say that they should have the fire out before dark. It might be well into tomorrow before what's left of the home is cool enough to inspect. There'll be more live coverage tonight. . . ."

Mary's pulse pounded so hard she could hear it in her ears. She put a hand to her mouth, to her forehead. The bartender, his young handsome face concerned, leaned toward her. His lips moved around those sharp white teeth. He seemed to be asking if she was all right.

"No, I'm not all right," she said. She gave him an incredulous look and flung out one hand in the direction of the television. "That's my *house*."

"There wasn't anybody at home, was there?" he asked.

"What?" She looked from him to her plate full of greasy food. Back to him again. Already in knots, her stomach lurched. The film clip had shown the blaze roaring out of every window and door. Even if the firefighters were able to put the fire out right after the broadcast, her work, the quilts, the paintings, her clothes, the few mementoes she had from her childhood, everything would be gone. "No. No, nobody was home, I live there alone. No pets. Just me in my house. And all of my things. Everything. Everything I own."

Mary and the young man stared at each other. The thick sticky film of shock began to evaporate, leaving raw incredulity behind.

This was a bad joke, she thought. Right? This was the beginning of an Arnold Schwarzenegger movie, like the one where the chick sits in a bar and finds out she's being hunted by a psychotic maniac, only he's not a psycho but a cyborg who sounded like he had a speech impediment, and he can't say her name right.

Right?

"I'm getting you a drink. On the house," said the bartender. He winced. "Shit. No pun intended . . . you just look like you could use a bit of brandy or something. I'll be right back. My God." He patted the air between them with both hands as if it might fix something, or mean anything, and he rushed away.

Mary watched him go. She knew what she was doing—she was having a Sarah Connor moment. Only this wasn't quite like an Arnold Schwarzenegger movie. It was a cross between an Arnold movie and *The Sixth Sense*. She was having a Sarah Connor moment, and she saw dead people. Mother Mary or Mother Teresa, or whoever the hell she had seen in her vision, told her she couldn't go home and she was in danger. Then she found her house burning on *Live at Five*.

Just because you're paranoid . . .

Several feet away, the bartender poured coffee into a cup and tilted some brandy into it. He waved another waiter over and spoke to him. They both looked at her.

Her ricocheting thoughts continued. In the Arnold movie, the cyborg went to Sarah Connor's apartment.

She knew she was mentally babbling, but it was an urgent babble because there was someplace she was supposed to get to, she could feel it, some appalled realization bubbling up out of the toxic sludge of her shock. She didn't want to deal with it but she had to.

Because in the movie Arnold the cyborg went to Sarah Connor's apartment.

Sarah wasn't there but her roommate and her roommate's boyfriend were. They died a horrible death.

And a neighbor called in the fire just after three o'clock.

Justin had said that he would come to pick her up around two thirty. She hadn't been home, but he wouldn't have left right away.

He was such a stubborn mule. He would have waited to see if she was late getting back from running errands. He would have stayed and stewed, paced and bitten his nails, and then he would have used his copy of her house key to let himself in.

Only when he was quite sure they couldn't make the appointment would he have given up and called Tony's office to apologize and say they were going to be late. Or maybe he would have said they were not coming at all that day and would have to reschedule.

But he would have been there.

She hadn't brought her cell phone, because she hadn't wanted to pick up a call from work. She lunged off her chair and grabbed her purse. The bartender hurried over to her with the brandy-laced coffee. She said, "Your pay phones."

He told her, pointing. She raced to the phone mounted on the wall near the restrooms and dug in her purse for coins. She didn't have enough for the long-distance call. She raced back to the bar and slapped down a ten-dollar bill. "Quarters."

"Right." He opened the cash drawer and handed her a roll. She raced back to the phone and fed it quarters until it let her place her call.

"Pick up and be mad at me, you dumb jerk," she muttered as she dialed his cell phone number. "Come on."

His phone didn't ring. Instead she heard his voice mail message right away, which meant that his phone was turned off. Maybe it was recharging.

Or burned? Was his cell phone destroyed?

She hissed and slammed the receiver back on the hook. She made a gigantic effort to think with some rationality. Somehow she had to shake off the feeling that some trickster god had turned into a graffiti artist and had tagged her with the message LIGHTNING STRIKE HERE, spray-painted on her forehead.

Who would want to harm her, or burn down her house, or possibly hurt Justin if he was inside? Nobody, that's who. She could think of a few people who probably disliked her in some mild way, but nobody who would burn down her *house*. That was insane.

Kind of like seeing a vision at the Notre Dame Grotto that told her she was in danger and she couldn't go home.

Yeah, that kind of insane.

She tried to think of anything that could explain the day's events in a reasonable manner and slammed into a mental wall. She knew she hadn't started the fire by accident. When she had been a teen, she had burned her arm on a clothes iron that her aunt had forgotten to unplug. As a result she double-checked everything to make sure she had turned off machines after she used them. When she was overstressed, sometimes she triple-checked appliances and the oven, which was actually another thing she should put on her fix-it list.

Who was it that had said when you have exhausted all possible explanations, you should next try the impossible?

She couldn't remember, although she was pretty sure it hadn't been Van Gogh.

She walked back to the bar and slipped into her chair. The bartender—Danny, she saw on his name tag—came over as soon as he saw she had returned. "A brandied coffee," he said as he pushed the mug toward her. "Did you make your calls all right?"

She shook her head, wrapping her fingers around the mug. "I couldn't get through. Thank you."

"The manager is going to stop by to see how you're doing," Danny said.

"That's kind." She tried a sip of the coffee and grimaced. The nasty-tasting liquid slithered down her throat to confront her already queasy stomach.

He handed her a sugar packet and a spoon. "Hey. Your house burned down. It's the least we can do. Can you finish any of your food?" She looked at the plate of cold greasy food and shook her head. "And you wanted it so much too. Want me to put it in a carryout container for you?" She shook her head harder. "Okay. You know, you look a little glazed. Why don't you just drink your coffee and take your time? Don't worry, I didn't put that much brandy in the coffee, but still—don't go anywhere until you feel steady enough to drive, okay?"

"Sure. I should call the authorities and tell them I'm alive." And tell them about Justin? Tell them what? That she had a vision, and thought of the film *The Terminator* and now she was worried about her ex-husband? She crossed her arms on the bar, put her head on them and groaned.

Someone farther down the bar called out. Danny turned toward him. "Hold on, I'll be right with you!" He looked back at her. "Look, it's just my opinion, but you know the authorities are still going to be available in twenty or thirty minutes. Take your time and let yourself deal with the shock."

She said, "Makes sense. Thank you, Donny."

"Uh, it's Danny."

"Right. Sorry." Those damn teeth.

"And you're welcome. Let me know if you need anything else."

Mary sipped at her brandied coffee until she felt the caffeine and sugar add a fresh spike to her bloodstream. She was borrowing energy against an inevitable crash, but there wasn't any other alternative. Her day had just become thirty times longer after watching *Live at Five*.

The restaurant manager came over, profuse with brisk concern and platitudes, but Mary didn't warm to the other woman. She could tell the manager was acting out of professional obligation and would rather be doing other things. Mary killed two birds with one stone and got rid of her by asking if the other woman would call the St. Joe police to tell them she was alive, if somewhat in shock, and she would be in touch with them soon.

Danny came and refilled her coffee. She thanked him, elbows on the bar, head in her hands.

Okay, she thought. She had to get at least a temporary grip.

What did she know?

She knew she was an intelligent woman. Her experiences were interacting with the outside world. Okay, so the incident with the dancing sticks and twigs from early this morning was pretty iffy, but her house really was on fire. She didn't know what it meant, but things were not just happening inside her head.

Psychic phenomena have been the stuff of myth and legend for millennia. She knew that for the last hundred years people had claimed to have experienced visions and have their prayers answered in the Grotto.

That was why she had gone there today. Even though she was not very religious, she had wanted to throw out a prayer. You know, just in case God did exist and would like to lend her a hand.

She wanted some answers. She couldn't very well complain when she started to get some, could she?

Maybe she lived in Gretchen's world after all.

The scientist in her tried to kick that thought out of her head. She frowned and held on to it.

Maybe . . . maybe all those years of med school were why she had started to doubt her own sanity in the first place. Maybe she was quite sane (there's a thought), and she just hadn't yet found the right explanation for everything that was happening. The doctor in her wanted clinical proof and scientific explanations, and maybe she wasn't going to get any.

For the last several years she had been trying to play by someone else's rules, and she felt more sick and unsure of herself than she had ever felt in her life.

"My dreams are real," she whispered.

In spite of the fact that she was worried about Justin and had lost everything she had in the world, a corner of her mouth lifted.

Where did she go from here? She should talk to Gretchen again. She needed to ask more questions, about the woman she saw in her vision and how weird she felt afterward, and what the hell was going on with her vision.

Maybe the Lady didn't say what Mary thought she had said.

Maybe Mary was in danger if she had tried to go home?

Maybe she would have been in danger if she had been home? The house might have caught fire from some bad electrical wiring, or even from vandalism.

In any case there was no reason for her to create a grand pattern out of everything. And Justin was fine. It was broad daylight. He would have been awake and alert, not asleep and in danger of smoke inhalation. He was pissed and he went back to work, so he turned his cell phone off. As for her, she needed to take things one step at a time and chill. Of course her vision had wonked out. She was chronically sleep-deprived.

She would need a week off to sort out her life. No other way around it. Maybe she would need two weeks. She had to deal with the insurance company and find a place to stay, buy clothes and essentials like toiletries. While she was dealing with all of that, she would get a script for Ambien, get some real sleep and reboot.

She started to feel almost cheerful, which was actually not too bad for someone whose life was in complete upheaval and who had lost everything she owned, aside from her car and what money she had in the bank. She waved Danny over. "I'm ready to leave now. Can you give me my check?"

"Forget it," he said. "You're good."

"But I ordered a lot," she said.

"You ate, what, three bites of your meal?"

"I had the salad, and the Coke and the coffee. . . ."

He leaned toward her. "I cleared it with the manager.

Like I said, you're good. She also told me to tell you that she called the police for you too. They're waiting to hear from you. Go do what you need to do."

"Thank you." She picked up her purse and slipped off the barstool.

As she pushed outside, she passed a group of people going in. She paused to take in a deep breath of fresh air, grateful to be away from the hot, noisy interior. As nice as the staff had been, she didn't think she'd ever eat at another Friday's again.

The sun was setting. The sky was lavender and gold, the edges near the horizon deepening to purple. She looked around with care. The Van Gogh effect was still present, but it wasn't as pronounced as it had been earlier in the afternoon. She lifted her face to a slight cool breeze.

It curled around her neck and kept circling, a jerky agitation of air.

She stopped breathing. She started to raise a hand to her neck and froze, not daring to move. Something was swirling around her upper torso but there was no weight or solidity to it. It felt as though she was wrapped in a puff of wind.

Then she heard a voice inside her head. *Danger.*

Seriously. Inside her head.

"Yes?" she whispered on a bare thread of sound. Her whole body tingled. "I know. I—Is it okay if I breathe?"

But then she had to. Stunned and feeling ridiculous, she clapped a hand over her mouth as she drew in air through her nose, as if that might help her to avoid breathing in whatever it was that swirled around her.

Must stay with you, keep you safe.

Gretchen had said that she had sensed someone was with Mary. Could this be BabyMama Two? She asked, "Who are you and how long have you been there? Were you in the car with me earlier?"

DANGER!

"Yes, I saw the news," she whispered. Could this creature or spirit understand television, or care? "I know my house is burning."

A couple approached the restaurant. Mary caught a sidelong glance from the woman as they passed. She started to walk again toward the parking lot.

The air grew more agitated. *Not there. Here and now!*

How can that be?

She rounded the corner of the building to the parking lot.

Two men approached. They were fit and tanned, in their thirties or forties. One wore a light jacket and jeans. The other wore khaki pants and a sport coat. Both were smiling. Preoccupied, she gave them the barest glance.

Something odd and subtle caught her attention. She lifted her head with a frown.

RUN! the presence screamed.

She jerked to a halt, caught between trying to make sense of what her small voice said, and—what was so odd about those men?

Purposeful and bland, they strode forward.

Toward her, not the restaurant doors. She took a step back, then another.

Then she figured out what was so different about them. Her eyes widened.

The edges of the men's bodies weren't glowing with that strange Van Gogh effect, as was virtually everything else. Instead they were surrounded by a dull smudge of darkness. Wrongness snapped at her with invisible fangs.

One of them called out with a smile. "Dr. Byrne?"

He reached inside his jacket.

Alarm jolted through her. She whirled to lunge back around the corner. She heard footsteps running after her. They didn't say anything further. That frightened her more. It frightened her badly.

She barreled into a family of four as they stepped outside the restaurant doors, a father and mother, a boy around eleven and an older woman. All were varying shades of blond. Mary's knees weakened with relief even as both she and the older woman staggered. The man grabbed their arms to keep them from falling. The wife yanked her son out of the way.

"Careful," the man said. "Are you two all right?"

The older woman shook free. She snapped at Mary, "You're going too fast."

"I'm sorry." Words tumbled out of her. "Two men are chasing me."

"Chasing you," said the older woman.

"I beg your pardon?" said the younger woman, who looked around with incredulity. "Here?"

Mary knew how the woman felt. Whoever those men were, they wouldn't do anything here at the front of the restaurant, not with the family as witnesses and all the cars whizzing by on Grape Road.

It was too public.

Just like Dairy Queen had been yesterday.

Fuck.

She knew when the two men rounded the corner. She felt their presence as a prickle along the back of her neck. She and the others turned to look at them.

"Let's go back inside, Christine," the husband said, putting an arm around his wife. "Just until this is sorted out. Right now."

Mary reached for the nearest door handle. Even as she jolted into movement again, she knew she was moving too slow.

She heard flat, popping noises and turned her head.

Crimson exploded in the middle of the man's forehead. The young woman Christine opened hazel eyes wide in surprise as she began a slow, graceful, downward pirouette. A spray of ruby stars appeared on the boy's soccer league T-shirt. The boy looked down and fingered one of the stars as his knees collapsed. The older woman's jaw shattered, bone and tissue flying.

Liquid warmth splashed over Mary's face and torso.

She knew that warm wetness well. Red was an important color to her. Four people toppled to the pavement like mown flowers.

"No," she said. She opened her mouth wide. Someone started to scream. She thought it might be her.

Her invisible presence screamed with her. *RUN RUN RUN!*

Still smiling, the man in the sports coat lunged at her and clamped a hand around her arm. The other looked around with a sharp gaze while he tucked his gun and silencer back inside his jacket.

She dragged hard against the fingers that dug into her flesh, still screaming.

"Come with us now, Mary," Sport Coat said. "You don't want any more people to get shot, do you? We'll kill everybody in the restaurant if we have to."

"Not that we'd mind," Spring Jacket added. "We like to kill."

But her body couldn't be reasoned with, or ordered to obey. It had a mind of its own and convulsed into wild struggles. Spring Jacket stepped over the bodies of the family to reach for her other arm.

She was a small, underweight woman. Both men had at least sixty pounds on her. Even as she bucked and heaved against the hard hands that sought to subdue her, her mind was a different engine that ran on its own track.

They didn't shoot me. They recognized my face. They called me by name. They want me for something.

What do they want from me?

Then she twisted into Spring Jacket's body and brought one knee up hard between his legs. As he groaned and doubled over, she jerked her arm free to stab at Sport Coat's eyes with stiffened fingers. He caught her wrist before she hit his face.

Sport Coat spun her around until she faced away from him. He forced both of her arms behind her back. She knew she was in serious trouble even as she tried to kick Spring Jacket in the head. He ducked to the side, and she missed.

With a grunt Spring Jacket stood upright. He backhanded her. Her head snapped from the blow. She bit her tongue so hard blood spurted in her mouth. Then she had to stop screaming because she started to choke.

"I'll pay you back more when we've got time," he said. She spat a mouthful of blood in his face. He wiped it off with a sleeve. "Keep it up, bitch. I'm running a tab."

Neither man had lost his empty mannequin smile. The four murders and the fight had taken less than a minute.

A short distance away, cars shot down a busy five-lane highway. She willed them to keep moving so that no one else got shot.

Even if someone noticed the fight and called 911, it wouldn't do her any good. The men picked her up, one at her torso and the other at her legs. They jogged with her toward a dark unmarked van.

That van was the embodiment of every kidnapping nightmare.

She couldn't go in there.

She was as good as dead if they got her in that van.

She bucked and kicked as hard as she could, and she barely made them stagger.

Panic enveloped her, a pure bolt that was as sharp and cold as a scalpel of ice slicing open a vein. It was followed by a blinding wave of white heat that filled her mind and body. A roaring madness took over the world.

She was aware, as if from a great distance, that both men had started to curse. They dropped her. She hit the ground hard and tried to roll into a ball. The roar of white noise filled her body and mind then began to recede.

She was being rolled on the ground, wrapped up in something.

Voices:

"Hurry up, goddamn it. Cover her legs with your jacket."

"I'm going as fast as I can. What the hell did she just do? Somehow she fucking burned my hands."

"I got burned too, ass-wipe, and I've got her shoulders covered. Come ON!"

The sound of a door sliding open. She stirred. Rough hands slid under her shoulders and legs. She opened her eyes. Felt herself being lifted. Looked up into two smiling mannequin faces. Liquid spilled out of her mouth.

A hawk with splayed talons plummeted out of the jewel-toned sky. It raked Spring Jacket's head from nape to crown, slashing him open to the bone. Wetness sprayed her again. The man rocked forward from the blow. He dropped her legs.

Spring Jacket wobbled and turned toward what hit him. A second hawk dove for Sport Coat's face. One of his eyes split like a grape under the slash of its talons. He lost his hold on her shoulders. She hit cement hard a second time. She would have whimpered if she'd had any breath. She managed to roll several times before she dared to lift her head.

Both men were bent at the waist, covered with dozens of attacking hawks. They beat at the air and slapped at the birds. Red streaked their flailing figures. One pulled his gun and fired blind. A few birds dropped to the ground. A dozen more took their place.

She struggled to her hands and knees but didn't dare rise to her feet, for a shrieking cloud of raptors wheeled and dove in the parking lot. Red-tailed hawks, rough-legged hawks, turkey vultures, Cooper's hawks, falcons, goshawks, harriers.

Calm descended on her for the space of one pulse beat.

She was not on earth. She was somewhere else where things like this could happen.

A breeze whipped around her damp neck, and that small voice said, *They die for you. Don't waste their sacrifice. Run!*

She ducked her head to crawl away from the battle. Gravel bit into the heels of her palms and her knees. Her hearing was filled with the sound of her harsh wet breathing.

Car. Keys. Purse. Where's the damn purse?

She had been carrying her purse by its strap. She had dropped it somewhere when she had been attacked. She crawled toward the front of the restaurant, searching the ground of the parking lot as she went.

She had to go back around the corner of the building. Her purse was lying close to the woman named Christine, near the dead woman's outflung arm.

She touched Christine's still-warm fingers and said in a harsh croak, "If your spirit is still here, I'm so sorry. I don't understand why this happened. I would have done everything I could to avoid your family if I'd known."

She snatched up her purse, struggled to her feet and ran, bent over, back around the corner and down the line of parked cars until she reached her Toyota.

Scrape, fumble.

Get the damn key in the lock. There.

She yanked at the door and fell into the car. Locked the door. Started the engine.

It stalled. A sob broke out of her. She tried again.

The engine roared. She jerked the stick shift into reverse, misjudged the distance and clipped an SUV as she pulled out.

Thunk!

Something hit her trunk. She screamed and twisted at the waist to look out the rear window. A blood-covered figure pushed off of the trunk of her car and fumbled along the driver's side toward her door, one arm curled over his head while shrieking birds continued to dive and rip his skin to ribbons. His raw, red flesh was unrecognizable as a face.

She screamed again, yanked her car into first gear and slammed down on the gas pedal. With a squeal of tortured tires, the Toyota shot away.

Chapter Eight

THE IMMACULATE INTERIOR of the back of the limousine was just as it should be, luxurious and contained. The man liked to have his environment comfortable and controlled. It brought him a sense of calm and peace, which allowed him to focus on his work.

The seats were made from butter-soft Italian leather. There was a small but perfectly stocked wet bar that included champagne and several bottles of a 1999 Royal DeMaria Riesling Icewine. The fridge was stocked with petit fours; smoked salmon pâté and organic whole grain crackers; boiled quail's eggs with a lemon-mayonnaise dip; melon balls made from honeydew, cantaloupe and watermelon; and several different kinds of fresh sushi. There was also a flat-screen HDTV that he kept on mute, perpetually tuned to CNN.

The man divided his attention between watching the ticker tape headlines running along the bottom of the screen and the spring scenery that scrolled past his windows.

His cell phone rang. It was one of his employees, and this was a phone call that he had been waiting for, so he answered and listened. "You're quite sure that he's dead? And it can't be traced back to you? Excellent. Thank the Senator for his help. Tell him that I too am looking forward to a mutually beneficial future." The man smiled out at the bright spring day. He asked his companion, "Do you play chess?"

"What?"

"Forgive me," the man said. "I thought I said that quite clearly. Do. You. Play. Chess."

"No, I do not fucking play fucking chess."

"Do you know anything about the game?"

"For Christ's sake, who cares?"

"Manners." The man kept his voice mild, but his gaze turned into spears of ice. "I do, and you would do well to remember that I am driving this conversation."

A pause. His companion said, "I only know the basic moves, and nothing at all about the maneuvers or strategies. I know just enough about the game to know that's like labeling primary colors to a master painter like Renoir."

The man was somewhat mollified. He relaxed back in his seat and chose, for the time being, to ignore his companion's truculent attitude. "Nicely put. Chess has been called the game of kings, you know, as it was deemed a worthy occupation for sovereigns."

"I presume you are driving this conversation to somewhere specific."

The man said, "Then there is the analogy as well. Politics is like a game of chess. There are the pieces, and then there are the players. Dorothy Dunnett, a well-known Scottish novelist, used the analogy in a series of historical novels filled with political intrigue. Have you read her work?"

"No." His companion closed his eyes, his expression indifferent.

"You should pay attention," the man said, his tone flat. "I am telling you the most important thing you have heard in your life."

His companion took a deep breath then opened his eyes and looked at him. "Fine. Do go on."

The man said, "There is another game beyond the game of kings. It is a shadow game, and it has been played for millennia behind the panoply of human things. Like politics, the board and the pieces of the shadow game have shifted and changed through time, but in this game, the players have remained the same. I have just removed a piece from the game. We should call him a bishop. Like any chess piece he could only make certain moves, but they were damn good ones. I'll give him that for his epitaph."

"You had a man killed because of a game in your head."

"No, I had a man killed because he could sense changes in spirit as he stood near his king and worked to protect him. With this man out of the way, I now have much more leisure and opportunity to take the king. All it will take is the highest-level security clearance, the right time and place and a handshake, and when I do it, it will strengthen my position in the game tenfold."

"Oh I see. So basically you had a man killed because of a game in your head. I suppose I could congratulate you," said his companion. "But I won't."

"Indeed," said the man. The corner of his mouth twitched. "The fact of the victory will have to be congratulations enough."

The ancient game, so long played, was coming to a head. There had been many peaks and valleys over the years, intense maneuvering and vicious skirmishes followed by periods of quiet and a wintering of conflict. Dared he hope they were at long last heading into the endgame?

The man remembered his first years on earth, that giddy rush of exhilaration he had felt after having been imprisoned for so long. He had been free at last and this whole world lay before him like a virgin with her thighs spread wide.

He had to admit it might have gone to his head a little.

He had not been a happy camper when he had found that a group of his people had followed him to earth. That first conflict . . . A frown marred his handsome brow. He didn't like to remember it.

It had begun so well, his first life in this place. He had lived in a golden land, and his childhood had been one long ascendant journey to self-discovery. He had been born to rule, not by birth but by ability, and by right, and he had taken that golden land of Babylon and made it his own. He became king and imposed his law, his order, enacting his own manifest destiny.

The group that had followed him had been fresh and at full strength, in the morning of their first birth into this world. They had just recovered their full memories from their earlier lives, and they had acted in concert to take him by surprise. Barely escaping with his life, he had been forced to go into hiding deep underground in the dark, airless catacombs of his city.

One of his enemies at the time had written: *How the oppressor has ceased! How his insolence has ceased! . . . How you are fallen from heaven, O Day Star, son of Dawn! How you are cut down to the ground, you who laid the nations low!*

But you are brought down to Sheol, to the depths of the Pit. Those who see you will stare at you, and ponder over you: Is this the man who made the earth tremble, who shook kingdoms, who made the world like a desert and overthrew its cities, who would not let his prisoners go home?

The author of that histrionic piece had been a stinking prophet with the burned gaze of the mad. He had come from an aggrieved and superstitious desert people that had been comprised of twelve tribes.

They had been too ignorant to realize the value of what he had brought to his kingdom, or the value of what he could have given to them, the education and learning, the technology and the civilization. They preferred to wallow in the heat and dust, and to plunge into constant petty wars as they worshipped their angry, vengeful God.

It had taken the man a long time to heal from the wounds he had gotten in that first battle on this world. But he had, and he could not forget, and he did not forgive. Among his many other projects and hobbies, he had made it his mission to hunt down the group who pursued him, and to destroy them. In fact, in that endeavor, he had enjoyed some degree of success.

The old bitch, though. He shook his head as he straightened his tie. She was a pistol. She'd gotten mighty dexterous at avoiding him throughout the centuries. But he had one huge advantage over the group that had come after him. He did not have their code of ethics. He had no ethics whatsoever that would hold him back from using his special talents in whatever way he wished.

The folks from home had liked to call him an aberration. He preferred to think of himself as unique. It had a much more positive spin.

As a result he was as strong and fresh today as a man in his prime, with all memories intact and all grudges well-nurtured. From what hints he'd been able to glean from the psychic realm, the old woman had let herself become frail as well as elderly. That wasn't the brightest of ideas when involved in a long-term war such as theirs.

Over the ages he had accumulated an awful lot of grudges against her.

Triumphing over her was going to be downright orgasmic.

But first things first.

About that chess piece he'd just removed. The bishop. Nicholas Crow had been too educated for a normal human, too much of an adept in things that most people knew nothing about. The old bitch had scattered her teachings like a virus throughout the first nations, so it was actually possible that Crow had been taught what he had known by a native elder.

But he had to wonder. Perhaps the old bitch herself had trained Crow. If so, the man might find a trail of breadcrumbs in Crow's past that would be advantageous for him to follow.

However, the very next thing the man needed to do was hunt down Dr. Mary Byrne, who had turned out to be a rather surprisingly slippery fish. And loud. Her psychic energy was blazing like a comet. At the rate she was going, she'd be a burned-out husk in a day or two. That was not the preferable option of events.

He had to find Mary fast if he hoped to get anything useful out of her. Just out of curiosity, he also wanted to find out what had happened to his two drones. They had almost gotten her, but then he had lost his connection with them.

Now he couldn't make psychic contact with either one. Neither was answering his cell, so the man had to assume for the moment that they had somehow been destroyed.

Also, the police reports he received about what had happened in Mishawaka were preliminary and confused, but rather interestingly freakish. He needed to get a more accurate account of what had happened, so he could determine what forces had been involved and decide what to do next.

He knew one thing for certain. Mary Byrne was acting in an unpredictable manner. Keeping track of her comet blaze in the psychic realm wasn't much of a problem, but actually catching her in the physical realm was going to be more of a challenge, which was why he relaxed in the back of his limousine while his driver took him toward northern Indiana.

Old adages became adages in part because they were true. If he wanted something this important to be done right, he was going to have to do it himself.

"Enough about me," he said to his companion. "Tell me about yourself. How are your teeth? Healthy? They look good."

His companion sat in the seat opposite him, a handsome dark-haired young male with a clever, narrow face. The male had been bound with expert care to ensure his captivity but minimize bruising and stress on the joints.

"Fuck you," the male hissed.

Oh dear. He was too bored to roll his eyes. He just could not get a decent conversation off the ground with this one.

He straightened the cuffs of his suit jacket. "Yes well, we don't have time for that. Tell me about your medical history. You look like you work out. Do you have cancer, a congenital defect, or a heart condition? How about an infectious disease?"

"You kidnapped me to talk about *chess* and my *medical history*?"

Yawn. "Very well. If you're not in the mood to talk about yourself, let's talk about your ex-wife, Mary. I want you to tell me everything you know about her."

"I'm not telling you a goddamn thing."

"That's what they all say, Justin. There have been so many of them over the years, and they have all been so very wrong."

Mary was another pistol. It had been simply ages since their last tête-à-tête. He missed talking to her. It was going to be a pleasure to get his hands on her again.

The sleek black car sped down the road, quiet as a bullet shot through a silencer.

Chapter Nine

SOMEHOW MARY MANAGED to pull away from the restaurant without clipping anybody else. In a crisis of shock and pain, her breathing erratic, she drove by rote until she found herself parked in front of a huge old Victorian house in an older tree-lined neighborhood close to Howard Park, near the St. Joseph River.

The house was more utilitarian than its sprawling gingerbread-trimmed neighbors. It was covered in beige aluminum siding, not painted, and fringed with sturdy plain white gutters. There were no perennials or shrubbery planted in its miniscule front lawn. It had been divided into apartments, and the backyard converted into an asphalt parking lot.

She had shared the upstairs apartment with three other women while attending Notre Dame. The rent had been cheap and there had been no cockroaches, so she had counted herself lucky although sometimes she had felt as if she would have been happy to sacrifice a limb for some privacy.

Muscle by muscle, she forced herself to unclench her death grip on the steering wheel. Then her body jerked as a new wave of dread hit. She twisted in her seat to search for any sign that she'd been followed or was being watched.

All she found were the peaceful sights and sounds of a quiet neighborhood settling into dusk. The adrenaline faded, to be replaced by bone-rattling tremors and the faint roil of nausea.

She was going to suffer from post-traumatic stress disorder over this day. She had earned it, she was planning for it and nobody was going to take it away from her.

What happened made no sense. Who would want to attack her? What was she running from?

How did those men know her name?

She didn't know anyone or anything. She certainly didn't own anything anymore. Nobody had whispered a mafia deathbed confession to her in the ER. The whole thing might be laughable except that four people were dead.

[struck, overpowered, carried to a black, unmarked van]

A wail built at the back of her throat. She clenched her teeth and swallowed the sound. If she started making noise, she might not stop. Worse, she would draw unwanted attention to herself.

[so many hawks, swirling like a storm in the jewel-toned sky]

She couldn't just sit here outside her old apartment. This street was too trafficked. Sooner or later someone would notice.

She inspected the abrasions on the heels of her hands and dismissed them as minor. Then she tilted the rearview mirror and checked the damage to her face, pressing light fingers along her swelling cheek and jaw. The damage wasn't too bad. If she were at the hospital she would order x-rays to check for bone fractures, but that would be just a precaution.

What hit her in the solar plexus, causing her mouth to wobble and eyes to blur, was the bright spray of drying blood that dotted her face and hair. She looked down. She was covered in other people's blood.

[flat, popping noises, the blossom of ruby stars on a child's T-shirt, and four people falling]

She pressed both hands to her sore mouth, panting, until the fresh wave of nausea had passed.

Oooh-kay. Okay. Usually she only dealt with that much blood in a medical facility where she was insulated with scrubs and the duties of her profession, and she wasn't clammy from shock.

She had to wash, but she couldn't walk into a public restroom looking the way she did. She looked around. The unopened bottle of water she had bought earlier lay in the passenger seat, where she had thrown it after the drive-thru. She also kept a first aid kit and a change of clothes in a gym bag in her trunk.

A block ahead of her, a car turned onto the street. Twin beams of light flashed across her face. The car approached at a slow pace. She twisted at the waist and bent down, drumming her fingers in a rapid tempo against the water bottle until the car had passed.

She had to move. Definitely.

She started the car and drove around to the back of the apartment house, and pulled into the parking lot. There was only one car parked in the slot closest to the house. A Dumpster squatted in the corner of the lot like a giant, bloated orange insect. She pulled the Toyota around and backed toward the Dumpster then popped the trunk.

Switching off the engine, she jumped out and limped to the back of the car as she glanced around. Dusk was deepening fast. The spring warmth from earlier that afternoon had fled, leaving behind a deepening chill. The windows from neighboring houses threw golden rectangles of light across the darkening backyards.

She didn't see or hear anybody outside.

Did that matter? Would she be able to hear anybody in time to avoid them? How paranoid should she be?

That woman in the Grotto said she had a powerful enemy.

She guessed that meant she should be pretty paranoid.

[We'll kill everybody in the restaurant if we have to. Not that we'd mind. We like to kill.]

Who talks like that? Nobody does.

She yanked her cotton sweater off and pulled it inside out, shivering as she inspected it under the dim light in the trunk. The only spot she could find that was not soiled was inside the back. She opened the bottle, splashed water on the material and scrubbed hard at her face, hands and arms, wetting the sweater as needed. While she worked to clean herself, she took a mouthful of water, rinsed her sore gums and tongue and spat out rusty liquid. Then she swiped at her braid with the ruined sweater, threw it in the Dumpster and yanked open the gym bag. A worn white T-shirt, a pair of jeans, underwear and old, blue canvas shoes were tucked inside.

Shaking from cold, she plunged her head and arms into the T-shirt. Did she need to ditch her jeans? She checked. The knees were wet with large, dark red patches.

[people toppling like mown flowers]

She must have crawled through blood to get to her purse. She didn't remember. She had been focused on the men, their guns, the hawks and her own terror.

The jeans joined her sweater in the Dumpster, and she hopped into the clean pair.

A small wind gusted into her face, and a thread of a voice said in her head, *Hurry.*

She froze. How could she have forgotten her daemon? She slammed the trunk, slid into the driver's seat and started the car again, letting the engine idle as she turned the heat on. Only then did she roll her window down partway.

The breeze blew in and bounced around the interior of the Toyota. Whatever it was, it seemed as upset as she.

Is there more danger? she asked. She locked her doors.

Not here. Not now. It swirled around her. It seemed as uneasy as she did about being motionless, but she could be projecting. If she followed her first impulse, she wouldn't stop running until she hit California. Then she would think very hard about getting on a boat.

But there's still danger, she said. *Close? Searching?*

Yes. We must leave.

Okay.

With her shock lessening so that she could more or less strategize, she said, *I need to go to the police.*

No!

Disappointment and fresh fear slammed her. *Why not?*

Her daemon didn't answer. Perhaps it didn't have the capacity to communicate the answer, or she didn't have the capacity to hear what it said. It continued to rotate in agitation around her so she turned her own thoughts to answering.

She didn't believe her house burned in a freak accident. Someone set fire to it. She didn't yet know why, so she set that aside for now.

If she had been followed from her house, those men would have taken her earlier in a much less public place—for instance when she sat outside Gretchen's house, or when she was alone in the Grotto. Nobody knew where she was, or where she would be next. They couldn't, because even she hadn't known. She had gone through her entire day on impulse and instinct.

How had they found her at Friday's?

The restaurant manager had done as she had asked, that's how, and had called the police. Whoever was looking for her either had contacts on the police force, or they could monitor police communications.

She blew out a shaky breath, more grateful for her small presence than she could say. Without it, she would be headed right now for the nearest police station.

Okay. No police. And visiting Gretchen again was out. She couldn't put the other woman in danger, no matter how much she wanted to see what the psychic would make of the hazardous Rubik's cube her life had become. For the same reason, she wouldn't be looking up old classmates in South Bend or coworkers in St. Joe, or go knocking uninvited on Justin and Tony's door.

A train wreck of a feeling clenched in her gut. Shit, she was more worried than ever about Justin.

Air caressed her cheek.

I know, she said to it. *I can't have a nervous breakdown in the parking lot. I'm a sitting duck here.*

The world had transformed into a weird mystery, and she was all alone in it except for a small puff of air that talked to her. It was such a quiet little voice, just something she heard in her head. For all she knew it was a splinter of her own overstressed personality.

If it was, it was smarter than the rest of her and had saved her life, probably more than once. It also seemed to be pretty clued in to what was going on, so she needed to pay sharp attention whenever it gave her any advice.

The thing was, she didn't think it was a piece of herself. Maybe if it had been just a small voice in her head, yeah sure, but it wasn't. Even now it plucked at strands of her hair and gusted against her swelling cheek as if patting the injury.

She whispered, "You've been with me all day, haven't you? I just wasn't aware that it was you I was hearing." The presence circled around her, like nothing so much as a small cat purring. She put a hand to her cheek. "Okay. As the Skipper might say to Gilligan, where to now, little buddy?"

North, her daemon said, flowing along her fingers in an insubstantial caress. *Go north. We must find the Grandmother.*

The vision at the Grotto had said Mary needed to travel north, but the woman hadn't looked anything like a grandmother. Mary chewed her lip as she thought back over the conversation. The woman had also warned her about danger and told her to take care.

Later in the restaurant she had tried to rewrite what had happened because she hadn't understood. While reasonable, that was a mistake that could have gotten her killed and had probably contributed to the murders of four innocent people.

She rubbed her eyes. She couldn't think about it right now. She had to channel Scarlett O'Hara, and think about that tomorrow.

Okay, she said to her only friend. *North it is. But I'm going to have a truckload of questions to ask when we find this Grandmother of yours.*

She put the car in gear and, her thoughts rambling through bits and pieces of TV and movie trivia, she pulled away from her old home.

Overhead, a couple of resting hawks took flight and followed.

* * *

HER GAS GAUGE hovered a millimeter over the red *E*. She had to stop and fill her tank. At least if she was being hunted, they already knew she was in town. A credit card trace wouldn't tell them anything new, and she could keep the cash she had for later. Thanks to the kindness of Gretchen and T.G.I. Friday's, she still had ninety-five dollars in cash.

What kind of response time would anybody have to tracing a Visa swipe? An hour? Half an hour? That had to depend, in part, on their resources and how close they were to the site of the transaction, and also on how secretive they had to be, because God only knew, the attack on her had been illegal six ways to Sunday.

Screw it. She didn't have a choice. She would have to go in with an agenda and get out fast.

She pulled into the first Marathon station she came to and leaped out, her abused muscles yelping in protest. She kept her head down as she shoved through one of the double doors and arrowed toward a restroom.

Once inside, she checked her appearance. She'd missed a couple of smears of blood. She threw handfuls of cold water over her face and neck, snatched paper towels from a dispenser and scrubbed herself dry.

The quick wash couldn't improve the looks of the hollow-eyed woman in the mirror with the lopsided, bruised face, but at least it removed the last visible traces of blood. When she was finished she strode through the convenience store, grabbing bottles of water, a large coffee, a tuna sandwich, a turkey sandwich, a chocolate bar, and a couple of bags of trail mix.

The cashier was a beanpole of a male around twenty years old. He held a cell phone between his jaw and one skinny shoulder and talked into it as he checked her items. She kept the bruised side of her face angled away from him, staring out the plate glass at the passing traffic as he swiped her card.

The countdown began.

While the kid bagged her items in transparent plastic, she pivoted and used the ATM machine opposite the cash register. She punched numbers to withdraw the limit as her heart rate picked up. The machine spat out green bills. She snatched at them, grabbed her bags and launched out the door.

Now that she was taking action, she found the focus she used in the ER. Her movements became smooth and efficient. She tossed the bags in the car, jammed the coffee cup into the driver's seat drink holder, slammed the gas nozzle into her gas tank and swiped her card again. As it processed she did a three-sixty.

All the traffic looked normal. A couple of cars pulled in and out of the gas station. The island where she stood was exposed by white halogen light. She imagined the barrel of a gun pointing at her from the shadows. There was no breeze.

Her card was approved. She cocked the nozzle, and the machine poured gas into her tank. Time bled out. She tracked it by the rhythmic pulse of the pump, which ran with excruciating slowness.

She wished she could try calling Justin again to see if he was all right, but all of her nerves were screaming at her to get on the move.

The pump clicked off, the sound overloud in the quiet evening. She nearly leaped out of her skin.

She had the gas tank capped and was in the driver's seat within the space of her next breath, and she forced herself to pull away from the gas station slow and smooth, like a normal customer. As soon as she was on the road she sped up.

Nothing could have induced her to go near the U.S. 31 Bypass or 31 Business North. They were too closely linked to the routes that led back to St. Joe. If someone was hunting her, those roads would be watched.

No doubt there were dozens of back roads that could also take her north, but she didn't know them, so she drove northeast, back toward Cleveland Road. She would take the 80 Toll Road East past Elkhart and turn north on Highway 131.

She'd driven that route before. The roads were fast, and she would be traveling in the opposite direction of St. Joe.

All her surviving material possessions were with her in the car. She had no other change of clothes. She had two hundred and ninety-five dollars in cash. After this, she wouldn't dare access her bank or credit accounts until she understood what was happening and, hopefully, was in some measure of safety again.

She had no idea where she was going, who was chasing her, why someone would try to kidnap her or why the attempt had been so violent. She was weaponless, she didn't know who she was supposed to find, or how, and she didn't understand the various psychic and/or strange phenomena she had experienced or witnessed that day. If she hadn't seen the cloud of attacking hawks for herself, she never would have believed it.

She rubbed at the back of her neck and sighed. That seemed to sum up her situation pretty well.

She reached the entrance to the Toll Road, rolled through a booth for a ticket, and pulled onto the highway. Then she stepped on the gas until she was traveling the speed limit. The last thing she wanted was to draw attention and get a speeding ticket.

Full darkness had descended. The sky was a latticework of thin clouds and clear starlight, hung over a dark, quiet countryside dotted with farmland and clustered lights from the occasional neighborhood. There was a half-moon. She glanced at the moon a few times to see if it was surrounded by the Van Gogh effect, but it was partly obscured by clouds so she couldn't tell. She gave up and concentrated on her driving instead.

She kept a back window cracked open. She was traveling at a speed that made the frigid wind knife through the interior but rather than close her window and perhaps trap her daemon outside, she turned up the heat. Welcome warmth blew over her damp hair. She sipped coffee and tried, as much as she was able, to let the tranquil scene soothe her jangled nerves.

She needed to regroup and gather her energy. It was difficult to do when she felt like someone had scraped her insides raw with the jagged edge of a grapefruit spoon. Whatever else happened next—and she truly could not imagine what that would be—she knew she was in for a long, hard night, and another long, hard day tomorrow.

Soon she reached the exit for Highway 131. She suffered a few bad moments as she pulled up to pay at the tollbooth. Her fingers were shaking as she handed money to the attendant, but the middle-aged man seemed bored and sleepy, and he hardly spared her a second glance.

Giddy with relief, she pulled up to the intersection and turned north. She made good time for a while as she passed through the small towns sprinkled throughout southern Michigan. Soon the highway broadened into four lanes. Then she picked up speed again, soaking up a fugitive sense of safety she felt at increasing the physical distance between her and South Bend.

Close to an hour later, she came to the outskirts of Kalamazoo and the traffic increased, and a horrified realization swept over her. I-94 was another fast highway. It hugged the southern part of Lake Michigan like a lover, curved north to St. Joe and then sliced due east across the width of Michigan.

It was a quick route, easy to drive. Someone could have traveled directly from St. Joe and already be in the Kalamazoo area, lying in wait for her arrival.

Wait. Did that even make sense? If she didn't have any idea where she was going, how could anybody else know? Was she panicking unnecessarily? The problem was, she didn't understand how they had found her in the first place.

Her attackers were somehow connected to the police, and she was vulnerable through the license plates on her car. But if someone had traced her that way, wouldn't they have already pulled her over? Or could somebody be following her even now? How could she tell in the dark?

She felt as if she had slammed into a guardrail doing ninety miles an hour. The lingering energy from caffeine and adrenaline drained out the soles of her feet, and her body began to shake. Her eyesight blurred, and she had to keep blinking hard to keep the heavy traffic in focus.

She didn't have a mind for this kind of existence. She glanced around, trying to spot any anomalies. All the traffic was traveling more or less at the same speed and going in the same direction. That's what people did on highways.

Her body reminded her that she'd been on the losing end of a fight and dropped to the pavement more than once. Her hands, wrists, arms and shoulders throbbed with a ferocious ache. Between the open window and the blowing heat and her own whirling senses, she couldn't sense whether or not she still had her airy presence.

"I can't go on any longer," she muttered. She flung out a question. *Daemon—are you there?*

I am here. Hang on a bit further, the small presence said.

At least that's what she thought it said.

Or maybe that's what she hoped it said.

She scrubbed at her face, turned off the heat and rolled down her window. The resultant chill sank into her bones and made her abused muscles ache even more, but at least it slapped her awake.

She reached the north side of Kalamazoo and passed the turn for a town named Alamo. A few miles north of that she passed the intersection for Highway 89. She was taking in hard breaths like a runner at the end of a marathon.

Then she truly couldn't do any more. If she didn't rest, she would pass out at the wheel. She looked for the next exit, took it and drove half blind until she reached a quiet side road. She slowed and turned, took the next road and turned again, until finally she found an obscure one-lane gravel road dark with overhanging tree limbs.

She pulled onto it.

Trees, darkness, the cold night air and the rustling sounds of unseen creatures surrounded her. She stopped the car and put it in park. The cold was so bitter it forced her to roll up her window, daemon or no daemon. Shivering in violent spasms, she tucked her jacket around her torso and huddled against the door. She had passed the point of balance long ago and couldn't unclench her rigid limbs. She felt as though she was bleeding out something essential, but she couldn't make it stop.

"I need help," she whispered.

Help help help.

The word went out from her in a gushing, rhythmic pulse.

She didn't fall asleep as much as plummet into a pit.

The pit didn't have a color. It was a wicked, lonesome black.

SHE WAS A daughter of one of the great houses in a city that sprawled like a lazy, tawny lion by the sea. Towers, minarets, domes and sails filled the horizon, all crowned by the gold and cerulean bowl of heaven.

The city was the center of civilization, turbulent with dust and heat and politics. The scent of spices, perfumes and rich foods mingled with the rank smell of animals and slaves. The cries of market hawkers were punctuated with the ululating call to prayer.

One of the five Pillars of Allah's faithful, the prayer that saved and sustained the world.

There is no God but God, and Muhammad is his messenger.

In a place where beauty proliferated, the people called her mother the Jewel of the City. They called her the Flower. She had thrived in a progressive court filled with musicians, architects, mathematicians, scientists, theologians and philosophers, physicians and magicians. Once she'd been considered an accomplished physician in her own right.

Now she lay in her bed, restless from dreaming of what once was, and what might have been. She never quite fell asleep and only sometimes managed to fully awaken.

Pain redefined the evening of her life and became her entire world, her lover, her friend, her enemy, her bedfellow, the child of her heartbeats, companion to her breath and her sovereign lord.

He came to her daily, and each time she would rouse.

He would raise her head with skilled hands and help her to drink the wine spiced with medicines and poppy. Then as she began to drift, he would unlace her stiff leather corset and open it wide. He would part the edges of the deep, jagged wound that ran from collarbone to pelvis. Abdominal organs lay exposed to his intent scrutiny. After probing the wound he would sprinkle magical powders into the crevices of her body and whisper words, or prayers, or incantations.

The sum of her existence had come down to this irreducible place. He knew her with a greater intimacy than did any of her family. She should have long since died from the wound, but his powers kept her alive.

As she endured the unendurable, he whispered to her how her family had abandoned hope. They had stopped searching for a miracle cure for her mysterious wound that would not heal. He whispered other dark things, a corrupt and insidious councilor sowing anxiety and fear at kingdom's fall. All the while he laced her tight in a perpetual bondage that held her torn body together and kept her spirit leashed to his hand.

Then he would leave and she would dream again, a bloodred petal drifting in twilight.

CRAMPED IN HER awkward position, her body aching, Mary surfaced from the black pit. She had a blurred impression of her car's interior, the edge of the steering wheel that dug into her hip, the lush purple and green of the dark forest. Her mouth was dry and her heart hammered, a rapid, skittish feeling. She groaned and struggled to find a better position.

Then she slid into another space.

She stood up, away from her body and out of the car, into the cool velvety colors of the forest at night. She felt light and airy. Looking back in the car, she pitied the young woman in the driver's seat whose abandoned body lay in an awkward huddle.

Mary held up her hands. She saw the shadow of tangled underbrush through her fingers.

She was like crystal.

She looked down at herself, or at least where her body should have been. She saw a transparent version of the woman that lay in the car, except in this version a jagged crack ran down the length of her torso. Light blazed like lava from the crack, illuminating the Toyota, the line of a tree, the gravel road. The crack didn't hurt. She almost poked curious fingers inside it, but an instinctive aversion made her stop.

A delicate cloud of lavender mist came to settle around her torso.

She caught her breath. *Daemon? Is that you?*

Yes. The lavender cloud swirled around her. *You must stop.*

Stop what? I don't know what you mean. She stretched, or perhaps she just pretended to, for her body was back in the car. Whatever she did, it felt as pleasurable and as expanding as a full-bodied stretch. She felt as if it was the first pain-free movement she'd had in days.

You are burning up. Her spirit companion turned in circles.

Am I? She glanced down at herself, at the crack in her torso that blazed like a sun. *I don't mean to be.*

Agitation. *You must find a way to stop.*

I don't know what I'm doing. Do you?

You're dying.

Goodness. She looked around. She didn't feel like she was dying. She had no idea dying could be so beautiful. *Okay,* she said. *What do I do to stop?*

The spirit wouldn't or couldn't answer. It twisted into endless, agitated knots.

She felt sorry for all the trouble she had caused it and started to apologize, but then it shot into the forest, disappearing so fast she couldn't tell where it had gone.

Saddened, she wondered if that was the last she would see of it, but then she realized that if she were dying, it wouldn't matter. She hoped her actual moment of death would be as painless and as pleasant as this. She experimented with walking, or pretending to walk. She loved the sensation of lightness and freedom.

Afrit.

The word popped into her mind, along with the memory of a mythology class she'd taken in high school.

Or was it afreet? She couldn't remember. Djinn. They were Middle Eastern mythological spirits of air, immortal, unpredictable, often mischievous and amoral, and not to be confused with angels or demons. That didn't seem like a fair way to describe her companion, which, if anything, seemed like an anxious, kind little thing. She preferred to think of it as a daemon, a supernatural being somewhere between a god and a human.

She heard a whisper of noise, a sound so slight that her physical ears would not have detected it.

She whirled. A wolf came out of the forest and took mincing steps toward her. Its head was lowered and its yellow eyes fixed on her—the crystalline, ethereal her and not the abandoned battered body in the car.

Oh, she said, or pretended to say, *aren't you gorgeous?*

Lady, the wolf said. *You called.*

Did I? She blinked. *I don't remember.*

Another wolf stepped out of the forest, then another, and then three more. Overcome with astonishment, she stared. What a lovely but incomprehensible dream. More wolves poured onto the gravel road. Soon her car was surrounded.

The one that had spoken was the largest and most powerfully built. It approached and sat near her transparent leg. It said, *You asked for help. We have come. We will do what we can to protect you.*

She flashed back to the cloud of hawks that had attacked her abductors. Some had fallen and hadn't risen again. *You mustn't try to help me*, she said. She looked around at the pack of wolves. They were so beautiful. *Don't risk yourselves. It isn't worth it. Apparently I'm already dying.*

The alpha wolf fixed its intelligent, lupine gaze on her. *Sister, we stay.*

Overcome by their generosity, she said, *My heart is full of gratitude.*

Only much later did she realize how stylized her words had been, as if they belonged to another place and another time.

Chapter Ten

THE PAIR OF hawks that followed Mary rode thermals high above the rolling landscape. They had hurtled in pursuit of the car as she turned east, falling back only after fresh hunters swooped in to take over the chase. If an ornithologist had been asked whether the aerial predators were capable of such a sophisticated tactical interaction, he or she would have laughed the questioner out of the room.

The hawks weren't finished with their task after they had been relieved by newcomers. Instead they winged west until they located a nondescript, battered blue Ford with a transplanted, meticulously maintained BMW engine.

Michael drove south on Interstate 94, which took him out of Wisconsin and along the outskirts of Chicago. As he wove through the crowded traffic, he rarely let the hybrid Ford's speed fall under a hundred miles an hour, even if it meant that he sometimes had to plunge onto the shoulder to pass snarls of slower vehicles. The pace was suicidal in the greater Chicago area and required absolute concentration and prescient reflexes.

While he drove he maintained a cloak of secrecy around the car, projecting a kind of psychic null-space, a void where the mind's eye preferred not to look. Troopers patrolling I-94 had radars flash with something inexplicable but their minds slipped away from the occurrence and they forgot it almost at once.

The man maintained minimal contact with his fellow hunters and companions, just enough to sense their presence without glancing away from the road, and to hear the simplest of messages. None had spoken after the first hawk had returned to make its presence known to him.

We have found her, it had said. *Follow.*

They came. They made contact.

It was enough. He followed.

All other questions and all other answers could be gleaned at a later time. If they lost her again, none of the questions or answers would matter, anyway.

As he drove, he thought back to another life and time, and another trip he had undertaken with almost the same desperation as this one. Another one of their group, Ariel, had been betrayed, captured by Burgundians and sold to the English.

She had begun that life as a peasant girl and fallen prey to the pitfalls their group faced as they grew to adulthood. Confused by her abilities and imperfect shards of returning memory, she became consumed by the voices she heard in her head. When Michael first made contact with her, she believed him to be a saint, and she laid claim to a holy vision. Even as a teen she had been a charismatic and formidable warrior, rousing the countryside to defeat their enemy both at Orleans and Patay.

Then their enemy's spies spread their poison well. Abandoned by her king, she had been tried for witchcraft and heresy by French clerics who worked in service to the English.

Spring in France had been a messy business that year. The roads to Rouen were churned to thick mud from the downpour of several days of rain. He remembered the heavy strike of hooves as his horse thundered along the treacherous route, and the stomach-churning sound of bone snapping.

He had roared with frustration as his horse went down and threw him from the saddle. He had been forced to slit the suffering beast's throat in the mud and the rain. And though he scoured every stable in search of another mount, and he had hurtled forward with every ounce of his considerable strength, he had arrived too late to prevent anything.

She should have been fine. He had told her to recant and keep quiet, to wait until he could break her out of prison, but their enemy had captured and tortured Uriel, her mate.

It had broken her. She had pleaded and demanded to be freed, had insisted the voices she heard in her head were real, and the frightened ecclesiastical court had burned her for it.

There had been no last-minute Hollywood appearance or rescue as the flames licked at the bottom of the woodpile. When he had arrived, there had been nothing left of her but the smear of ash and the memory of an outcry on the wind.

Thus was the sum of a noble life: loss and pain and defeat in a foreign place, and the strange, empty gift of sainthood almost five hundred years later, long past when she and her mate had been destroyed, and their real stories and original identities had been buried under the weight of human superstition and history.

Goddamn, he had forgotten how much he had loved that horse. He had raised it from a colt. It had given him everything it had, including its life.

Michael was forced to stop just past East Chicago to refill his depleted gas tank. The pause was agonizing.

Throughout the day as he traveled, the psychic realm rustled and whispered. Ethereal energies were more agitated than usual by the day's disturbances. Dark beings as well as lighter ones crossed the landscape at the edge of his awareness. Once something fled past him, sobbing inconsolably.

Through all of it, he could feel the woman's psychic presence radiating with uncontrollable force, a star blazing into a supernova before it died. Creatures attracted to such extremity moved with purpose and stealth toward her, hopeful for an easy kill.

Murder was a child's picture drawn in bright crayon

compared to the savagery he felt. In contrast to his current mood, his former state of rage had been pastel.

Night fell. His speed never lessened except once, briefly, to make the turn north. After an agony of waiting, his current feathered guide said, *Turn here*.

He was traveling at such a high speed that he shot past the exit. The Ford screeched onto the road's shoulder. He reversed and gunned the engine until he could take the ramp. Then he drove the side road with more care as he followed the terse commands, for he had to translate everything from a hawk's perception into information that he could use on the ground.

At last he cruised down a country lane. In the sweep of headlights a red-tailed hawk sat motionless on a low-lying limb of a huge oak. Huge golden eyes flared as the hawk turned its head and stared at his car. The oak tree grew beside a one-lane gravel drive.

He made the tight turn gently onto the gravel road. The forest was thick with night sounds, tangled underbrush and overhanging trees. His headlights picked up a dark parked Toyota yards ahead. At least thirty wolves surrounded the car. They rose to their feet and turned to face his vehicle with bared teeth. A few were half-grown pups.

He took a careful breath, put the Ford into park and killed the engine. Whatever he might have expected, it hadn't been this. He touched the nine-millimeter in his shoulder holster then opened his door and got out, leaving the car's headlights on.

Along with the quiet rush of chill spring air came the flutter of a small wind spirit. It batted around him like a trapped and bruised butterfly.

Dying, it said. *She's dying—*

Hush, he told it. He brushed it away gently with his mind.

The alpha wolf of the pack paced toward him. He stared down into the powerful male's steady gaze. The wolf said, *Warrior.*

He replied, *I will pass. Let me do so in peace. I do not want to hurt you.*

The alpha male said, *We have answered her call for help, and we have promised to protect.*

It was another loyal beast. His mouth tightened. *Your clan is an honorable one. Can you heal her as well, or save her life?*

The wolf remained silent.

I will pass, he repeated.

The alpha male turned to his pack. One by one the wolves moved out of his way. He walked to the Toyota and looked at the woman who curled in a crumpled heap in the driver's seat. She was small with a snarled braid, her shoulders two thin, vulnerable points under her jacket, but he couldn't make out any other details in the indirect light.

The old woman had taught him well. Staring down at the woman, he remembered the eight-year-old boy he had been. He thought of all the reasons that his old mentor had for being ready to kill him should it become necessary.

Those same reasons applied to this young woman.

He must be prepared to kill her if she wasn't salvageable.

Chapter Eleven

DRIFTING.

A bloodred petal in twilight.

She felt as empty and dry as a drained chalice. An abundant golden river flowed into her. Her parched soul soaked up the current. It was as strong and rich as burgundy wine, and as warm and nourishing as summer.

She surfaced from the black pit and became aware, as if from a great distance, of details around her. She was no longer hallucinating an out-of-body experience. Instead, she lay on the cold gravel between her Toyota and another parked car. Her body felt heavy and weak on the sharp rocks.

The unfamiliar car's headlights threw a slant of harsh illumination on the scene. A pack of wolves ringed the area. Someone knelt over her, dark head and broad shoulders silhouetted against the angled light. Large, heavy hands rested flat on her torso, one at her sternum and the other on her abdomen.

The car headlights seemed thin and white, and as dim as shadows, compared to the man who shone from within like the sun.

The golden river poured into her.

A powerful sense of recognition flooded her, along with an incandescent joy. She took a breath and sighed, an easy expanding movement, for the moment free from fear and pain. Moving one hand across the uneven gravel toward the man, she smiled with relief at waking up from the long dark.

"There you are," she said in a blurred voice to the radiant silhouette. "I've missed you so. I had the strangest dream. . . ."

Déjà vu swept over her, and her half-conscious mind groped after the feeling. Hadn't she said this before? Hadn't she said it many times as a small child, as she blinked up at her mother's bewildered, frightened face?

Mommy, I had the strangest dream.

I dreamed I was—

She slammed awake for real. The brilliant radiance faded.

An unknown man knelt over her, silhouetted against the headlights of a car. She looked from the strange man to the ring of watching wolves and knocked away the hands that rested on her torso. Quick as a cobra, he grabbed her wrists and pinned her to the ground. She strained against the restraint, her heels scrabbling for purchase on the loose rocks.

The man shook her once, then again, harder, as she continued to struggle. "Stop it," he ordered. His voice sounded harsh and rough as the rocks upon which she lay.

She was bewildered at the strange tricks her own mind played on her. She didn't recognize this man. She had never seen him before in her life.

He was not Spring Jacket or Sport Coat. He was someone different. Someone new, bigger. Stronger, more deadly.

She made a terrified sound, bent her head and tried to sink her teeth into one of those iron hands shackling her wrists.

With an agile twist the man avoided her bite. The world pitched as he heaved her body up and around. He was so strong and fast, panic surged all over again at how easily he manipulated her weight.

She kicked and clawed for his eyes but somehow ended up sitting between long, powerful jeans-clad legs, crushed back against the man's hard chest, her arms crossed in front of her while he held her wrists. She tried to butt her head back into his nose. He hugged her tight and buried his face in her neck.

She recognized the position. It was a safe restraint hold, and it was as effective as a straitjacket. The whiskery skin covering the man's jaw abraded her neck, but no matter how she yanked or struggled, she couldn't budge his long, tough body.

Finally, defeated, she stilled. Her blood pounded in her ears, her breathing serrated in the cold quiet night. Her captor's breathing was unruffled. Gradually she became aware of the wolves' sharp animal interest in the fight. She stared. The wolves, while a quieter presence, were as much of a bizarre image as the attacking hawks had been.

Hardly aware that she spoke aloud, she whispered, "I don't understand."

"Maybe now we can get somewhere," the man said. His voice was rough velvet in her ear, the proximity mimicking a loverlike intimacy.

She shrank as far away as his tight hold would allow. The sense of profound recognition still beat at her, along with an upsurge of revulsion at his unwelcome nearness. She *knew* that she had never heard his voice before. The contradictory impulses were so strong, she felt like she was going insane.

"If you fight me or try to get away, I will tie you up," the man said. "If you promise not to, I will let you go. If you break your promise, I tie you up and you stay tied up. No second chances."

If he tied her up she was helpless and as good as dead. If she was free at least she had choices, and a chance to get away. Of course she said, "I promise."

"Right," he grunted. She knew he didn't believe her, but he let her go anyway. She took the opportunity to scramble away from him, her shoes digging into the gravel until he warned her with three soft-spoken words. "That's far enough."

She'd only managed to get a couple of yards away, while her nerves screamed a chaotic, contradictory nonsense. She was still too close and needed to scramble farther away. But at the same time, she was too far away and needed to fling herself forward, into his arms.

And just as she had known about his voice, she knew that she had never seen his face before in her life.

INSANE INSANE INSANE.

The screaming in her head cut off abruptly as he raised himself up on one knee to strip off a battered jean jacket. He wore a gun in a shoulder holster. She froze.

[We'll kill everybody. Not that we'd mind. We like to kill.]

Her breathing sawed at the air. Nails ripped as her fingers dug into the gravel. She clutched handfuls of the rock, ready to throw them while her gaze darted around the edges of his body.

She could see no sign of the smudged black that had surrounded Spring Jacket and Sport Coat.

But she didn't even know what that meant.

The man flung his jacket at her. It settled over her head and shoulders. She dropped gravel to yank it off her head. A huge wolf padded over to her and sat down nearby. She froze and tried to control her jagged breathing. Her gaze slid sideways to the wolf then back at the man. The man was watching her with an intent gaze.

The harsh flood of light threw a mask of crags and hollows onto his face. Underneath the mask he was neither handsome nor ugly. He was not a young man, although he was still in his prime. His hair, cut military-short, was so dark it seemed black in the harsh light, and his eyes were colorless like moonstones.

She might have passed him on a busy street without a second glance, except for the lithe bulk of muscles that strained against his dark T-shirt and the taut material of his jeans, the piercing intelligence in those light eyes and the razor's edge of toughness he wore as comfortably as a second skin. He bore himself with a soldier's competent assurance.

He knelt on one knee as he faced her, the lines of his body strung as taut as a bow. Her gaze fell to the clenched fist resting on the upraised knee where broad scarred knuckles shone white. He looked ready to spring at her at the slightest provocation. Whoever he was, and whatever his motivations, this man was a whole different kind of danger than Spring Jacket and Sport Coat.

And he had that gun.

Her gaze left him again and traveled back to the wolf. The man and the wolf seemed to have something in common. At first she couldn't pinpoint what. Then she realized what it was. They were both looking at her with the same expression.

She became aware she was shivering only when the man gestured at the jacket she held and said, "Put it on."

Her shivering increased until uncontrollable tremors racketed through her body. She felt as hollow as a reed. After a frozen moment she shrugged into the jacket.

The material still held warmth from his body. It smelled like him, which set off the cacophony in her head again. Some part of her that felt horrifically starved wanted to bury her face in the material and inhale that clean, fresh male scent. At the same time, she wanted to tear it off and throw it screaming back in his face.

She struggled to find the soft calm voice she used to de-escalate violent situations in the ER. The only thing was, she wasn't sure which one of them needed to de-escalate. She managed to say, "Thank you."

He tilted his head, eyes narrowing. Then he rose with a light, fluid movement that made her recoil as her heart kicked. He must have decided that she was a pathetic flight risk, for he only moved to her car. He returned a moment later, the plastic bag from the convenience store held in one hand as he pocketed her keys with the other. After rummaging through the contents of the bag, he took one of the sandwiches then handed the bag to her.

She clutched the shopping bag then sat frozen. Shit, he took her keys.

He knelt near her again, tore open the wrapper on the sandwich and ate it in quick, strong bites. She watched every move he made out of the corner of her eye, her face half averted.

He nodded to the bag. “Eat something.”

She said, “I'd rather not.”

He frowned and shot a glance down her huddled figure. “Do it anyway. You need the calories, and it will help you warm up.”

Stung by his critical look, resentful that he was right and mindful of his greater strength and the gun, she dug out the second sandwich, opened the wrapping and snapped off a bite. As she tasted tuna, her stomach threatened to revolt. Then it settled and she managed to eat most of the sandwich until she caught sight of the wolf again.

She turned to look at the strong, powerfully muscled animal. The wolf's yellow impassive gaze regarded her. Obeying a half-formed impulse, she took the last corner of her sandwich and placed it with care on the ground between them.

He held her gaze for a long moment. Then with slow deliberation and a remarkable delicacy, he bent his head and ate the offering. The strange man watched the interaction with an unreadable expression.

“Huh,” she grunted. She bent her head and knuckled her eyes. Sharp points from the gravel dug into her ass. Her body started to ache again in places where she had forgotten she had been hurt.

She must have pulled onto private property. The wolves had to be trained. Maybe they were wolf-shepherd hybrids. They must belong to the man. They would probably run her down if she tried to get away

Her flimsy attempt at logic crumbled. She spoke to the alpha wolf in the same way she spoke to her daemon. *I had a dream about you. You said you had answered my call for help. You said you're here to protect me?*

Silence unfurled in the clearing. She felt like a fool.

Then the wolf said, *Yes.*

The simple word came into her head from a place outside of herself. Her lips parted. This was far beyond her daemon, which could, after all, be explained away as a construct of her own mind. She reached out to the wolf but didn't quite dare touch him. *I am . . . very grateful. Thank you.*

Sister, the wolf said.

Beyond trying to make her experiences fit into any logical scientific framework, she thought of the hawks that had fought off her attackers, and rapid words burst out of her. *I don't understand what's going on. Please don't let this man hurt me—*

The wolf lowered its head. We can only protect, he said. We cannot heal. The warrior can help you more than we can. You must let him.

*But—but—*Her gaze went back to the man who watched her with hard, expressionless eyes.

He had pinned her down. He scared her.

He pinned her after she woke and started fighting him. She had tried to bite him too.

But he didn't have to pin her down. Why didn't he just back away? He threatened to tie her up, and no amount of rationalizing could make that okay.

The man remained silent, as if knowing better than she the kind of thoughts that raced through her mind.

She said aloud, again, "I don't understand. Who are you? What do you want?" An avalanche of questions piled up behind those two. She had to bite her lips to keep from shrieking them.

The man said, "You can call me Michael. What I want is irrelevant."

He reached out a hand. The panic hit her low and hard, slamming into her gut. She cringed from the hand and scrambled away. She didn't stop until she had put several feet between them.

Only then did she realize that he hadn't moved. She huddled into the overlarge jacket, head down, and dared to look sideways at him.

He knelt frozen, his hand outstretched to her, palm up. Nothing moved in the clearing, not even the wind through the trees. The stoic expression in his hard face and blank eyes never changed. He looked prepared to take any blow and not budge.

It took a moment before she realized he was silently asking for her plastic bag of food. She hesitated then inched forward to offer it to him, holding the bag as far away from her body as she could.

Moving only his hand, slow and easy, he took the bag from her. He pulled out a packet of trail mix, tore it open and shook some into his hand as he said, "I hear you were attacked and some people were killed. Where did this happen?"

She pulled his jacket tighter around her torso. "How did you hear that?"

His colorless gaze lifted to her. "A wind spirit. Hawks."

"My daemon talked to you?" She lifted her head but couldn't sense any ethereal presence hovering nearby. "Where is it? You didn't hurt it, did you?"

His glance admonished her for the question. "I sent it to someone, with news." He chucked the handful of mix into his mouth.

She felt a sharp pang of loss. "You had no business doing that. It can't leave me—I needed it. It was going to show me how to get somewhere." Part of her found room for amazement. She laughed. "Listen to us. We sound like lunatics. We're talking about something that can't exist. The two of us are the same kind of crazy."

"I'm not crazy," the man named Michael said. He shook more mix into his mouth. He didn't look crazy either. He looked like a tired man after a long, hard day. His gaze speared her. "But I figure you've got to be pretty close to it. I'm just trying to decide how close you really are."

A fresh thrill of fear jangled along her nerve ends. She reached for her tattered dignity. "Whether I'm crazy or not has nothing to do with you." She added bitterly, "And you had no right to send my daemon away."

The man continued to study her. "What's your name?"

"That's none of your business either." She hugged her knees, her muscles in knots.

His lack of expression was chilling. "Listen to me carefully," he said. "We don't have a lot of time to debate this at length. You can't afford to take weeks or months to decide whether or not you're going to like or trust me. I can either help you or I can kill you. There is no middle choice. I will not let you go."

His words echoed in her head.

I can kill you.

He actually said those words to her.

She sucked air. "So what am I now, some kind of hostage?" she hissed.

"I didn't say that, did I?"

She shook her head hard. "You want me to tell you things but you don't tell me anything, is that it?"

"I didn't say that either. All I said was that what I want is irrelevant, and it is." He paused then added in an abrupt clipped tone, "You are mixed up in something far greater and older than you can understand at present. Right now you're a danger to yourself and to others. You're a danger to me. And you are dying, unless we can get you help from someone that I know."

Even her daemon had said she was dying, yet she had no visible wound. She panted as if she had been running hard, but she couldn't get enough air in her lungs. Her composure broke. She flung both arms over her head, and rocked back and forth. "I don't understand!"

The man named Michael rubbed his face, his mouth held in a tense line. He said, "You don't understand. I have answers. You're in danger. I'm a fighter, a good one. You're dying. I know someone who can heal you. This is not rocket science. Are you going to cooperate or not?"

She stopped rocking, lowered her arms and looked at him with eyes hollow from trauma and weariness. "Or you'll kill me."

His light, colorless gaze seared her. "No. Or I tie you up

and take you with me. I'll only kill you if you're not salvageable, and we're a long way from determining that. And I'll kill us both before allowing us to be taken by the other creatures who are hunting you. Death is preferable to being at their mercy. But we have a greater chance of surviving if you cooperate."

"Well isn't that a goddamn comfort." Her voice sounded like the rest of her, stretched too thin.

He stood. "Are you going to come willingly or not?"

"You're not giving me much of a choice, are you?"

"No."

She looked at the Toyota. First she lost her sanity, then her home, and now her car. Soon she would end up with nothing. "What are we going to do, just abandon my car?"

"Yes. With any luck, ditching it will slow the hunters down. It could buy us some time." He didn't sound like he had much hope for that to happen. He walked over and held out his hand.

She ignored it and forced her aching body upright. His hand fell to his side. He had a good foot on her in height. She came just to his shoulder and had to tilt her head back to look him in the face. She said cautiously, "I was supposed to go north to a grandmother."

"I know where you're supposed to go," he said. "That's where we're headed."

He knew? The lure of that pulled her more than anything else.

She was going to cooperate with a man who stood ready to kill her because—he said—the alternative was worse. Shuddering as the wind swept through the tangle of strange forest, she felt more lost than ever before. She longed to see a safe and friendly face, someone who genuinely wished her well. Someone who was not an enigma.

She told him, "I want my purse."

"I'll get it."

She glanced at his gun. "I also have a first aid kit in the trunk. I want that too."

"I have a first aid kit."

She raised her eyebrows. "Are you a doctor?"

His tough, expressionless stoicism shattered. He looked stricken, as if she had knifed him without warning. She watched, uncomprehending, as his throat muscles worked. He whispered, "No I'm not."

"Then I'm guessing mine's better."

A muscle in his jaw bunched. He gave her a short nod. He walked away to retrieve her purse and the canvas bag that held her first aid supplies.

Then he strode toward her. Even though his large body was heavy with thick muscles, he was so light on his feet he was a symphony of graceful movement.

Something about the fluidity of his body reminded her of the abundant golden river from earlier. His hands had rested flat on her torso as the shining stream had poured into her.

"Wait," she said, instinct driving her words. "When I woke up you were trying to help me in some way. Weren't you?"

He held the purse out to her, his gaze steady on hers. "I did help you. I bought you some time. But I can't heal you. That's beyond my abilities."

Their eyes met. She experienced a moment of light-headedness at the intensity of the connection.

She almost said, I do know you. Don't I?

But her gaze dropped to the gun in his holster, and she didn't. Instead, silently, she took her purse.

He turned to the alpha wolf. *You have fulfilled your promise with honor. Go in peace, brother.*

Warrior, the wolf said.

She stuffed her hands against her mouth, filled with excitement and wonder for she had heard both of them as clearly as if they had spoken aloud. Even if she felt like she had lost her mind, she wasn't creating *everything* that she was experiencing. The wolf looked at her.

She said, *I'll never forget you.*

He paced forward and nosed her hand. Then, before she could stroke his head, the wolf whirled to leap into the forest. The pack poured after him.

When the last of them had disappeared, she looked at Michael. “My name is Mary. I have two hundred and ninety-five dollars in cash. I haven’t used my checks or credit cards since I was attacked.”

“Good.” He regarded her, his hard expression thoughtful. “And don’t worry about money. I have plenty. We need to go.”

She walked with him to his car and climbed into the passenger seat.

THE INTERIOR OF the Ford was worn but spacious and comfortable, with old-fashioned bench seats and much more modern installed seat belts. The backseat was piled with things that were unidentifiable in the darkness, but the front seat was clear. The car smelled faintly of engine oil, leather and the faint clean scent of aftershave.

She tucked her purse and the plastic bag of snacks between her feet. They were now the sum total of her worldly possessions. After she put her seat belt on, she rummaged in the bag for a bottle of water and the chocolate bar.

Michael twisted to look over his shoulder, and he backed the car onto the paved road. She caught a glimpse of a large red-tailed hawk perched on a low-hanging limb of a tree and craned her neck to stare as it launched into flight. It was soon swallowed by the dark night.

After a few minutes they approached the entrance ramp to Highway 131. Michael took the northbound ramp. The car accelerated to just under the speed limit and held steady. She sagged back in her seat with a sigh and unwrapped the chocolate bar.

The duality in her emotions continued. As afraid of him as she was, she was also intensely relieved to be on the road again. Losing her independent transportation worried her, but leaving her car behind meant that they also left her license plates behind, and she became a little more difficult to track.

They traveled in silence. Apparently you-can-call-me-Michael was a man of few words. He drove with competence and appeared relaxed, but she noticed that he checked the rearview mirror often and his expression remained a closed vault.

He didn't offer to turn on the radio, and she didn't ask. She looked out the window at the moonlit landscape and the occasional traffic, sucking on her candy. She didn't offer him any chocolate, and he didn't ask.

In the privacy of her own mind, she admitted that it was a relief to sit passive for a while with someone who seemed strong and capable, who wore a gun and knew how to use it and who appeared to understand the dangers they faced. At the same time her bruised, hypersensitive nerves jangled with awareness of the tough, dominant presence at her side. She could not get beyond her fear of him, or the threat that he had made.

Hawks, wolves, wind spirits and the strange haunt of inexplicable dreams. Two grotesque men and casual murder. The vision at the Grotto. Her house in flames. She was dying.

Why was she dying?

She was walking and talking like a normal person, but something was terribly wrong with her. She didn't need to take Michael's or her daemon's word for it. Deep in her bones, she could sense that it was true. It felt like she had torn something open, some unseen spiritual ligament, and it was vital in some way to her existence. In the meantime everything she thought she knew about the world had crumbled into dust.

She said aloud, "It's like all my life I've lived in some kind of painting. There was a lot of color and detail, and the painting seemed to make sense, but either somebody has smashed the frame or I've fallen out of it somehow. Now I'm in a totally different reality. The color and detail seem similar, but everything's changed. I can't go back into the painting. It's two-dimensional, and I don't fit. I don't even know how to try. But I don't understand this new reality either, or how to survive in it."

The atmosphere in the car changed. She could sense his attention sharpening on her as she spoke. She paused, but he said nothing.

Anger sparked. She said, "If you're not crazy, then I'm not crazy. I heard you speak to that wolf. I heard that wolf speak to me. Someone burned down my house. I saw it on the news along with other people in a restaurant, so I know I'm not making that up. Hundreds of hawks attacked two men who murdered four innocent people right in front of me. Those men called me by name. They were kidnapping me. Those hawks were the only thing that kept me out of their van. *These things happened.* I have the bruises to prove it. And I resent like hell that I might need you, but you might kill me for some mysterious unknown reason. As far as I know, maybe you'll kill me on a whim—maybe just because you get indigestion and you feel cranky and trigger-happy tonight. By the way, you never thanked me for that sandwich you took without asking. And if I'm already dying, which you say, I don't know why you'd even bother to kill me unless you just get cranky and trigger-happy sometimes. Maybe you're the crazy one, and I'm the one who's sane. Did you consider that, Mister Enigmatic?"

As she twisted in her seat to glare at him, a startled smile flickered across his face. By the dashboard's dim illumination she caught how the brief smile shifted the planes and angles of his face into something quite different from his former grim endurance. He glanced at her, his light eyes glittering like a flash of bright gems glimpsed under a shadowed cloak.

"I'm sorry," he said.

She waited again, but he fell back into silence. "That's it—you're sorry?" she said after a while. Bitter anger scalded her words. "Thank you, everything has become crystal clear, and I feel so much better now."

"I'm thinking," he said. The trace of a whip was in his voice.

She shrank closer to her door, her temper chilling. Great,

Mary. Release all your stress on the guy with the gun. You know, he really might kill you just because he's got indigestion. How much more of an idiot can you be?

It was time to force some conciliatory words out of her mouth, whether she actually felt them or not. She said, "I shouldn't have said all those things. It's just that I've—"

"You've had a rough day, I know," he said. "I should never have said anything about killing you. It was a cruel and useless thing to say, and I'm sorry. Let's just say I've had a rough day too and try to get past it, all right?"

She mulled on that and found it unsatisfactory. She said, "Is it true?"

The fleeting smile was gone. In its place was something darker, much more savage. "Yes," he said. "But you didn't need to know it."

"But why?" The thin-voiced plaintive question hung between them.

"All I can do is repeat myself," he said. "There are some things that are worse than death. Someone is hunting you. If he captured you, what he would do to you would be far worse than death."

She rubbed her face and forced herself to focus. "There were two men who tried to kidnap me."

"They were dangerous in their own way and destructive enough, but ultimately they're unimportant. They're just tools for the person you need to worry about. If he had gotten hold of you, you wouldn't have escaped, hawks or no hawks."

She shuddered at the thought of someone worse. "Who's that?"

"I don't know what name he goes by these days. But he is quite old, powerful, inventive and wicked. I've dedicated my life to his destruction. So has Astra, the woman that I'm taking you to see."

"The Grandmother."

"Some call her that." His voice had turned measured and expressionless, giving away no hint of his own thoughts or opinions.

She remembered that she was thirsty, opened the bottle of water and drank. After she'd had enough she hesitated then held the bottle out to him. He took it. "Why do I feel that you and the—wind spirit, as you called it—are right and I'm dying?" she asked. "Aside from some scrapes and bruises, there's nothing physically wrong with me. And what did you do to me, back there by my car?"

"As far as the difference between you dying, and me killing you goes . . ." He blew out a short sharp gust of air, an exhalation of frustration, and she tensed in dread. "If I killed you, I would only be killing your body. What you're suffering from is much more serious than a wound of the flesh. Somehow you've taken a wound of the spirit. If you expire from the spirit wound, you will be destroyed. Gone. You won't exist any longer, so you could never be reborn."

Spirit and body. Death and rebirth. Her lips felt numb. She rubbed her mouth. Gretchen had talked of spirits. "Are you talking about reincarnation?"

"Yes, or at least some form of it." He glanced at her. "We don't exactly lead typical lives."

"We." Her hand migrated upward. She rubbed at her dry eyes. He was grouping her with himself, and with this woman named Astra. Who were these people? Who did he think she was? Did he believe they were some kind of soul group that chose to reincarnate and live their lives together? Disorientation yanked at her. She felt unmoored and drifting, like she was coming apart at the seams.

He continued, "If your energy is dispersed, you—the spirit essence of you—will be gone forever. There would be no rebirth for you, no chance at another life. So you see, there is the physical death. Then there is the real death, the permanent one, from which there is no coming back." He took a deep harsh breath. "What I was doing to you when you woke up . . . picture an arterial wound, only it's a spiritual one and you're bleeding to death. I gave you an infusion of my blood, or my energy, in the real sense. It's strengthened you and we've gained some time, but it hasn't closed the wound or stopped the bleeding. For that, we need the woman we're going to see.

She understands far better what has happened to you. She has the skills to heal you."

The physician in her took over. "Wait, to use your analogy, if you killed me," she said, "wouldn't my spirit still bleed to death, so to speak?"

"Actually," he said in a tired voice, "in some ways your spirit would be easier to heal if you were dead. You could make the journey north to Astra in a matter of moments. She could heal you. You could rest and then you could be reborn. But there are . . . other reasons why that isn't an attractive option."

Outrage held her frozen for a moment. Attractive option. How about like I don't want to die, you son of a bitch? Is that one of your reasons? Struggling with her unruly emotions, she wrapped her fingers around the edges of the jacket he'd lent to her.

Finally she managed to say, "I'm pretty tired of being scared."

"I know it's asking a lot but try not to worry too much, at least about that," he said. "As long as you are with me, I can infuse you with energy when you need it. When we get to Astra, she can heal you. You won't die of that wound if we have anything to say about it. And we have a lot to say about it."

"Astra," she murmured. She was not just tired of being scared. She was also just plain tired. She leaned her head against her window. Astra, in Greek, meant star. "Do you know how I got injured in the first place?"

"What I know is that it happened a very long time ago," he said. The caution had come back into his voice. "Lifetimes ago. It might be better if you tried to remember what happened for yourself."

Somewhere along the line she had stopped being quite so terrified of him.

That might or might not be a good thing. She simply didn't have the reserves to sustain such an exhausting emotion. Whether or not she believed anything he said was a different matter. She shelved that for another time when she could think about it in private. For now she suspended disbelief and tried to absorb what he chose to tell her.

"I went to visit the Grotto at Notre Dame University today," she said. "Do you know where that is?"

"Notre Dame is in South Bend, right?"

"Yes. Anyway, I—well, I prayed for help, and I had a vision," she said. "This lady told me I had to remember who I was, and that I needed to find her. She said I needed to travel north. At the time I wondered if she might be the Virgin Mary."

"Maybe she was," Michael said, surprising her. "But from what you're telling me, it sounds more likely that she was Astra."

Wait—was he saying that the Virgin Mary could actually exist? She stared. Concepts were coming at her too fast. Was she intrigued or disappointed that her vision might not have been the Holy Virgin? She caught up with what he said. "Astra could do that, make some kind of bodiless visitation?"

"Astral projection? Yes. But it's exhausting, especially across long distances. She would only do it in an emergency, and if she was safe enough to recover from it afterward. She's too important to risk."

"Astral . . . But . . . How would she know to find me?"

"You've been blazing like a beacon in the psychic landscape ever since this afternoon. She might have traced you that way. I focused on finding you in the physical realm. I couldn't afford the time or the energy on an astral projection." He shook his head, took one hand off the steering wheel and rubbed at his neck. "We've been afraid something like this would happen. We've been looking for you for a long time."

Blazing like a beacon since this afternoon. She remembered the sense of something vital tearing open and shuddered.

"How long were you looking?" she breathed. Was he talking years?

"Lifetimes," he said. The brief reply blasted away her assumptions and shook her to the core all over again. "We know our enemy has been looking for you too, but it's been like you've been hidden behind a veil. We've gotten brief glimpses of you and your life, but we never got quite enough information to find you until today. Today it felt like you ripped past the veil yourself. My guess is that's what reopened your spirit wound, because you couldn't have been bleeding like this your entire life. If you had been born like this, you would have died in a matter of days."

"That beacon you mentioned. Is that how those two men were able to find me? No," she said, in answer to her own question. "That doesn't make sense. My house had to have caught fire before I prayed in the Grotto. The blaze was too far along by the time I saw it on the news."

"It could be that your house isn't connected to this," he said. "Maybe the fire is just a coincidence."

She heard the lack of conviction in his voice, and she was not reassured. "You think it's more likely that your enemy was closer to finding me than you two were?"

"Anything's possible," he replied. "Especially that."

"Why burn down my house? Wouldn't it have been smarter to wait until I got home? It's not," she said in a caustic voice, "like I've had a clue about what I've been doing, or what's really going on."

"We don't have enough facts yet to answer that question. But if your house fire was arson, most fires are started to hide something. It could also have been set to draw you back home, although that reason on its own seems excessive when all someone would have to do is wait for you to return."

"I saw the fire on the news. I had contacted the police and was starting to return home when those two men attacked." She rubbed her shaking mouth. She whispered, "What they did was excessive. There was no reason for it. They didn't have to kill those people. They were brutal because they liked it."

"Our adversary is like that. He enjoys cruelty, and he feeds on pain." His profile had turned harsh, the bones of his face slicing through the shadows thrown by the dashboard lights. "When he creates his tools, he destroys something essential in their souls. They can still function but they no longer have a moral code, or creativity or any real free will, or whatever it is that makes them human."

She closed her eyes. What kind of creature had the power to destroy someone's soul? It was appalling, too much. She had to give up on the puzzle for now. She thought she ought to give up on all of it and try to rest. Her body and soul, or spirit, as Michael had said, felt frayed almost to tatters. Even though she had fallen into that black pit earlier, it had only been for a couple of hours. Her dreams had been so restless and vivid she had gained no real refreshment from it.

Her dreams.

A sudden flood of memory brought back the dream of the wounded woman. Like the sacred poison dream, the wounded woman was another recurring dream that she'd had throughout her life. Blood-shot and filled with disturbing imagery, she had tended to dream it only in times of great stress.

And her dreams . . .

Her breathing roughened, became erratic. Michael's jacket no longer provided welcome warmth but became a stifling restriction. She couldn't get enough air inside her lungs. She fumbled to unlatch her seat belt and struggle out of the jacket, and she began to claw her way out her T-shirt.

"Okay, easy," Michael said, his voice sharp. "You need to take deep, slow breaths. Try not to fight it."

She heard his words but not their meaning. All her attention was focused inward where an immense heat blazed up. She was burning to death. She felt suspended in time as though she had waited all her life in a silence so profound it seemed to roar, waited to hear the first sonorous clang of a terrible gong.

Remember who you are.

My dreams are real.

And she was racing back in her mind to the small child she had been, and what that child had said to upset her mother so badly, she had learned to bury it and eventually forget, and how ever afterward her mind would slide away from that memory because it was such a bad, bad thing. . . .

Mommy, I had the strangest dream, she had said.

I dreamed I was human.

Unspeakable loss welled up inside her again, only this time it was deeper and stronger than ever before. This time it wasn't held at a distance or tucked behind a veil. It roared into her like a tsunami, and she cried out and doubled over from the force of it.

Chapter Twelve

EXHAUSTED BY HER long-distance astral journey to talk to Mary, Astra rested on her narrow bed under a pile of every blanket in her bedroom, but she still couldn't get warm. A deep chill had settled into her aching bones last winter, and it had never gone away. Despite all her best efforts, her body was wearing out. She knew part of the reason why was her spirit was as worn as her flesh.

There used to be some things that mattered to her more than existence. Sometimes now it seemed neither existence nor those things mattered at all.

Time and again the group had struggled, and for what? They died and they died, and now some of them were gone forever.

Raphael and Gabriel. Ariel and Uriel. All destroyed beyond reclaiming.

A tear rolled down her cheek, sliding down the furrows and creases of her face.

A gentle tap sounded at her doorway. "Grandmother?"

She wiped the tear away and turned her head. "What is it?"

Jamie still refused to lift his head and look directly at

her. "Your light was still on," he said. "I wanted to ask you if you needed anything."

"No." She needed nothing this kind child could give her. "How is your grandpa?"

He shuffled his feet and cleared his throat, and said hopefully, "He's resting well. I think his color looks better."

"Good." She said it like she believed that Jerry's condition would improve, or like she cared anymore. Jerry wasn't getting better, and she didn't. He would be dead in a week, and she didn't care about any of the people on this earth anymore. She wanted to go home. "Go to bed, boy," she said in a rusty-sounding voice. "You'll not be of any use to your grandpa if you don't get some sleep."

"Yes, ma'am." He hesitated as if about to say something else but then, for a mercy, he kept silent and turned away.

At last, filled with dread, she crept into sleep.

She dreamed. She had known she would.

She stood in a dry wasteland devoid of any green or growing thing. There was no wind, no day or night, just a vast barren grayness. Even when her dream self closed her eyes, she saw the image of the gray landscape. If she had been in control of the dream, she would have changed the landscape to add color and life, but she wasn't in control. This wasn't her dream.

She waited in despair for what would happen next.

A figure appeared and strolled toward her. It shone with a ferocious black light. In its hands it held an agonized slip of lavender mist.

Old woman, the Deceiver said.

She looked at the wind spirit he held and recognized it immediately. It was the one she had sent to help Mary. She said, *This is unbelievably petty, even for you.*

I promised you a long time ago, the figure said. *You remember, don't you? I will destroy every creature that you hold dear, even down to the smallest one.*

Creator, have mercy, not for me but for your fragile child who is in such pain.

Forgive, forgive.

She didn't bother to try to gather her strength. She had none, and she couldn't have acted even if she had. Neither she nor the Deceiver could actually hurt or touch each other in this dream, for it was merely a sending, a message filled with events that had already occurred. He liked to show her his executions.

The black radiant figure took the wind spirit in both hands and savaged it to shreds. The delicate creature had no defense. It made a muffled whimper as it was destroyed almost instantly.

The Deceiver showed her its empty hands. *Until next time, bitch.*

How many times must she be summoned to this killing field?

The world wasn't large enough to contain her grief.

Chapter Thirteen

WHEN ALL WAS said and done, Michael found himself surprised that he was walking and talking with any semblance of coherency.

He had prepared his entire life for this very encounter with Mary, and still the reality of coming face-to-face with her blew through all of his expectations. He had never quite found his equilibrium after her scream in the psychic realm, and internally he was still reeling.

He had to get grounded and centered again, to reconnect with his sense of purpose. He knew how to do that when he was alone, but he didn't know how to do it in her presence.

When he had opened the door to her Toyota and looked upon her unconscious face for the first time, he felt as if he had been dealt a body blow.

She was young, possibly as much as ten years younger than he, and she had fine-boned features and a honey-toned skin color that had turned pallid. Her face was lopsided with a swollen bruise that had begun to turn a dark purple. Her tawny hair was kinked with curls that were confined in a braid. She was dressed in nondescript, comfortable clothing.

Her looks didn't matter in the slightest. He knew she

could have been old or young, or of any nationality, and before he had laid eyes on her, he would have said that he'd had no expectation or desire for her to be anything but what she was.

But this . . .

She was beautiful.

He spiraled down into a place of astonished enchantment and did nothing to try to stop it. Instead he embraced his fall.

He gently laid the tips of his fingers on her cheek, and the impact of that first touch sent him to his knees. She was warm, living and embodied, and it was such a goddamned miracle, his eyes flooded with moisture.

He, who had experienced relatively few emotions in this life, was overcome with a feeling so powerful, it shook his body to the marrow. Blinking hard to clear his eyesight, he traced her soft, lush lips. The delicate warm brush of her breath on his hand thrilled him utterly.

She was revolutionary, transformative. He had not known beauty before he looked at her. He had not known desire, until he touched her face.

Connecting with her hemorrhaging energy shocked him back to the present, along with the realization of the real extremity of her situation. Then every emotion that had exploded into life inside of him seemed to redouble in reaction: rage and fear, hope and determination, and a wicked hate for the one who had damaged her.

He fought to keep his expression and manner neutral, to hide what went on inside of him and to give her as much room as he could to deal with her own reactions. The last thing he wanted to do was to escalate her before they were able to get help from Astra, and precipitate a crisis that neither one of them would be able to handle on their own.

But he had not counted on how hard that would be, when the reality of his own reaction to her was so volcanic, it eroded his own reasoning and his control.

And as it turned out, there was nothing he could do to stop her anyway.

When Mary cried out and doubled over, Michael checked traffic, yanked the car onto the shoulder and slammed on the brakes.

Cars shot past, headlights blazing like comets. He turned to his passenger. Although the car was filled with night shadows, he could see quite clearly with his psychic senses. Mary's spirit wound was bleeding bright, feverish gouts of energy.

He tried to shift her. She was rigid, clamped in a fetal position. He twisted in his seat, got a firmer hold and hauled her toward him. Her skin felt burning hot and dry. Her spirit wound was affecting her physical body. He wondered how high her temperature had spiked. If it went too high for too long it would kill her.

Stopping for any length of time on the side of a major highway was all but suicidal. He gave up on trying to conduct any risk assessment and instead focused on the problem at hand. Slipping one hand under Mary's chin, he tried to turn her face up. She was locked in place, the tendons in her neck standing out against his palm. He didn't want to force her head around in case he hurt her.

Awkward in the cramped space, he wrapped his arms around her. He put one hand to her forehead and pushed his other hand under her arm, laying it against her sternum. Then he rested his cheek against the delicate protrusion of bone at the nape of her neck, closed his eyes and sent his awareness into her mind.

The psychic landscape was the land of spirit, which lay interlocked with the physical world. The interior of the mind was quite a different matter. It was a small, private realm comprised of perception, memory, thought, emotion, dream images and imagination. After pushing into her mind, Michael paused to let her adjust to his intrusion while he attempted to get oriented.

Tattered scraps of images drifted around him. He kept from focusing on any one image and allowed them to continue drifting, as he spent precious time forcing himself to settle into the calm, aware state of utter mindfulness. He could not help her if he was in a panic.

When he was centered and still, he extended his senses throughout her mind.

Turbulent emotion buffeted him. Trauma, shock, horror, fear. Incredulity. The sour taste of guilt.

Why guilt?

The question almost snared him, but at the last moment he let it go and let it wash through him. These were her surface emotions, connected to recent experiences and relatively shallow. He could not sense her active, aware presence in any of them.

He reached deeper and sank into an agony so raw and acidic it burned. He had to force himself not to recoil but to push further until he could sense her presence.

"Mary," he said to her. MARY.

He found her presence. An image slammed into him. This time he was unable to let it wash past. Since this was the image he had been searching for, the image that held her awareness, he embraced it and entered a scene.

Mary sat in a room hewn out of rock. Intricate carvings, gilded with silver, covered every inch of the walls. The carvings flowed and looped together in never-ending spirals. On one wall two stylized and graceful, inhuman figures reached out to each other. Where they touched their hands melded together.

Michael recognized the room. This was where they had died their first deaths and left their original home forever.

Mary's mental self-image was dressed as she was in the physical realm, in jeans and T-shirt. Her tangled hair, held back in a lopsided braid, looked dull and lifeless. She curled over her knees, head bent.

He looked down at himself. He, too, had automatically replicated his own physical appearance down to his gun, which was nothing more than a useless image in this place. He walked over to kneel in front of her.

This close he could see that her skin was as transparent as paper. She glowed like a Japanese lantern. The force of her emotion beat against his skin. He put a hand on her shoulder and despite the burning pain that shot through his fingers he gripped the slender bone and muscle in an unbreakable hold.

"Mary," he said again. He projected the full force of his urgency through the touch of his hand.

She lifted her head. Her eyes shone from within. She uncurled her body.

A jagged cut slashed down the front of her torso. It bled an ectoplasmic light. In her hands she cradled a crystal goblet etched with an inscription in a language that Earth had never seen. He recognized that goblet from ages past when he, along with a group of seven others, had drunk poisoned wine in one last deadly communion.

His breath caught. He reached out and touched the goblet's rim with a finger. She had remembered and re-created it with perfection, down to the slight nick on the bottom of the stem.

Neither he nor Astra had expected her to be capable of anything like this. They had always assumed that if they found her again, retrieving her memories would be a slow and challenging process that might encompass lifetimes. Instead she was retrieving her memories all on her own by the side of a road.

He touched her cheek. It was just as petal soft to his senses as it had been when he had physically touched her the first time.

"Where are we?" she said. She sounded dazed. "How did we get here?"

The question jarred him. He asked carefully, "Where do you think we are?"

She gestured with a listless hand and bent her gaze down to the goblet. "I've been dreaming of this place my whole life," she said. "I never imagined that these creatures might be real. They were so alien and beautiful."

"Yes," he said. He was uneasy with this new, foreign desire to be gentle, but he worked to keep his voice quiet as he knelt beside her. "We were."

They had been creatures of fire and light, a race of beings forever mated, each one having a twin of essential contrast and compatibility, yin and yang, a harmonic completion of universal balance.

She frowned and rubbed her forehead with the back of one hand. "You were one of them?"

"Yes." He stroked her tangled hair. "We had to leave our physical bodies behind in order to come here to this world. We're born to humans and we die like humans, and like humans, when we're reborn we forget who we are. For a while. It's actually a mercy, most of the time. It gives us a chance to rest in between awakenings."

"This happened a very long time ago, didn't it?" She stared at him, but he knew she wasn't seeing him. "A long, long time."

"Over six thousand years."

Sometimes the humans who were native to Earth had helped in their battles. Corrupted fragments of the resulting stories had survived and been embellished over the millennia. One of the most famous and inaccurate was the story of Satan's fall from heaven and the group of rebellious angels that had followed him.

They were no angels. They didn't even make very good humans.

She whispered, "Do you remember it?"

He said, "I haven't bothered to try recovering those first memories of Earth. I figured I would sometime if I needed to. But Astra remembers. She remembers everything. She has had to, in order to help the others of us remember."

She shivered. "How could she bear to do that?"

He had often wondered that, how Astra could stand to remember every minute of their unending exile. "I don't know. Maybe she can because she must."

"There were seven in my dream," she said. The goblet image her mind had manufactured melted away with the change in her attention. She leaned forward to grip his arms. "Where are the others? You haven't talked about them."

"They're gone," he said in a flat voice. He hated to witness the fresh horror and grief on her face. "There are only four of us left—you and I, Astra and the criminal. The Deceiver. He destroyed the others. And you've been missing for so goddamn long—"

Her body stiffened and her gaze snapped into a sharp blue focus, locking with his. "Wait. You think I'm one of you, that I belong in your group?"

His gut clenched, and he went to red alert. Carefully he took her by the shoulders. "Don't you see that's why you keep dreaming of this place?"

Her body arced away from his touch. "Let me go. You're wrong. This is a mistake. I'm not one of you. I can't be one of you."

His fingers loosened immediately, and he let her go. She scrambled back until she hit the wall. Her face was filled with horror. "It's all right," he said. He held a hand to her, palm out. "You're going to be all right."

She screamed at him, "I'm human!"

"Of course you are," he said. He fought his own sense of horror. This was beyond disastrous. None of them had ever recovered so much of their memories before without realizing their real identities. "You need to calm down. You're safe."

"I'm safe until you decide to kill me?" she said, her voice hoarse. She pushed to her feet and turned to face the wall, looking up at the carving of the two inhuman figures, and she made an inarticulate sound that was so wounded and afraid, it scalded his senses.

He straightened, keeping his movements slow. He kept his voice soft as he said, "I made a mistake. I'm sorry."

"You're not sorry," she said in that stranger's voice. She began to feel along the wall, running her fingers over the carvings as though reading Braille. As though the scene was a prison that she was trying to escape. "You meant it. Where is this place? How did you bring me here?"

Step by step, with seeming effortlessness, she peeled away all the layers of indifference that he had built up over the centuries until he felt raw with agony. Fighting every instinct he had to move forward, to take hold of her again in a grip so tight she would never get away from him again, he took a step back then another. Then he waited until she looked over her shoulder at him.

He said, "You'll have to figure that out on your own."

Fresh devastation flared in her eyes. Steeling himself against the expression, he turned away, unable to talk in this mental landscape and hold his energy separate from hers, unable to stand the sight of the unnatural gash down her psychic body.

Exiting her mind with as much care as he could, he pulled his gun even as he opened his eyes to look around. They had been motionless for perhaps a half hour.

When he had pulled to the shoulder of the road earlier, he had refrained from putting on the car's hazard lights, hoping they would look like an abandoned vehicle to those passing by at high speed. Whether by luck or by his design, they had been left alone.

Mary's body rested against his chest. He had been quietly feeding her energy the whole time he had been in her mind. Despite her confusion and anguish, her body felt relaxed and more natural now, no longer feverish. She seemed to be asleep.

In a stealthy movement he pressed his lips against her shoulder blade and rubbed his mouth lightly on the thin, warm cotton material of her T-shirt. Then he eased her over more to the passenger seat, tucked the jean jacket around her and buckled her seat belt into place. She sighed, shifted and went still.

Cars and trucks shot by, providing quick flashes of illumination. The psychic landscape was restless with movement as whispers tickled the edges of his mind. Despite all his instincts screaming at him to get moving again, he took another stolen moment to lock in his memory the sight of the precious curve of her living cheek.

Then he faced forward and acknowledged some hard truths. He gripped the steering wheel with his left hand, gun clenched in his right. Holding rigid was the only way he knew to survive.

There was no road map for where they were in their history. He still didn't know what had been done to her to cause the kind of wound that she had. All he could tell was that her energy was skewed somehow, different than it had ever been, and every time he looked at her with his psychic senses she looked cracked wide open like an egg. The evidence of such a violation, the sheer wrongness of it, made him feel like roaring.

He thought about what it would be like to put the gun to her head right now and pull the trigger. Death was just one gentle move and a click away. It would be good to do it while she was asleep, and it would be over with so fast, faster than she could comprehend. She wouldn't experience any more pain. Then it would be so simple, the work of a moment to turn the gun on himself.

His head ached so ferociously, he thought he might split apart from the force of it. He rubbed the barrel of the gun against his temple.

MARY OPENED HER eyes. She leaned against the passenger door, wrapped in the warm jacket. She was still overtired and her body hurt, but mercifully the raw feeling had eased in intensity.

Why had they stopped moving? What had just happened?

She must have had another hallucination and passed out.

No.

Somehow, somewhere along the line, she must have crossed over into sleep without realizing it. That was odd but not impossible for the dangerously sleep-deprived, and boy howdy the dream she'd just had was a rough one.

No, that didn't work either.

Then she heard a quiet sound. It was Michael, whispering.

The fine hairs at the back of her neck rose. She gave him a surreptitious look between her lashes.

He rubbed the barrel of his gun against his temple as he whispered, "It was too a mistake. I'm sorry. I didn't have any choice. I'm sorrier than I can say."

The sight of him struck her hard, like a slap in the face. Some of the words he used were straight out of her hallucination, her dream.

She took a deep, careful breath and didn't give herself time to think. Slowly she reached toward him and touched his arm. A flash of emotion seared her, and it was not her own. She got a sense of suffering so intense it felt like a mortal wound. She let her gentle fingers trail along his arm, keeping the motion unhurried and nonthreatening, giving him plenty of chance to react and pull away.

He did neither. Instead he froze when she touched him. His big, tough body was so taut it felt like he might break.

At last her fingers curled around his clenched hand. It was so much bigger, so much more powerful, than hers. She put the lightest pressure on him, a silent request more than anything to ease the gun away from his head. He let her, until the nine-millimeter rested against his heavy, muscled thigh.

"It's all right," she murmured. She didn't try to take the gun from him. Instead she stroked the back of his hand and his thick, corded wrist. "You're all right. You're safe."

Reassuring him just as he had reassured her in her hallucination, her dream.

He opened his eyes and looked ahead at nothing. His eyes were bloodshot. He said, "I'm really tired."

How crazy was this? Her heart twisted for him, this big, strange, dangerous man. "I know you are."

They sat quietly, her hand resting on his wrist. Then his taut body relaxed. He took his hand out from under hers and holstered his gun. He said, "Have you figured out yet where you were?"

She was completely unprepared for the question.

Realization blasted her back against her door. Her hands went out in front of her. She grasped at the dashboard as her world reeled yet again. She gasped, "You were in my head. Just now. You were in my fucking head."

He said nothing.

"You've had the same dreams," she said. The words kept

coming and coming, a deluge pouring out of her mouth. "You know that place. You think I'm one of that group. You think I'm one of you. *Who do you think I am?*"

EVEN THOUGH WE'RE trying to take care with each other, Michael thought, we're still tearing each other's barriers to pieces. He couldn't find a way to slow down the revelations. Instead they came in an uncontrolled convulsion.

Without warning, his own burden of agony, which he had transformed to rage in order to survive each killing day of an interminable existence, welled to the surface. A deep groan broke out of him like the girders on an overstressed bridge.

"Michael?" she asked, searching his face.

He'd told himself he wouldn't. He had imagined a thousand times or more various scenarios like this one. He had coached himself on how he would behave. None of it meant a goddamn thing.

He grabbed her and yanked her to him, bowing his head and shoulders over her slender body. Holding her so tight he felt some of her bones shift under the pressure, he put his face in her hair and shook so hard he thought he would fly apart from the force of it.

He said in a hoarse voice, "You were my mate. The other part of my soul. And you have been missing for over nine hundred years."

A couple of heartbeats thudded between them. For a wonder, she didn't struggle to free herself. He felt her arms encircle his waist in a light, tentative hold. She leaned into him, and for a moment he recalled with shining clarity what it was like to cradle his second half, to rest against a luminous being of grace and beauty.

For a moment to his parched and destitute soul it felt like he had come home, after wandering in a strange and hostile wilderness for such a long, long time.

After a moment she whispered, "I have no idea where to put that, on top of everything else."

Despite her guarded and rational words, he felt her arm

muscles tense, until she was holding him with as tight a hold as he held her. He rubbed his face in her hair, savoring every fleeting sensation.

"You don't have to put it anywhere," he forced himself to say. "It was millennia ago. We were quite literally different creatures then."

Her head moved under his cheek. "You believe that."

"Belief has nothing to do with it," he said, his voice flat. Just as what he wanted had nothing to do with it. "It's the truth. When the Deceiver escaped, there was only one way we could follow him. We had to leave our lives behind in order to travel to another dimension, or another universe, if you will."

"That's why we had to die. It was the only way to transform," she muttered. She seemed to recoil from what she had just said, as if it sounded too real. She added quickly, "I mean that's what happened in my dream."

"We became hybrid creatures when we grafted on to Earth's ecosystem," he said. He forced himself to speak as clinically as possible. "In order to regain a physical existence, we had to become part of this world's cycle of death and rebirth. We were forced to adapt and evolve beyond our origins. On top of that, you and I have survived something unprecedented. No other mated pair has been subjected to and survived nearly a thousand years of separation. We are, quite literally, not what we once were."

Somehow he had to remember that. Somehow he had to come to believe it.

Chapter Fourteen

MARY HUDDLED AGAINST him, soaking in the illusion of strength and safety his big body offered as she considered everything that he had told her.

Of course the whole thing was outlandish, outrageous. It was also the only explanation she had ever encountered that explained everything she had experienced in her life.

Someone else knew of her dreams. Someone had walked inside her head, had looked at the bizarre images and said, Yes, I remember that too.

Damn, it made all the puzzle pieces fit. That didn't mean she had to like it. She wasn't sure she believed in it. It just . . . fit.

She muttered, "I have to think."

"You do that. In the meantime we've been sitting here like stationary targets on an open-air shooting range. We have got to move." He gripped her by the shoulders and pushed her away.

For a moment her traitorous arms resisted letting go of him. Then her muscles loosened and they separated. She settled back into her seat, her gaze lingering on the lines of his face that had settled back into his earlier expression of grim endurance.

He started the car, checked behind them and pulled onto the road.

She huddled under his jacket and leaned her forehead against the cold glass of her window. She wasn't ready to talk again so she pretended to fall asleep. She wasn't ready to sleep and risk another dream, so she fought to stay awake. She labored under the burden of too much information that had come at her too fast. At the same time her need for answers had built up to such a desperate extent her mind kept racing on to the next question, and the next.

The physician in her realized that she wasn't out of triage yet.

How she felt about Michael was a question she wasn't ready to examine, so she set it aside. At first his withdrawal had pierced her with a strange hurt. Then she was grateful for it. If he was right—*if* he was right—and she was not quite human, she was still no longer that creature from her sacred poison dream.

When she had put her arms around Michael, for a few brief moments she might have felt that she held her mate in her arms, her essential twin, the missing piece of her soul. But that feeling, if she believed it—*if* she believed it—was an anachronism, like feeling phantom sensation from an amputated limb. It had to be. She knew nothing about him in this life, or what kind of man he had become.

She stretched and felt her companion's attention snap to her. She remembered her first impression of him, that physically he was forgettable, nondescript, like a thousand other tough soldierlike men.

Now she couldn't connect in the slightest way to that earlier impression. He was not conventionally handsome, but the lines of his face were stamped with intelligence, and he radiated forcefulness like the blast of heat from a volcano. The heavy muscles of his long, hard body rippled, sleek and sinuous, under his tanned skin.

Watching him was a hypnotic experience. Every

movement he made flowed like water. If he stood in the middle of a crowd, her eyes would be instantly drawn to him. *She* was drawn to him—to the magic encased in his physical form, to his masculine scent. Something about his hands caused her body to pulse with awareness.

With a slow sense of incredulity she realized that she was sexually drawn to him. And they might not be twinned souls any longer, but she basked in the vitality of his strong presence.

Even though she already knew she had his attention, she said, "Michael."

"Yes." He was curt.

She wanted to touch him. She frowned at his profile. "Did you have a rough time recovering your memories?"

He stirred. "No, but my circumstance doesn't compare with yours. I was eight when Astra found me. I was able to recover my memories over time. She both shielded and taught me as I grew up. It was a good thing she found me when I was so young. I was not, shall we say, headed down the right path. Whereas she and I are pretty sure this is the first time you've incarnated since you sustained your spirit injury. It may be the first time that you've been strong enough."

The first time she'd been strong enough in over nine hundred years. Her breath whistled between her teeth. "That bad."

"Yes," he said, the word a quiet hiss. Then he continued, "This is all happening for you in a much more traumatic setting, as an adult in a dangerous situation. To be frank I'm amazed you're as sane and intact as you are. We didn't know what we would find when we recovered you. We had to be prepared for you to heal in stages—over lifetimes—and we didn't dare hope for more than a chance to help you heal in this life as much as you could."

"Talk about taking the long view," she muttered. She stared at the night sky. The earlier clouds had dissipated. Now a hard edge limned the landscape as if it were cut from sapphires and diamonds. When the sun rose later, the jewels would melt in a gush of heat and light.

She was disturbed by how Michael talked about dying

and being reborn with such apparent dispassion. It seemed as if a part of him didn't connect with the miracle of being alive in the present.

She tried to look at it from his point of view, to consider the realities he had been forced to endure. The woman Astra had influenced him from an early age. Was that the elder she remembered from her dream? She wondered what kind of person Astra had become.

Then she realized she was falling into a thought pattern of acceptance. The realization made her stiffen. She said, "Do you think I'll stop dreaming those images, if I accept what is happening?"

He lifted a shoulder in a shrug. "Who knows? Maybe after you're healed you'll go on to dream of other lives and other things."

The words he used triggered something else.

"I was a healer," she said. "Back then, in the first life. Wasn't I?"

He paused as he shifted track with her. "Yes. It was one of the ways in which you and I balanced each other."

Healer and warrior. Yin and yang. The two aspects would provide a sometimes tense balance. She chewed her lip as she considered. She wondered if they had managed their partnership without conflict.

In her dream of that first, strange life she had been a fine healer, a really good one. She didn't remember much, but she remembered that.

Had she always been a healer? It seemed like such an essential part of her. Her mate in the dream had been very much a warrior, just as he was now. How much had they changed? How much had they remained true to their core identities?

"I need to think," she muttered again. They fell silent.

She rebelled at the thought of going to someone else for healing. She frowned, aware that the feeling was not quite sensible. After all, if she needed an appendectomy she would go to another doctor.

This shouldn't be any different, but it was. This was, as

Michael said, a spiritual wound not a physical one. When she met Astra, she might feel welcome and safe, like she was reuniting with a lost long friend or a mother, but that hadn't yet happened.

She didn't know the other woman. All she had were too-brief dream images of Astra, or what had once been Astra, and Mary was tired of being vulnerable. She was tired of feeling broken.

She would much rather heal herself, if she could. Michael was an overwhelming presence all on his own, and her reaction to him was complex and bewildering. Astra must be just as overwhelming in her own way, if not more. When Michael and Astra were together, the effect would be multiplied. They had worked together as a team for a long time, long enough that they would know each other well.

Mary would rather be whole and independent when she dealt with them together. And what if she and Michael ran into more trouble before they reached Astra? She would like to be more useful than she had been when she was last attacked.

Huh, listen to her. When she was last attacked. She shivered as she realized that she had accepted just how much danger they were in.

"Where are we?" she asked.

"Just south of Grand Rapids," he replied.

He was back to being Mister Enigmatic again. She tried to search his expression in the dashboard's dim light. His eyes were shadowed, and lines bracketed his mouth. "Are you all right?" she asked. She added quickly, "I mean you said you were tired. You're not too tired to drive?"

"I'm fine," he said, his tone terse. "I just need food and coffee. We'll go through a drive-thru when we hit the city."

"Stopping for a real meal would be nice." She bit her lip when he looked at her. She sounded like a wife on some kind of crazy-bad vacation. She muttered, "I suppose that wouldn't be a good idea."

His voice remained level. "That wouldn't be a good idea."

"Makes sense," she said without enthusiasm. "I guess."

"Things don't feel very friendly in the psychic realm," he said. "I'm pretty sure the Deceiver knows somehow that you and I have connected. It feels like he's picked up the pace of his hunt."

"About that," she said. "Why is he called the Deceiver? That's not just your nickname for him. We called him that in my dreams too."

"For one thing, we shouldn't call him by his old name. When we talk and think of him, we open conduits in the psychic realm where all things are connected. We don't really know for sure what he can sense, and we don't want to draw his attention to us."

Shards of ice moved in her veins. She looked around at the already familiar interior of the car, not feeling nearly as secure as she had just a moment ago. "All right, that's creepy."

"For another thing, we call him that because that's what he is. He lived under a cloak of deception for years as he betrayed our laws and our people. He did something unheard of and turned his back on his mate. He was a moral and spiritual deformity, a sociopath in a race that had no concept of what that meant, or a word in our language with which to define him."

She swallowed hard. "I see."

He told her, "You should rest while you can. We don't know what's ahead of us, but I would bet my shirt that the rest of the trip to Astra's isn't going to be easy. We may be caught in a situation where I can't take time to lend you strength."

"Understood," she said.

Actually, that was another good reason to see what she could do to heal herself. She couldn't rely on Michael being available to keep her stabilized.

She folded his jacket into a pillow and made herself as comfortable as possible. She closed her eyes.

She thought about the wounded woman in her dream. Maybe she could make herself go back in a dream to that life before she was injured. Maybe she could remember what it was like to be whole.

She wasn't sure she would be able to, but she was tired enough that she fell asleep as soon as she closed her eyes.

HER FATHER WAS an accomplished politician and merchant, a powerful diplomat and a kind man. Her mother was clever, well-educated, happy and lovely. It was not hard to be a dutiful daughter under their doting parentage. Surely their family was the most blessed of all the Faithful in a city fabled for its wealth and beauty, where people came as supplicants from all over the world.

She had been educated as well as any man, and better than most. When she became troubled by mystical dreams and visions, her father searched for sorcerers, soothsayers and magicians of all nationalities to help decipher their meaning.

Many were charlatans. A few were true adepts, and she learned from each one. She became skilled in a variety of disciplines, although each teacher puzzled greatly over the mysteries that she presented to them.

One day, her father came to her and said, "Daughter, I have found a kind man for you, for it is past time you married."

By then she understood enough of her own nature to know what answer she must give him. "Father," she said, "I cannot."

"It is your duty," he said. He frowned, though she could tell it was from concern and not anger.

She knelt before him and bent her head. "Am I not a good daughter and a faithful child of Allah?"

"You are."

"And do you know that I love you?"

"Most assuredly." He passed a gentle hand over her hair. "You are second in my heart only to your mother."

"Then know this, my father. I would give my life for you if you asked. But I cannot marry your kind man, for I have a task to do. Allah in His infinite wisdom has seen fit to make me incomplete. I must look for the other half of my soul. . . ."

Her father listened and believed, and so they searched again, and tales spread of their inquiries.

[Mary stirred as an echo of a bone-splitting pain throbbed in her chest. She surfaced partway from the dream, pressed her hands against her breastbone, and pushed the memory of pain away as she fought against the pull of awakening.]

. . . And she pulled out of her body.

Marveling, she stood beside her physical body, which was dark-haired and strange looking, and clad in a plain tunic and trousers of homespun cotton. Her physical self sat, eyes closed, in a relaxed cross-legged position, mirroring the posture and position of her elderly teacher.

Then she held up her hands and stared at them in wonder. They appeared crystalline in the heavy amber afternoon. The astral replica of her teacher's slight, frail body joined her. "Celestial Daughter," her teacher said. "You have done well. I am pleased."

She gave her teacher a polite bow as she observed the niceties of his culture. "This person is unworthy of such high praise," she said. "It is much easier to talk in the mind voice when one is skyborne, honored one."

"It is easier once one masters the technique," said her teacher. "But practicing when one is skyborne can be hard on one's chi, or life force. Therefore we shall continue to work on the mind voice when we are in body. Aiyyee."

She turned her attention from the window. "Yes, honored one?"

The replica of his face shimmered, as he seemed to smile. "I could see that you carried yourself with grace and light. Like this you shine like the morning. This humble person is honored beyond measure to teach the Daughter of the Sun."

She returned his smile. "You dismiss yourself much too fast, honored one. Of all the would-be teachers who have made such great claims to my father, only you have shown that you have the true wisdom of the realms."

"No, child," he said. "I only have some small store of knowledge. The mysteries you present have shown my true ignorance. It has been a marvelous teaching, for which I am grateful. I can but pass on to you what little I know. Now we must get to our lesson before we tire. As you know, there are four realms—the inner realm, the physical realm, the psychic realm and the celestial or heavenly realm. Each realm is distinct, yet they are intricate in their entwinement."

"And humans are connected in some aspect to all four levels," she murmured. "So true healing must occur on all four levels as well."

"Correct. There are creatures native to each realm. As in the physical realm, some are beneficial and others are not. All are in balance. In the psychic realm we have some of the greatest, most beneficent forces on earth. Here we have the dragons. . . ."

[The amber afternoon faded as Mary half surfaced from sleep again. She stirred, her pulse sounding loud in her ears.

The car slowed. Cold air rushed in as Michael rolled down the window. There was the exchange of voices and the greasy smell of fast food and coffee. She waited until the car sped up again. Then she reached for sleep and the dream images once more, yearning for the spacious home in the city by the sea, the nurturance of tranquility and learning, the love and understanding of a family, all long since gone to dust.]

. . . And she stood in her sumptuous bedchamber. It was furnished with thick patterned rugs, mahogany tables inlaid with ivory and gold, brass lamps and glazed pottery, embroidered cushions, a divan and her bed surrounded by gauze curtains.

Carved, ornate shutters were thrown open to the breeze that blew in from the sea. Beyond the shutters she could see a cloud-studded sky and a wide, private terrace.

The terrace was one of her favorite places, suspended above the city like a jeweled pendant above a woman's breasts. She spent much time on the terrace, gazing at the fishing boats and the merchant ships that sailed in the harbor. Sometimes she took her meals there. Often she sat reading, or in thought.

The morning was drenched with sunshine and the

promise of heat. Her maidservant had laid out a breakfast of fruit and bread and sweet tea on the outside table. It was an ordinary morning like so many others, filled with many tasks, and she had grown hungry.

She took a step toward the terrace. Dread swept over her body, an unreasoning gush of terror that dried her mouth and froze all rational thought. A trembling set in her bones as though she were a deer surrounded by hounds.

It might be an ordinary day but something terrible waited for her on the balcony, something so terrible everything inside of her wailed from it.

But it was such an ordinary day her feet took another step and then another, and no, no, no, she couldn't go out on that balcony, she couldn't bear it, and she couldn't stop it either, because the terrible thing had already happened—

A male figure, radiant as a black sun, stepped from the balcony into her room. "Mary, Mary, quite contrary," said the figure. "You've started to mess around with things you might have been happier to leave alone."

She gasped and gasped, but there was not enough air.

On the balcony the sword had come down. It had almost split her in two. She'd wrapped her arms around her torn body and held her own intestines as they spilled out. Her maidservant had screamed, the whole world had screamed, and the household guards had come running but they had been far too late—

"You see," said the figure as he walked toward her, "after this afternoon I rather thought you'd begin digging around in the past. So I thought I would help you out and send you this dream. You know, do my bit to nudge the memories along because you've made a bad mistake, Mary. You're putting your trust in the wrong man. He used to be your mate, but he's been insane for centuries. He tried to have you kidnapped in South Bend today, and he's the one that slaughtered you like a cow in this past life. While I might not have had the most altruistic reasons for doing so, I was the one who tried to save your life. Have you remembered any of that yet, Mary Mary?"

She stood hunched over, arms wrapped around her violated torso, head turned sideways to stare at the black diamond man. The crack in her body shone like a golden river. He glittered in its reflection. Her face contorted in a scream but no sound emerged.

"Oh look." The figure cocked his head. "You're bleeding energy again. And it's already been nine centuries. A wound of the spirit as deep as yours can only come from your mate. I would work hard at getting away from him if I were you."

Chapter Fifteen

WHEN THE MAN had completed his agenda in the spiritual realm, he anchored himself back in his body and opened his eyes.

He had stretched out on one of the limousine seats, and he bit back a groan as he struggled to sit up. Every joint ached, even those in his fingers. He put his elbows on his knees and rubbed at his face, taking heed of the warning. Already, after just a few days, his current body was almost worn out.

Strange noises penetrated his awareness. He looked over his hands. He had left Justin handcuffed to one of the doors. The young human was eating sushi and melon balls, eyes glued to the flat-screen that no longer played CNN but instead a black-and-white Japanese monster movie.

The man looked from the television to the plate of food on Justin's lap.

"What?" Justin said with his mouth full. He shrugged. "You locked me up with a fridge and a TV."

"I sure did, didn't I?" the man said.

He started to chuckle. Come to think of it, he was starving. He took one of the plates from a nearby container and served himself salmon and crackers, sushi, a few melon balls and a petit four. He offered the plate of petit fours to Justin, who took one and put it on the plate at his knee.

"You know," Justin remarked with a flash of those charming dimples, "I've been awfully curious about that Royal DeMaria."

The man grinned as he tucked into his meal. "Have you ever had icewine?"

"Yes, but not one of that caliber. How much did it cost, a thousand a bottle?"

"Closer to four."

Justin's eyes widened. He chewed, swallowed and said, "Why the hell not."

The man opened the bottle and poured them each a glass. Justin thanked him, took a sip and breathed, "Wow."

"Yes," the man said, smiling. "Wow."

They finished the bottle. The man opened a second, and they finished that one too. Then, although he cut Justin off from having any more alcohol, the man moved on to the champagne while Gamera and Godzilla rampaged across the flat-screen.

Some time later, after he had gorged until he could not eat another bite, the man confided expansively, "People are idiots, you know."

"Why's that?" Justin asked, rubbing his eyes.

"Only the human species would produce so many nuclear weapons they could destroy the world not once, but many times over." Champagne sloshed as the man gestured with his wineglass. "They're bright enough to make them but too stupid to quit. I don't get it."

"You might have a point there," Justin admitted. Stress had deepened the lines bracketing his eyes and corners of his mouth, and his face was smudged with weariness.

"You look tired," said the man. "Did you get a nap?"

Justin's eyes narrowed. He said, "That's an awfully damn solicitous question for a kidnapper."

"I have my reasons." Ignoring a queasy sense of nausea and how his stomach felt stretched and overfull, he took another drink and continued. "Only the human species would continue to landfill reusable products in a world of diminishing resources, and spray millions of acres of arable land with pesticides until the land is virtually dead and nothing, not even earthworms or insects, can grow or live on it any longer."

"Okay, let me try one for you," Justin offered. "Only humans would haul their garbage out to the oceans then fish in the same oceans and eat what they caught."

The man laughed. "That's a good one. Only humans would mow down miles of rain forests while maundering on about the need to develop and produce clean energy and cut down on air emissions. All of this, while at the same time they fight to keep from bringing their current power plants up to reasonable safety or cleanliness standards. I ask you, how logical is this behavior?"

"I must admit, not very."

"Honestly. I could go on, but it's clear I've had too much wine." He pointed at Justin. "Not that I don't like people. I do. I just believe in calling a spade a spade, and people are fucking morons. Their pets have more sense."

"Yeah, I miss my dog." Justin sighed. "My bed, my Tony, my life."

The man squinted at the last of the champagne. An inch of liquid fizzed at the bottom of the bottle. What the fuck. He was already drunk. He took a swig and swiped at his mouth. "Then you gotta smile at groups like SETI who search so hard for extraterrestrial intelligence. They're constantly sending out messages of greeting to the cosmos. Is it any surprise no one's responded when you look at the current conditions on Earth? For Christ's sake, the human race isn't even toilet trained."

"You sure don't sound as if you like people much," Justin muttered. "In fact, you sound just like a predator."

The man finished off the bottle. "Go ahead, tell me—how does a predator sound?"

"Oh, you know, they talk of their prey with a certain amount of contempt." Justin's smile was edged, his dark, intelligent eyes hard. "It's like how abusers justify their actions in their head. It's never the abuser's fault. They like to maintain the fiction that they are victimized and put-upon. Those they abuse are too fat, or too stupid, or too infuriating, or unworthy for one reason or another. That makes it all okay for the abuser to crack someone across the face, or to attack someone verbally."

The man's eyebrows rose. "You have a point. Maybe I'm just getting old and crotchety."

"You're what, all of twenty-eight?" Justin laughed.

The man said in a soft voice, "I thought Sodom and Gomorrah were kicking towns. I helped to destroy the city of Troy, and I taught vivisection to the Babylonians. I'm probably the only person left alive in the world who could be called an expert in ancient Egyptian torture techniques."

Justin's eyes had widened as the man spoke. "Ooh-kay."

"You got to love that Middle East," the man murmured. He licked a smear of chocolate off of one thumb. "Those folks know how to put a special spin on their cruel streak."

"I tell you what," Justin said. "I'm going to write a book. Forget about *Interview with the Vampire*. I'm going to entitle mine *Drunken Binge with a Murderous Whack-Job*. Think that could sell?"

The man considered. "I think it has a certain ring."

"When I hit the *New York Times* bestseller list, I'll style my hair in a pageboy and wear lots of black and lace. We'll have to sell the condo and get something with more atmosphere so I can drape myself broodingly around on the furniture. Tony should start writing poetry. We'll be all the rage, new to the literary horror scene, you know, yet somehow soothing in our familiarity."

The man threw back his head and burst out laughing. "Damn, I do like you."

"That is not as reassuring as one might think," Justin said.

As they talked, the limousine had reached Grand Rapids. Guided by GPS, the car cruised through the streets in the quiet predawn. It pulled into a motel parking lot and stopped outside the office.

"Excuse me," the man said to Justin, who had turned silent and grim. He reeled out of the vehicle. The nausea grew worse, so he stuck his finger down his throat and vomited the contents of his stomach by the back wheel. Once he was sure that he had his equilibrium back, he walked into the office, while his driver waited with the engine running.

Inside he hypnotized the sleepy desk clerk and rifled through her memories. He was still too drunk to be as careful as he should, so unfortunately, she might end up with brain damage after he was done. Once he determined which room was farthest away from potential witnesses, he took a master key and walked to it. Tame as a housecat, the limousine purred behind him as the driver kept pace.

He was so close behind Mary, he could taste it. He hated to take time away from the direct hunt, but it couldn't be helped. He had been expending too much energy. He had coordinated the hunt for her on several different levels, sent two dreams and committed various murders, and he hadn't rested in over a week.

Originally he had wanted to keep Justin as leverage, but the kind of marathon output he had been engaged in took its toll. He had to use whatever means he could to recoup his flagging energy.

At first running into Justin at Mary's house had appeared to be a windfall. It seemed like a sensible strategy to take Justin hostage, and to throw his old dead host into Mary's house and set it on fire. The news of her burning house should have brought her racing back home, where he had been waiting, ex-husband in tow.

Things hadn't gone as planned. Mary had not only been acting unpredictably, but she was now reunited with the warrior. Worse, they were moving faster than he had anticipated. With the first dream, he had been keeping his promise to Astra. That second dream he sent to Mary had been a judgment call in terms of energy expenditure, but if he had managed to rattle her enough to slow her down, it might have been worth it.

In the meanwhile, he needed to take some much needed time to recoup.

He had learned a lot by experimenting in the early years.

In more mellow times he could inhabit a healthy adult body with relative safety for up to twenty or even thirty years. When he was able to take his time, he could groom a future host and harvest not only a body but also the host's finances and resources at his leisure, adding them to his own separate estate, which he maintained with numbered Swiss accounts, property managers and accountants.

In periods of crisis he rushed through his hosts at a more precipitous rate, especially when he indulged in his tendency to overeat and drink during times of stress.

He found that the ideal method was to take over a body and rest for a few days or a week, to let the meat recover from the death of its natural spirit and adjust to its new owner. When that couldn't happen, the body didn't have time to adjust properly and tended to fail at a faster pace, especially when he was involved in strenuous activity. In fact, the more energy he had to expend, the faster the meat deteriorated.

Everything came with a price, but it was still worth it. By taking over a body, killing its native spirit and inhabiting it through its prime years, he avoided the cycle of death and rebirth. He bypassed that very critical, vulnerable period of forgetfulness involved in starting a new life. He reduced the risk of forgetting his own identity and the identities of those who hunted him. It gave him an edge.

He had suffered through some tough times and narrow escapes, but he had managed to leap from body to body for most of the last six thousand years. He had only gone through a natural birth three times.

The first time had been the inevitable result of his escape from his home world. Once he had been killed, and the last rebirth had happened when he had died by accident. Each birth and new life had involved years of dreams and confusion, ambitious study, the single-minded pursuit to understand his nature, and to recover his memories and his power. They had been harsh vulnerable times when his enemies had come closest to annihilating him. He didn't like to think about them.

When he had reached the motel room he wanted, he used the master key to open the door. In the meantime, his driver parked the limousine, pulled Justin out of the backseat and force-marched the male to the room.

"Let him loose," he told the driver, who did as he ordered.

The man looked in a mirror to bid adieu to his current body. His host had been a handsome young computer salesman and a fitness fanatic, perfect for his purposes. He strolled over to Justin as the young man shook free of the driver's hold and rubbed one wrist.

"Wait outside," he said to his driver.

The driver left the room, shutting the door gently behind him.

Justin's clever, narrow face was tight with tension as his gaze darted around the room and settled on the bed.

The man sighed. "No, we're not here for that. I already told you, there's no time."

In the end Justin looked at him, all satire and mischief gone. It was clear that the young man knew what would happen, as most prey did.

Justin said, "You don't have to kill me."

The man felt an unexpected pang and tilted his head in acknowledgment of it. He said in a gentle voice, "But it is to my advantage if I do. I do like you, but players of the shadow game cannot afford to make decisions based on sentiment. I wish I could promise this won't hurt, but the truth is, I just don't know. No one has ever survived to tell me. I will try to be careful though."

He shot out a hand before Justin could reply. His host's hard, strong fingers gripped that clever face as Justin fought to punch him, and he sent out a black spear of energy that impaled Justin's head. Justin's body convulsed as his spirit died.

Timing was crucial when he took over a body. He had discovered there must still be a spark of that mysterious, vital thing called life, or his own spirit couldn't take hold. It was impossible to inhabit a host that was already dead, futile to inhabit one that was dying. In the process of experimenting on how to transfer from body to body throughout the centuries, he had discovered how to create his drones, killing off just enough of a body's essential spirit to allow for his control yet leaving enough of a life spark so that the body could continue to behave like a normal human.

He lowered Justin to the bed, slipped out of his old host and into Justin's body. The body of the computer salesman fell discarded to the floor.

He had to ride out the last of the convulsions. Uncomfortable, but necessary. The meat always sustained some trauma at the death of its original spirit.

After the convulsions had run their course, he took a power nap. Then, although he could have wished for more rest, he made himself sit up and get out of bed. He had too much to catch up on, phone calls and e-mails to make to various employees, and then he needed to redouble his efforts on the hunt. Plus, he was happy to discover that he felt hungry again. Justin had been careful not to overindulge in what he ate.

He didn't bother to glance at the computer salesman's body that lay sprawled by the bed like cowboy Woody from *Toy Story.* Instead he went to the mirror again and inspected his new residence with the clever, narrow face, and the well-kept body.

He tried out one of Justin's charming smiles and felt another pang. Whatever had caused that adorable, mischievous twinkle was gone. Still, he did like the result.

He widened the smile to watch the dimples deepen. This could work out better than he had expected. Justin cared about his ex-wife. Depending on what abilities and memories she recovered, Mary might actually trust him for a short, critically important while.

"Man, you're hot," he said to the image. If he ended up occupying this body for any length of time, he would have to visit his tailor.

He had a particular style he favored. It was killer chic.

Chapter Sixteen

MARY WOKE UP hard from her dream. She sucked in deep, ragged breaths as she stared at the battered interior of the car, at the grim man beside her, at the highway.

Memory settled into place. She scrubbed her face with both hands. Christ, she was getting tired of being tired.

"What's wrong?" Michael asked. He shot her a sharp, pale-eyed glance.

She shook her head, not wanting to answer him. She looked instead at the bags of fast food on the seat between them. "Is some of that for me?"

"Yes. The coffee in the holder is yours too. It's probably cold by now. I didn't want to wake you. I figured you needed to sleep." His mouth tightened, a pale, grim line. "What's wrong?"

To avoid answering him, she ducked her head and rummaged through the contents in the bags. There were a couple of large lukewarm hamburgers, French fries that had congealed and stuck together, and a piece of cardboard with a picture of apple pie on the outside. She opened the plastic lid on the coffee cup and sipped at it. The brewed liquid tasted harsh. It was cooler than the food. She sighed.

"I want a month in a hotel by a beach," she said. "I don't want dreams. I don't want to ask a single scary question, and I don't want anyone to tell me anything useful. I plan on practicing the art of cheerful incuriosity. And I want room service to bring me a mushroom and asparagus omelet, a fruit salad and fresh-ground French roast with cream."

Steel entered Michael's voice as he repeated, "What's wrong? If you dreamed it might be important."

She snapped, "I'm sure it is important, but I'm not ready to talk about it. Quit pushing me."

He blew out a breath between his teeth in a sharp, impatient sound but fell silent. She forced herself to eat some of the starchy food while she thought. Then she drank all of the coffee, grimacing at the bitter taste.

She could no longer summon even a pretense of disbelief at what was happening. A bleak resignation settled in her chest. It rested in a lump where the assassin's sword had cut into her, all those many centuries ago.

"There isn't going to be any month on the beach, is there?" she said. "This is the sum of our existence. We're born, we're haunted, we work to understand what has happened to us, to remember and to find each other, and we try to destroy the Deceiver. Then we die and are reborn, and it starts all over again. Over and over."

Michael gave her a long, thoughtful glance, clearly assessing the change in her attitude, although he didn't remark on it. Instead he said, "That's not quite true. There can be years of peace at a time. It's possible to have a good childhood. This life has been harsh for a lot of reasons."

She thought of the sprawling, gracious home in that ancient city by the sea, of the people who had been so mystified by her and who had loved her anyway. Her eyes pricked with tears. "Yeah," she said, her voice thick. "When was the last time you knew peace?"

He remained silent. Somehow she knew he would.

She said, "I need to go to the bathroom. Can you stop as soon as possible?"

"We'll make a quick stop at the next rest area. It should be in about ten minutes."

"Thanks." After a few minutes she said, "Do you even think it can be done? Destroying him, I mean. It's been such a long time."

"It can be done," he said. "He's powerful, but he's not a god. This world is a big place, and he has gotten talented at hiding. We spend a lot of time just hunting him. And not all of us have been involved in every conflict. I was alive when the Deceiver destroyed two of the group in the fifteenth century, and Astra's told me something about the other two and how their lives ended. She doesn't know for sure exactly what happened to Gabriel and Raphael, only that they died together."

Shadowy memories of people ghosted through her head. She asked in a hushed voice, "How did they die? But I guess that's the wrong way to ask the question, isn't it? How were they destroyed?"

He rubbed the back of his neck, and the lines of his face settled into that habitual grimness. "One of his favorite tricks is to capture one mate and use torture to try to control the other. Ariel and Uriel were the two he killed when I was alive. He caught Uriel while Ariel was imprisoned by the English. It—the local politics of the time don't matter. He destroyed Uriel, and Ariel's spirit dissipated as well. I couldn't get to her in time. I couldn't get to either one of them." The bones of his face stood out in the dim light of the dashboard. "They both died alone."

"I'm so sorry," she whispered. The back of her throat felt thick with unshed tears.

He glanced at her. "This situation we're involved in right now—it's important for a lot of reasons."

Then he fell silent. She didn't ask anything more about the other pair, rubbing her arms as she thought. "Is it important because the four of us are all in one geographical area?"

He nodded. "That's part of it. You've managed to resurface, which is another part. Also, early yesterday morning one of our allies in the Secret Service was assassinated. That means the Deceiver is preparing to try to take control of the U.S. Presidency."

"Good God," she uttered. She stared at the lines of his hard-edged profile. "You can't be serious."

Michael said, "It's another one of his favorite tricks, to either assume the identity of a head of state or, failing that, to control one. He's not yet in a position to make his play, but it won't take him much longer to get there. The good news is that he has to try to take control in person. The bad news is, we no longer have someone in the White House with the ability to sense his presence and with the authority to act on it."

Maybe a month on the beach had happened in other lifetimes, but it didn't sound like it would be happening here soon, or even in this lifetime. She let her head fall back on her headrest.

Mary, Mary, quite contrary. You're bleeding again.

And it's been over nine centuries.

A wound of the spirit as deep as yours can only come from your mate.

The black diamond man was such a liar. Of course he was. He was a mean-spirited malcontent who used words to manipulate and wound. She couldn't let him worm his way into her head.

But there was Michael who had just hours ago rubbed at his temple with the barrel of his gun. Michael had looked like a man standing at the edge of a precipice, like a man bereft of a single reason not to plunge over that edge and shatter himself on the jagged rocks below.

She held herself tense, closed off from the occasional searching glances that he gave her, until he slowed the car and turned onto an exit ramp. Then she looked around.

Dawn had begun to turn the eastern part of the sky rose-colored while the western horizon darkened to a royal purple. Close by, a cluster of gas stations, fast-food restaurants and diners huddled together. The buildings looked dingy and tired of their codependency. Michael pulled into one of the gas stations and parked in the lane closest to the road.

"I'll get gas since we're stopping." He spoke in his terse voice. "Don't take long."

"I'll take as long as I have to." Her reply was just as terse. She could feel him looking at her but she refused to turn her head. She got out and walked inside, feeling as tired and shabby as the buildings looked.

The station attendant was a pimply young man wearing earbuds. Mary could hear the rap music from across the counter. She struggled to find a friendly smile and asked in a loud voice, "Where are your restrooms?"

The smile was a wasted effort. He didn't glance up from his magazine. "Outside. You need a key."

She waited a moment, but he didn't move. Her friendly expression vaporized. She slapped her hand on his magazine and snapped, "May I have the key, please?"

The attendant gave her a nasty glance. She sneered back at him, feeling as if she had regressed to a snotty teenager. He shoved the key across the counter. She snatched it up and stomped outside.

Michael stood by the car pumping gas. He had shrugged on his jacket, no doubt to hide his gun, and he stood hipshot, hands resting at his waist. He looked haggard as well, the lines of his hard face jagged.

She felt a ghost of compassion stir at the sight. This life had not been kind to him. In the glow of the station's lights his eyes were the color of pewter. He watched her with his Mister Enigmatic expression.

She forced herself to walk at a decent speed around the corner of the building. Once she was out of Michael's line of sight, she rotated her shoulders and stared at the open field that bordered the gas station. The ever-present forest lay just beyond. She felt the urge to run until she couldn't run any longer, just for the illusion of freedom for a few brief minutes.

"Mary, Mary, quite contrary," she muttered. "The freaky son of a bitch got that much right."

She jabbed the key into the lock and opened the door. The restroom looked as bad as she had expected, with a broken mirror, and a rust-stained sink and toilet. Her gaze bounced around, taking in the filthy floor and the lack of paper towels. At least the dispenser had toilet paper.

Her hotel on the beach would have gorgeous bathrooms with designer soaps and lotions, fresh-cut flowers delivered daily and Jacuzzi bathtubs. Populations of small island countries could live in those bathrooms. Hell, forget about the beach. Give her a bathroom like that, and she would take her entire vacation in it.

She shut and locked the door, and used the facility. Then she washed in cold water. There was no hand soap. Of course. When she finished, she studied the door. At least that was adequate for what she wanted, constructed as it was of sturdy metal. Better yet, it had the kind of lock that bolted from inside.

She gritted her teeth and lowered herself onto the floor in a corner as far away from the sink and toilet as she could get. Leaning against the wall, she closed her eyes and took deep breaths as she concentrated on relaxing and remembering how easy it had felt in her dreams to slip away from her body, like sliding a knife through whipped cream.

She could do this again. She remembered how.

She breathed in deep, slow breaths, and after a few moments, she slid away from her body. As the first pounding began on the door, she stared at her transparent hands, then at the crack down her torso that continued to bleed light.

Michael's deep voice reached her through the door. "Mary? Mary!"

She smiled and walked through the door.

She hadn't counted on Michael's thirty-plus years of experience, or his psychic sensitivity. His head snapped around as she passed him, his hard-angled expression incredulous. They stared at each other. He said, "Jesus. What the hell are you doing?"

She told him, *I can't heal myself. But I remembered someone who can.*

"Astra can heal you." He bit off each word. "We don't have time for this."

Tough, she said. *We'll just have to make time. I don't know either you or Astra any longer, and I'll be responsible for my own healing.*

He punched the door, a short, savage jab. "You don't know what the fuck you're doing. There are predators in the psychic realm as well."

Then you'd better stop distracting me, don't you think?

He punched the door again. "If I get inside that bathroom," he snapped. "I can make you get back in your body. Just remember that—and act fast."

She hesitated. *That's it? You want me to try?*

"If you think you can heal yourself, by all means do it," he said. "We need you strong and well, and the sooner that can happen the better. But pay attention. You are very visible to anyone who has the ability to sense you. The longer we sit still the closer our pursuers get, and you're using up strength you can't afford to lose. Now *hurry.*"

New questions crowded her mind. She shoved them aside. He was right—she was using strength she could ill afford to lose. She could ask questions later.

She moved away from Michael, the gas station and the parking lot, until she stood in a clear wide space of field. Even with the sun-filled space around her she could hear whispers and rustlings. Dark things flitted at the edge of her vision, but she could sense that none of them quite dared to draw close in the full light of morning. Not yet.

She faced the eastern sky. The first tip of radiance appeared above the horizon. She caught her breath as she found she could stare at the sun full-on. Then as her centuries-dead Asian teacher had once instructed her, she called a long lyrical, physically unpronounceable name.

Then she waited. Michael, her body and a growing collection of furtive dark creatures in the psychic realm waited as well. After several moments her bright and eager hope started to dim. She became aware of her waning energy and their increasing danger, all of which she had gambled in this desperate foolish experiment.

Goddammit Mary, Michael roared. *Come back.*

She shook her head. *No.*

Whatever you tried didn't work.

Just a little longer, she gasped. Her astral presence began to flicker.

Come back now!

A hollow boom sounded as he threw his shoulder against the restroom door. He stepped back and began to kick it in.

She was about to admit defeat and return to her body when something far-off snagged her attention. She had the sense of an archaic being lifting its head to look in her direction.

A tremendous power shot toward her. It came from an impossible distance, moving with the speed of a lightning bolt. Even though she had left her physical body behind, her astral projection fell to its knees. The gathering of dark creatures hissed and fled.

The dragon flew across the rose and gold of the dawn. Her spirit leaped at the sight of its immense, undulating body and a wingspan that draped the sky. A creature of pure elemental energy, it was one of the monarchs of Earth's psychic realm. It plummeted to land before her. Then it raised its huge lion's head and regarded her with an ancient, tranquil eye.

She bowed her head. *Honored One, this unworthy person's heart is full of gratitude that you chose to answer her humble request.*

Celestial Daughter, said the dragon. Its voice was a bell that shook the bones of the world. *You have slept long and long. And you bleed.*

This person will cease to exist unless someone wise in the arts of the realms should honor her with healing. Her astral presence trembled from the strain of being so long away from her body. She abandoned formal speech as she gazed up, into that swirling, alien eye. *Our group owes a debt to this world that has not yet been paid,* she gasped. *I would not want to leave . . . without paying it. I thought you might help . . . for the love of my old teacher who was once your friend. . . .*

I would for the memory of my old friend, and that would

be reason enough, said the dragon in a gentle voice. *But I would also help for love of the memory of your brightness that has now grown so dim. Come.*

The dragon scooped her up in massive, gnarled claws and bent over her. Feeling cradled in a strength that was as old as time, she abandoned all strain, all fear and pain, and rested in total trust.

Then the dragon breathed on her.

She plunged into a deep pool of lava. Her entire being caught on fire. The pain was a horrific, immeasurable shock. After the first few moments it also felt necessary, as it purified, strengthened and nourished her energy rather than destroyed.

Poisons, injuries and old soul scars smoothed away. Something in her that had been crippled long ago straightened gently into place.

When she had been burned to an essence beyond form, thought or words, the dragon stopped. Still she kept glowing, but it was no longer in gouts of uncontrollable, hemorrhaging energy. Now she glowed with a healthy bright color like a new-minted coin.

She had a dim awareness of Michael approaching with her body in his arms. He and the dragon spoke to each other, but she did not try to understand their exchange. Then the dragon deposited her back into her physical self.

Her head lolled. She managed to crack open her eyes. Michael held her against his chest, supporting her upper body while her legs sprawled on the ground. With her psychic sense, she could see the dragon looking down at her. Not yet capable of words, she pressed a hand over her heart in a silent gesture of thanks.

Now you are as you were meant to be, Daughter of the Sun, said the dragon.

Before either she or Michael could say anything, it launched with a forcefulness that buffeted them to the ground. When it winged away, the trees in the nearby forest bent and swayed as though from a violent wind.

She lay limp in the circle of Michael's arms, at first too

replete and weak to move. She had forgotten the simple miracle of feeling whole.

She had, in fact, never known the feeling in this life. Tears spilled down her face. A muscle in Michael's lean jaw worked. He turned from watching the dragon's flight to press his lips against her forehead. His arms were clenched so tightly on her, she could feel his heart beating, too fast, as if he had been running for miles.

She looked up at him with pity and thought, he doesn't remember that he killed me.

Chapter Seventeen

MICHAEL KNELT ON the ground and held Mary, her head cradled in the crook of one arm as he stared into her eyes. They were as beautiful as the rest of her, jeweled and bright, a vivid, aquamarine blue. She gazed back at him, her expression grave, even compassionate, although he did not understand why she would look at him like that.

She was a game changer. *This* was a game changer.

He became aware that he gripped her too tightly again. He clutched at her as if he were afraid she might melt into nothing. He forced his arms to loosen.

She gave him a small, tentative smile. "It's better now, isn't it?"

He ran a hand down her slim torso, probing mentally at her energy. To his careful scrutiny, she felt burnished and whole. She felt magnificent. Sharp terror for her had spiked then vaporized, leaving behind a vast, dizzying void that made his ears ring.

He whispered, "It's so much better now."

She put a hand over his as it rested on her flat abdomen. "They can't trace me like this anymore, can they?"

"No, they can't," he said. "You're no longer shining like

a beacon in the psychic realm, which means our day just got much better." He lifted his head to study the field and the nearby buildings, frowning.

Her smile vanished. She sat up, out of his arms, and looked around too. "Then what's wrong?"

"You know how I said there are predators in the psychic realm?" He glanced down at her. "Some have gathered around, hoping to feed, but they can't hurt you now. Still, we need to leave this place."

She struggled to get to her feet. Her movements were slow and clumsy, and it was clear that she was hurting. The dragon's healing had been purely psychic, so she still retained all the physical soreness from her earlier injuries. Before he thought about it, he slipped an arm around her and lifted her upright.

She gave him another guarded glance, murmuring thanks. Why did she look at him like that?

His head was splitting. The pain was so bad it made his eyes throb. Despite the fact that she had changed the game, and they were no longer in quite the imminent danger of discovery that they had been, the sense of an oncoming crisis crushed down on him. He shook his head to try to clear it, to expand his senses to check their immediate surroundings. It was a mistake, and it made his head pound worse than before.

He managed to say, "Get in the car. I'll be right there."

She hesitated and looked as if she were about to say something. Then she must have changed her mind, because she limped toward the car without a word.

Changing the game. Changing everything.

I don't know you and Astra any longer, she had said. *And I'll be responsible for my own healing.*

Grimly he went into station to pay for the gas and buy yet more coffee, along with a travel packet of pain reliever. He tore the packet open with his teeth and dry swallowed the pills before scooping up the coffee cups and pushing through the door.

Mary's declaration was an outright statement of distrust.

He couldn't blame her. What she said, after all, was only the truth.

But how would Astra respond to Mary's unpredictability, or her rejection of reliance on either one of them?

MARY CLIMBED BACK into the passenger seat of the car, still trembling and moving with care. She watched Michael step outside the station with two disposable cups. His expression was set in bleak lines, the skin around his eyes tight.

When he climbed in the driver's seat, she held her hand out for her coffee. She said, "I'm sorry."

"Sorry for what?" He didn't look at her as he started the car, glanced around and pulled onto the road.

"For what I said about you and Astra." She sipped the steaming hot liquid and lifted her eyebrows. The filthy little gas station produced a delicious cup of joe. Who knew?

"You only spoke the truth. You don't know Astra or me any longer." His voice was toneless. He was back to the stoicism of the soldier survivor. The car sped up to the speed limit and held steady.

She fastened the lid back on her cup. No matter how good it was, she couldn't face another swallow of coffee. Then she put a hand on his thigh. Under the covering of his jeans, his powerful muscle tightened at her touch. "What I said was only one version of truth, which can sometimes be as hurtful and misleading as a lie. I trust you."

"Maybe you shouldn't." His expression remained closed, harsh.

"Maybe I didn't," she said. "But I do now. Or at least I trust you far more than I did a few hours ago. But we've still had a long separation, and we've all changed. We need to get reacquainted with each other, with who we are right now."

There was a pause. He drank coffee and watched the road. "How are you feeling?"

"Indescribable," she said. She stretched and took a deep breath. "I feel clean and straight, like everything inside me has come right again, even things I didn't know were damaged. This might sound funny, but I've defined myself through a sense of being injured or incomplete for so long that I'm not sure who I am without it." After a pause, she said, "The dragon helped with my memory too."

His gaze shot to her. "Do you remember any more about the past?"

She chose her words with care. "The dragon didn't help bring back everything, but I remember bits and pieces. Some of my recurring dreams were from the life when I was wounded. What he really did was to help clarify everything. I understand better now some of the things that have happened. I suppose if I want any memories from other lives, I'll have to work at retrieving them like you did."

"Tell me." She heard buried in his quiet voice a desperate hunger. "I need to know what happened."

"I will," she replied. Her voice was as hushed as his. "I promise. But I'm not going to have that conversation with you while we're on the road."

His mouth tightened, and he rubbed his forehead as if it hurt. "It's too important to wait."

Why did he feel such urgency? Was he close to remembering for himself? She didn't want him to recover those memories when he was behind the wheel of the car.

"If that's so, then we need to find a safe place to stop," she said steadily. "We need real rest and real, nutritious food. I have no idea what happened to you before you caught up with me, but you had to have expended a lot of energy to find me."

His reply was slow in coming. "I did."

"I'm not surprised," she said. "I don't know about you, but I need recovery time. I worked a twenty-six-hour ER shift, and after that, there's been one crisis or epiphany after another. Half-hour naps on the run aren't helping. Coffee isn't doing a thing for me anymore. It's just making my stomach hurt. My body has had the crap kicked out of it, I ache all over and I've had enough."

He glanced at her in thoughtful assessment. She also

didn't like how he looked, but she didn't mention that. A small vein throbbed at his temple. His gaze was too bright and somehow feverish, his expression stark. She wanted to put her fingers on his wrist and take his pulse.

"A game changer," he muttered.

"What do you mean?"

"When you healed, you changed everything." His chest moved as he took a deep breath. "We need to reunite with Astra before we fight him. We stand the strongest chance of winning if we're all together. But you're not traceable in the psychic realm any longer, and we've ditched your car. As long as nobody recognizes you, we can afford to pull off the main roads for a while."

"We'll both be better for it," she said.

"Agreed." Thoughts moved like shadows behind his eyes. "I know a place where we can stop. I go there as often as I can. It's secluded and it should be safe enough. We can rest and talk there."

"Are you still okay to drive? You look like you're in pain."

He covered her hand with his own larger one. "I'm fine. I just have a headache. No need to fuss."

Her whole body reacted to his touch. She felt the rasp of calluses across the back of her knuckles, and she focused on the weight of his hand on hers. A self-conscious heat tinged her cheeks. She coughed. "If you think this is fussing, you don't know fussing. This is self-preservation. I don't want you to drive off the road. If I start fussing, you won't be able to mistake it."

A glint of amusement entered his overbright pewter gaze. "So you're a talented fusser?"

"I have my moments," she said.

"When can I get the full treatment?" he asked.

Her breath caught. Maybe she wriggled a little. "When do you want it?"

A slight smile eased the haggard lines of his face. He said, "Anytime you feel like starting."

Slowly she turned her hand, underneath his, and the sensation of his skin sliding over her sensitive palm was so shockingly erotic, her heart started to pound. She whispered, "That's a dangerous thing to say to someone who might have compulsive fussing tendencies."

"A woman with a hint of danger." His voice had deepened and turned rough. Moving his hand over hers, he rubbed her forefinger with his thumb. "That's pretty hot."

She thought, I am flirting with a man who wears a gun and knows how to use it.

That was just about as alien to her as, well, discovering she was an alien.

She had the impulse to remove her hand. She didn't, but she did back away from the flirting. "Okay, maybe I am fussing a little," she confessed, her voice turning serious. "I have things I need to tell you, and I'm concerned."

"I know," he said quietly. "That's one of the reasons why I agreed to stop."

She nodded, biting her lip. "How far away is this place where we're going?"

"It's about an hour away. We've got to go through Big Rapids first."

They fell into silence. She watched the growing dawn. They were allies now. All it had taken was one long, strange night. She hadn't even known he existed two days ago. She hadn't known who she was. How can someone exist in such rampant ignorance? She had stepped out of the painting, and the painting shattered.

The early morning traffic thickened as they neared Big Rapids. They passed through the city at a quick pace and into the quieter landscape beyond.

"Tell me what your life has been like," he said. "You said you worked an ER shift."

She stirred. "I work—I worked at a community hospital. Cue back to the fussing. People got better out of self-defense."

"You're good at your job."

He hadn't phrased it as a question. She gave him a quick glance and a wry, lopsided smile. "Actually, yes. I had my choice of residencies at more prestigious facilities, but I liked the idea of contributing something to an underprivileged area."

The rare pleasure that had lightened his expression vanished. He became the hard-edged soldier again. "You said your house burned down."

Her fingers jerked under his. "That's right."

He flicked a finger in the direction of the dashboard. "I heard about it on the news too. Missing doctor's house burned in the St. Joe/Benton Harbor area. In the news segment on the radio, the police had yet to—" His words cut off.

His abrupt silence had her twist in her seat to face him. She searched his profile. "Police had yet to, what? What happened?"

He gave her a quick glance under slanted brows, his mouth grim. He said, "The police have yet to issue a positive identification on a body they found in the house. All the newscast said was that it was a six-foot male between twenty-five and forty-five years of age."

"Oh shit," she said. Her eyesight blurred.

His long hard fingers curled around hers. "You know who that was?"

"It had to have been Justin, my ex-husband." She pinched the bridge of her nose as hot tears spilled over. After a moment, she could speak again. "He—we—it's a long, stupid story, but we figured out fast we never should have gotten married, and we ended up friends instead. I knew he was going over to my house yesterday afternoon, but I left anyway. I've been so worried about him."

After a blank pause, he said, "I'm sorry."

She bent her head to wipe her wet face on her shirtsleeve. "Why was he killed? What purpose did that serve?"

He tightened his hold on her hand, a sure steady grip. "We may not ever know the answer to that. But when we can, we'll try to find out."

Silence descended in the car. She looked out the window as she struggled with grief and rage. Finding comfort in the contact, she kept her hand on his thigh. He covered it with his own whenever traffic allowed.

Some distance north of Big Rapids, he signaled and exited the northbound highway, turning west. A large portion of Michigan was National Forest. With the turn, they entered old-growth woods then they turned north again onto a gravel road. Soon she saw a small cluster of cabins and buildings, and a sign that said Wolf Lake.

Michael pulled into the gravel lot of a small building with the words WOLF LAKE STORE painted on the side. He said, "Stay in the car. Your photo may have been released in the news. I'll be right back."

She nodded, sliding down in a self-conscious hunch in her seat as he strode into the building. Even though she kept a wary eye out, she didn't see anybody.

Less than ten minutes later, he stepped outside, carrying two full grocery bags in each hand. He set the bags in the backseat before climbing back into the car. They drove at a gentle pace in silence for a few more miles, until he turned onto a drive that was guarded by a weathered NO TRESPASSING sign.

She had rolled down her window in the growing heat of the morning. The forest was alive with an old green presence that wrapped around them in welcome.

They pulled up to a rough-looking cabin. Michael turned off the engine, and even though the car ran at a soft, powerful purr, in that quiet place the change seemed loud.

She sighed at the peaceful sounds of birds singing, and the soughing wind as it braided fronds of leafy branches. The sunlit, green clearing emphasized a huge absence as the weight of stress lifted off her body.

"I'm never living in a city again," she said. "This place is wonderful. Is it yours?"

"Yes. I come here when I can. The lake is about a third of a mile down a path that ends behind the cabin. Sometimes I fish."

He got out of the car and she followed. He handed her the four grocery bags. As she took them, she saw that two of the bags were filled with food, and the two other bags were stuffed with simple, new clothes. She caught a glimpse of a gray sweatshirt, and a packet of white women's socks.

Then he reached into the backseat again, and he pulled out two large black canvas bags. One of them seemed an ordinary bag one might pack for a weekend. The other was longer and he hefted it with more effort, so it had to be heavy. She looked at that bag for a thoughtful moment.

He turned and walked up the porch steps to the door, warning over his shoulder, "The cabin is pretty rustic."

"Is there any chance of hot water?" She followed him onto the porch.

He unlocked the door and shoved it open with a foot. "In about a half an hour."

"Then it sounds like heaven on earth to me," she said.

He stood back and let her walk into the cabin first. She stopped in the middle of a large room, pivoting to look around as he brought in his bags and tucked them out of the way.

He was not exaggerating when he called the cabin rustic. The walls were wooden with a few built-in bookshelves. A table and a few chairs sat in the middle of the floor. Two corners at one end of the room were filled with a wide bed and a dresser.

Against the far wall a counter, a small stove, sink and refrigerator comprised a kitchenette area. More bare shelves were under the counter, stacked with a variety of canned foods. A large fieldstone fireplace took up most of the third wall, with wood stacked in a nearby box. A package of long matches sat on the mantel.

A closed door was in the last corner. Michael walked over to the door and disappeared. He stepped back in the room moments later.

"This is the bathroom. I've turned the water heater on," he said. "We'll be able to wash in comfort soon."

"Thank God," she said. She felt like she had picked up twenty miles of road dirt. "I like your cabin. How long have you owned this place?"

"Eight years. It's only a day's travel from Astra's place,

and it's private and independent. Sometimes I need to get away from everything, even her. Especially her." He walked over to the refrigerator, opened the door and looked in the freezer. "The fridge is working fine. Aside from what I picked up at the store, I have some frozen stuff, mostly steaks, ground beef and vegetables. I keep the coffee in the freezer, and there's the canned stuff under the counter."

"It all sounds terrific," she said.

She set the grocery bags on the table and unpacked the food he had bought. Most of the items were off-brand, just good, plain food, enough for several meals. There were containers of flavored yogurt, eggs, a small tub of butter, another small container of half-and-half, apples, cheese, a package of pasta noodles, a jar of spaghetti sauce, crackers, a loaf of bread and a few packets of fresh vegetables and fruit.

Asparagus, mushrooms and strawberries.

Her eyes moistened as she stared down at the fresh produce. He had bought ingredients to make her wish breakfast at a dream hotel: a mushroom and asparagus omelet, fresh fruit and coffee with cream.

She gathered up the perishables and tucked them into the otherwise empty fridge.

Then she rummaged through the other full bags. He had bought a petite-sized pair of jeans, two T-shirts, a hooded gray sweatshirt, the white socks she had glimpsed earlier, a packet of pink underwear and a set of three sports bras. There was also a new toothbrush, antiperspirant and a travel-sized tube of toothpaste.

The sports bras looked a bit big, and the T-shirts and sweatshirt would be baggy but useful enough, and hopefully the jeans might fit. The socks and underwear should be fine. They were all treasures.

"I already had soap and shampoo. Is it okay?" he asked. He had picked up the lighter of the two black bags and paused with it in his arms. He was watching her with an uncertain expression that looked odd on his normally confident, decisive face.

"It's more than okay. It's amazing. Thank you so much for thinking of it." She looked with longing at the bathroom door. "Do you think the water has warmed up enough by now?"

He shook his head. "I doubt it. If you want, you can shift things in the dresser to make a space for your clothes."

"Thanks."

She rifled through the dresser. It felt odd to handle his clothing, adding another layer of intimacy to their already convoluted and confusing relationship. She took one of the new T-shirts and a pair of underwear from the packet then tucked the rest of the clothes, still in their plastic packaging and labels, in the top drawer. The T-shirt looked like it was long enough to reach her upper thighs.

Clutching the clothes in her hands, she turned to him. "I can't wait any longer. Do you mind if I go ahead and use the bathroom?"

He raised his eyebrows. "Help yourself, but I'm sure the water isn't warm enough yet to bathe in comfortably."

"That's okay. I've got an agenda," she said. His well-cut mouth widened in a smile. His unshaven jaw lent his features a rough appearance, and his wide shoulder and chest muscles flexed under his black T-shirt as he moved around the cabin.

She was fascinated by all the evidence of his existence, by the sight of him, by the quiet sounds he made as he moved around, his warm fragrant male scent, by her own response to him. It took an effort to yank her gaze away and slip into the bathroom. Once inside, she leaned against the door and shook her head back and forth.

Too much, too much going on.

On the bright side, a lot of items on her fix-it to-do list had been wiped out. She didn't have a dirty house any longer that needed cleaning. She couldn't feel guilty about not finishing any of her quilting projects, and going to work was out of the question.

On the dark side . . . She thought of Justin again, and her eyes filled.

Then she shuddered and scrubbed her face with one hand, closed the door on her grief for the time being, and looked around. The bathroom was utilitarian and somewhat outdated, with the water heater in one corner, and a bath and shower, and a white sink with a small mirror, but it was mercifully clean, which gave it a five-star rating in her travel book for this trip. A small cabinet hung over the toilet. When she opened it, she saw towels and washcloths on the two shelves inside.

Stripping naked, she scrubbed her panties, bra, socks and T-shirt in the sink. Then she tackled washing her dirty jeans, wrung all of the wet clothes out as best she could, and hung everything along the top of the warming water heater so it would dry faster.

Cleaning her teeth with her new toothbrush was nothing short of heavenly. By then the water had heated enough to make bathing comfortable, so she ran a bath and stepped in as soon as she could. The various scrapes she had acquired throughout the previous day and night stung as they came in contact with the water, and her bruises throbbed. Still, soaking in hot water eased some of the aches. When the water began to cool she soaped her hair and body.

The soap and shampoo in the bathroom were as utilitarian as the rest of the place. She knew she would pay for that later as her unruly hair dried, but she was so grateful to be clean that she didn't care. She would have to wrestle the tangles into submission while her hair was wet and then braid it back. With any luck—she paused in the middle of rinsing and her breathing halted—with any luck she would live to wash her hair again with a decent conditioner soon.

The small bathroom had warmed to a toasty temperature by the time she dried, slipped on the new T-shirt and panties and wrapped her hair in the towel. As she walked into the main room she discovered that Michael had built a fire that crackled as it banished the damp chill from the cabin.

He had made even more coffee with an old-fashioned percolator on the stove, and he sat at the table with a cup near his elbow. She had thought that the challenging years of her residency had turned her into a heavy coffee drinker, but he had her beat by a mile.

Any pretense he had to domesticity ended at that point. Her steps slowed as she took in the various weapons he had laid out on the table. The long black bag that had seemed so heavy was open at his feet. A large Kevlar vest draped the back of one chair. He was cleaning his handgun.

As she approached gingerly she caught a glimpse of something in the bag that looked remarkably like a sword.

Easing into a chair, she watched his deft, large long-fingered hands manipulate the gun, her body tense.

"What are you so upset about?" Michael said, his tone brusque. "The weapons? You've got to know by now it's what I do."

"What crawled up your ass and died?" she said. She threw him a nasty glance, pushed to her feet and went to the kitchenette area to rummage for a glass. "I've had so much shit hit my fan in the last three days, you take your pick. Four people were gunned down in front of me, for no reason I can tell except that I bumped into them and my attackers liked to kill things." She couldn't find a glass, so she took a coffee mug, filled it with cold water and drained the contents. As she filled it again, a betraying quiver ran through her voice. "A lot of people have died on me in the hospital, but I've never seen anything like that—not in real life, not right in front of me—so you go ahead and do what you need to do, and you have my blessing. But yes, it upsets me." Needing to leave the room, she turned toward the bathroom. "Do you want a bath? I'll run you a bath."

His hand circled her wrist as she tried to walk past. She tugged, trying to free herself, but he yanked her toward him, into his arms. Giving in to the simple, animal comfort he offered, her arms slipped around his neck, and she cried for the murdered family, for Justin and for the cruel, unapproachable look that had been on Michael's face and the life he must have lived that made him look like that.

"I'm sorry," he said. One large hand rubbed up and down her back.

"Me too. For the meltdown, I mean," she said, leaning against his long, muscular body. He had so much strength it was easy to believe that he had survived so many centuries. She laid her cheek on top of his head and fingered his short military-cut dark hair. "I'm okay. I just haven't had time to cry for them before now and I needed to."

"I'm sure you did," he said. He pulled her onto his lap, holding her tight. "It's going to get uglier."

"I know. It's not fair," she said. She put her head on his shoulder. "I feel like a whole person for the first time in my—in this life. I want to, I don't know, celebrate. Play. Put on a pretty dress, go out on the town, go dancing, maybe see Paris. Then I look at the terrible things *he* has done to other people, and I feel like such a whiner."

"Well, you are a whiner," he said. He gave her a light pinch, and in spite of herself, she chuckled. He said in a more serious voice, "You should be able to put on a pretty dress, go dancing and see Paris. But that's not what we have in front of us right now. I'd say you're entitled to some whining." He tilted his head and looked down the length of her body. "Your knees are all bruised and scraped."

She looked at her knees too. "It doesn't matter."

"It matters. Poor knees." To her utter shock, he bent and twisted, and pressed warm lips first to one knee then the other.

He lifted his head. They looked at each other. His eyes had dilated until they appeared black. Sexuality shimmered between them, a silvery, shining heat. Then he carefully, firmly put her on her feet again.

"Sit over there," he said. "And tell me what you need to tell me."

Even though the room was comfortable and warm, she shivered away from his body heat. Rubbing her arms, she huddled into herself and tried to adjust. "It isn't pretty."

"Very little of this is." He snapped a piece of his cleaned gun back into place.

"Yes. Well." She was grateful he had created a physical separation between them, yet unsettled as well.

Was it her human self that felt the urge to sink her fingers into his flesh so deep she could never let go again? Or was it her alien, earliest self that whispered in the crevices of her soul that he was the part of her that had been missing for so long? She felt as though a stranger had slumbered deep in the subterranean recesses of her mind and was now finally coming awake. That stranger had impulses and motivations she didn't fully understand or trust.

There you are, she had said to his radiant form upon waking up. She had felt such unutterable relief, such incredulity and joy.

But there was the weight of what lay behind them, and between them.

So much, so much.

She slipped into the chair and looked away from his pewter gaze, trying to concentrate on what she should tell him. He needed to know only so much, and then no more.

"About my last life. I was a member of a wealthy family. We were Muslim and we lived in a large Mediterranean port city. I'm not sure where, maybe Constantinople. I guess it could have been Cairo. Anyway, my father was not only powerful but he was progressive, and I was loved and educated quite well. Earlier, before we had stopped at the gas station, I had dreamed of the best of my teachers from that time. He was the one who taught me about the Eastern dragons. That was how I knew to try calling the one I called. The Eastern dragons aren't anything like the Western concept of dragons. They are very wise."

"So I saw. You are certainly full of surprises." He laid the gun aside.

"Yes, I've found that I'm full of surprises to me as well," she said in a dry voice. She pulled the towel off of her head and tried to run her fingers through her damp, curling hair. "Anyway, in that life I was in the process of recovering some sense of my real identity through dreams and meditation. I knew about you, or at least I knew enough to start looking for you." She dug the heels of her hands into tired, scratchy eyes. "We searched everywhere we could for clues. My father interviewed anyone who claimed to have any magical arts or esoteric knowledge. One morning someone tried to assassinate me." Even though the dull ache was gone, she pressed a hand to her chest, hyperaware of the still, tense man beside her. "It was a sword." She gestured down her own torso. "You saw the path where it cut."

"Yes."

"For anyone else it would have been a mortal wound. Maybe it would have been mortal for me as well. I know I tried to start healing myself, and the household was in a panic. My father had been interviewing some petitioners that morning. One of them claimed to be a magician and a physician. He was the Deceiver, but nobody knew that, nor would they have understood what that meant if they had."

His fists pushed down on the tabletop. "And you would have been too injured to be sensitive to his energy signature, or unable to protect yourself if you had."

"Yes." She frowned. "I don't know where that wonderful teacher of mine was that day. Maybe he had traveled back to his homeland or maybe he had died. In my dream he was elderly and seemed pretty frail. He was also wise, and an adept at psychic nuances. I think he would have known not to trust the Deceiver."

"What happened?"

"My family was desperate for any chance to save me, so the Deceiver became my physician. God knows what he used to treat the wound." A convulsive shudder shook through her body, and his gaze jerked to her. "One of my recurring dreams was about him sprinkling the wound with some kind of powder and probing at it with his fingers. I was disoriented from the drugs and the constant pain. I'm not sure how long that lasted. It felt like a long time. Weeks, maybe months. The understanding I got from the dragon's healing was that he was somehow poisoning me."

Michael flattened his hands on the table. His face was the color of old ivory. "If you had died, he would have lost you," he said. "If you had healed, you might recognize him. He could have just destroyed you, of course, but then he couldn't use you as a pawn, and besides you would have been no danger to him as long as you were so badly injured."

"Yes." She frowned. "There was something, too, that the dragon showed me about the poison. It was alchemical in nature. He wasn't just keeping me from healing or dying. I think he was trying to turn me, or to break me in such a way that he could control me. And I think the whole thing was a setup, starting with the attack."

Michael took a breath. "Why didn't it work?"

"It might have worked eventually, but a—a friend realized the truth of what was happening. He helped me to die." She looked away. "You see, by then I was too damaged for my body to heal. Besides, I was so tired from the pain I was ready to go."

When the silence became prolonged, she looked back at Michael. He had closed his eyes, and he rubbed his temples again as though his head still pained him. "Who was this friend?"

When it came right down to it, she couldn't tell him. "What difference does that make now?" she said. "After a while, somebody was perceptive enough to see that something had gone horribly wrong, and he was brave enough to help, that's all. It happened a very long time ago."

He shook his head. "You said that you had a teacher who would have known not to trust the Deceiver, but that everyone else did. They were your family and they loved you. They would have been too full of hope to kill you."

"Michael, please let it go." She kept her voice calm and quiet. It was her ER voice, used in times of crisis.

White teeth showed as he bit out, "I can't."

She watched him with shadowed eyes and hurt for him. She couldn't make herself tell him what she knew, yet she understood instinctively the struggle going on inside him, how in spite of all reason, he was driven to know.

He lifted his head and met her gaze. His face was stark. "I did it, didn't I?"

In the gentlest way she knew how, she said, "Yes."

When he stood, he knocked his chair over. When she

would have laid a hand on his arm he jerked away. "I can't see it," he said. "I don't remember."

"Don't you think that's for the best?"

He didn't answer. Instead he strode into the bathroom and slammed the door.

Chapter Eighteen

THE CREATURE CLUNG to the underside of the car outside the cabin. It was a tattered handkerchief of shadow, a dark spirit from the psychic realm that liked to feed on the negative energies of pain, anger, hate and despair. Intelligence or species didn't matter to it. Pain was pain.

The dismal cluster of gas stations had been an adequate feeding ground for it, where it lay in wait for travelers. Plenty were either strong, happy or well adjusted enough, but there was always someone passing through who was grieving or suicidal, or riddled with the wormwood of hate and resentment.

The creature had first been attracted to the woman who had bled with such beautiful, agonizing brightness, but it had been afraid to approach too close to the fierce, dominant presence that traveled with her.

Then the dragon had come and it had healed the woman with its terrible, shining power. The creature had cowered underneath the Ford, staying still and silent, for, other than the ability to drain creatures that were already weakened, it had almost no power. It was nothing more than a small scavenger. One exhalation of the dragon's breath could incinerate it in an instant. When the dragon left, it had nearly left as well, but it was a greedy little spirit and the two people it followed were not only potent. They were volatile as well.

Unable to leave the promise of such alluring pain, the creature had attached itself to the undercarriage of the car. It sniffed at the emotions of the people inside and hoped to catch them unguarded.

When they stopped traveling and went inside the cabin, it continued to wait, for it could sense the ferocious emotions that swirled around them.

Then there was a maddening, delicious upsurge of pain, and it came, not from the woman, but from the man. The creature detached from the car's undercarriage and drifted over to the cabin window, hovering at the hot psychic scent, too frightened of the warrior to draw any closer and too far away to feed.

Chapter Nineteen

MICHAEL PUT HIS hands on the bathroom sink and leaned over it. The pain in his head that had been plaguing him all day turned excruciating. He fought waves of nausea, and his body shook while his eyes watered until they overflowed.

He felt like he stood at the edge of a hot, howling darkness. He saw everything else as though at a distance, through blurred vision. Compared to the howling dark, everything else was pastel.

In their long search for clues about Mary's disappearance, he and Astra had worked hard to recover his memories of the last time he had made contact with her, but they could not glean anything of significance. Why hadn't anything surfaced?

For a long while they had believed that something must have happened to Mary in a lifetime before she had remembered who she was, or before she had been able to make contact with anybody else in the group.

But he knew better now.

They hadn't recovered his memories because he couldn't bear to remember. He couldn't bear it, but the darkness was rising, and he couldn't hold it off any longer. He sank to his knees, rested his head against the cold, hard porcelain sink and the memories came.

They hit him like shards of flying glass, a disjointed attack from within that cut him to shreds.

He had been a mercenary soldier, a captain in command of his own company. They wintered in his home base in Italy. Otherwise his company roamed throughout Europe to fulfill the contracts he accepted.

In that lifetime, he had recovered his memories and had known who he was. He took jobs from various principalities that were both lucrative and wide ranging, which helped to fuel his search for others from the group.

One spring, he heard a tale through traders, of a ruling family in Constantinople that looked for answers to arcane mysteries and paid good money to honest men. Trusting his instincts, he began to journey to the city.

One morning, early at his campsite on the road, he bolted awake to a sharp thrust of pain, though he had sustained no physical injury. The sharpness soon faded, but the pain stayed with him, a ghostly ache that infused him with urgency.

Leaving his company to follow as fast as they could, he rushed ahead to the nearest port city and boarded the first ship he could find. A couple of weeks later he arrived in Constantinople, only to hear a story of an inexplicable assassination attempt that had left a cherished daughter lingering near death, and her wealthy family shocked and grieving.

In the bathroom, Michael shook his head, his breathing growing heavy and uneven. He fell, and the howling dark consumed him.

Mary pounded on the bathroom door with the flat of her hand, a quick, urgent staccato. "Are you all right?"

"Leave me alone," he said in a hoarse voice.

The memories continued to slice at him.

Try as he might, he couldn't gain an audience with the wealthy family. They had closed themselves off from the public and were surrounded with a small private army.

"I can't," Mary said. "I'm worried about you. Talk to me."

"Go away," he managed to say.

So he had to break in to their citadel. He felt the cold stone beneath his hands as he scaled their walls, night shrouding him in a purple gauze of shadows. Combing patiently through the halls and apartments, and hiding when necessary, he eventually found her sickroom.

The guard at the door had been one of the Deceiver's tools. He killed the man easily enough, but he knew that the Deceiver had sensed his presence. He entered the room and barred the door, but it was only a delay. Death rushed in a rage to snatch back its prey. They did not have much time.

Inside, the room held a scent like violets and putrefaction, and the air was tainted with the twist of her suffering spirit.

He walked over to the bed and lit a lamp.

The images. After being buried for so long the images assaulted him, as vivid as if they had happened yesterday.

The black fan of her long hair on the silk cushion. The haggard beauty of her face, carved with the graciousness of her spirit. The gorgeous, dark eyes that opened, immense with pain and dilated with opium.

The smell. It came from her body.

"Do I know you?" she asked. She could only manage a mere thread of sound.

He stroked her hair. She was so lovely. She was a treasure beyond the price of all princes. "We've known each other for a very long time," he told her in a tender whisper. "I've come to help you."

Her gaze lit with the fragile luminosity of wonder. She breathed, "I've been looking for you."

He caressed her cheek, her dry lips. He whispered, "I've been looking for you."

When she smiled at him, it lit the entire world. "Where have you been?"

Where have you been? Not, where are you from? Because even in those first few moments of reconnection, it was clear that they both knew where they were from.

"Florence," he said. He smiled back at her. How could he

not? His was an old, savage soul, and she had, in an instant, become the single, shining jewel that lived inside of him. "I'm sorry it took me so long to find you."

"Have you found any of the others?" Cold, delicate fingers like twigs touched at his weathered face.

He shook his head. "No, only you." Time winged away from them. He wanted to lunge after it and capture it in both desperate hands. He closed his eyes, touched his lips to the tips of her fingers, and with every ounce of passion inside of him, he willed everything to be different. "I don't even know your name."

"Maryam," she murmured. "You?"

"Michel."

No matter how desperately he tried to capture it, time would not halt its precipitous flight. Guards shouted outside in the hall, and the pounding began at the door.

He had still hoped against hope at that point. He entertained wild thoughts of tying her arms around his neck and scaling the outside wall, until he peeled back the covers and saw the leather corset. He slit the laces and opened it, and as the support fell away, he saw the long purple-edged wound gape open. He caught a glimpse of glistening muscle or organ before he wrenched his gaze away.

Curled on the bathroom floor of the cabin, Michael gagged.

The tiny movements of her rib cage, the ruined breasts, were a torture to witness.

The household guard began to take an axe to the door.

"I'm not going to get better," she said in that ghost voice. "I'm so sorry. I would for you, if I could."

He kissed her forehead, her eyes and her beautiful mouth.

"You're going to get better," he said. He settled on the bed beside her, moving with infinite care so that he did not cause her any more pain, and he laid his head on the silken pillow beside hers. At the same time, he pulled his stiletto and held it tucked against his arm so that she could not see what he did. "You will like my home, I think. I have cows, and a few sheep. In the winter, there is snow on the fields and nothing to do but laze abed with a fire roaring in the fireplace."

She breathed, "I would like to see snow."

The guards were halfway through the door. In a few more blows, it would splinter. He touched his lips to her temple. "A noblewoman nearby has gardens filled with irises and azaleas. We will make love in the winter, and I will steal flowers for you in the spring."

"And I must learn how to milk a cow." For a few fleeting moments, amusement and tenderness had banished the shadows in her thin face.

He rose up and leaned over her. "We will live until we are very old," he said against her lips. "And we will be happy right up until the moment we die."

"I love this dream," she whispered. It was the last thing she said to him.

As the final blow from the axe splintered the door down the middle, he slipped his stiletto under her ribs and pierced her heart. Her spirit slipped so easily from her body, with a relieved sigh and the lingering brush of an insubstantial caress.

He'd had a few moments in which to decide against escape, when the realization of empty years stretched ahead of him. While he knew he had done the only thing he could, that he had been right to release her from her torment, something broke inside him.

Nothing mattered anymore, not their eons-long struggle, not the destruction of the Deceiver, nothing. Guards poured into the room. With an expert flip, he reversed the stiletto in his hand, positioned it and thrust it into his own heart. The gush of warm liquid flowed over his fingers, and his body settled beside hers on the bed.

Then he knew no more.

In the bathroom, Michael curled on his side and pressed a hand to his chest as his heart kicked in wild arrhythmia. He was aware, as if from a great distance, of strong, slender arms circling him, a feminine body pressing against his side and fingers pressing against his carotid artery.

Michael, Mary said in his head. He turned his head away at the intrusion, pressing his sweating cheek against the cold, tiled floor.

Broken.

Radiance cascaded into him. It surrounded and filled him, and soothed his heart back into rhythm. He gasped as it drenched the raw shards of darkness inside, and his spirit gulped at it with ravenous eagerness. He didn't think he could ever get enough.

Michael. She pulled him onto his back and passed a hand over his hair. *I have been looking for you.*

Her serious, blue gaze was very different from those great, lovely dark eyes from so long ago, but he would still know her anywhere. Anywhere. He gasped, *I have been looking for you.*

She was stronger than she looked. She drew his upper body up and cradled his head against her shoulder. *I would have loved to learn how to milk a cow.*

And I would have loved to make love in the winter, and steal flowers in the spring. He closed his eyes. He had never been a man of peace, except with her.

She rocked him. *The memories are terrible, but they are in the past. Don't let them consume you. Acknowledge them, and let them go.*

He nodded. Her physical scent and psychic energy mingled in his senses until he didn't know where one began and the other left off. It was all the same: warm, fragrant, golden. It nourished him with a lavish, lustrous generosity. Twisting up, he wrapped an arm around her neck. "This was why you didn't want me driving."

She laid her warm, soft cheek against his. "You didn't seem to remember, and—well, I knew how hard my memories have hit me. I would have protected you from them, if I could."

"I needed to know." He nosed her neck and rested his lips against the healthy, vital pulse in her throat. Alive, she was alive again.

She pulled back and cupped his whiskery cheek. "I'm

going to run you a bath," she said. "And I'm going to find you some clean clothes. Are you hungry?" He shook his head. "No? All right. Then afterward we're going to rest, Michael. Mike. Does anyone call you Mike?"

Nobody called him anything. Only Astra knew that his name was Michael. He stood when she stood and let the soothing patter of her voice wash over him like a gentle rain. "You can call me whatever you like," he said.

She put the lid down on the toilet and pushed him toward it. Obediently he sat.

"Can I? Mike," she said. Her voice was thoughtful as she turned to start the water running in the bathtub. She bent to test the water's temperature with her fingers then adjusted one of the knobs. The new T-shirt came just over the curve of her ass. She glanced over her shoulder with a small, calm smile. "Trevor."

"Aloysius, even," he said. "Or hey you."

Whatever she called him, he would always answer.

She straightened and flicked water from her fingers. "I think Michael suits you best. We'll stick with that."

"All right." He leaned against the back of the toilet and let exhaustion sweep over him.

"I found your razor and shaving cream earlier," she said. She pulled the items out of the medicine cabinet behind the mirror over the sink. Her gaze ran down his lax posture. "You're too tired to shave, aren't you?"

"Yeah," he admitted. He was so tired, he could lie down and die if he thought it would offer him any chance at peace.

"Not to worry. I'll do it for you, if you'll let me."

Incredulous, he watched her wet a washcloth with warm water. After coaxing him to tilt back his head, she placed the cloth on his cheeks and jaw. Then she squirted a mound of shaving cream into one small, capable hand. She lathered his face, rinsed her fingers, turned off the bathwater, and started drawing the razor over his skin with such a light, deft touch he barely felt it.

He regarded her in mute amazement. He couldn't remember anyone doing such an intimate, caring thing for him before. Certainly no woman had ever done so. Perhaps one or two might have wanted to, but he had always rejected female overtures with a clinical efficiency. Relationships bred vulnerability, and he had known from a very early age he wasn't going to lead a normal life. Besides, all the women he had met had been too pastel.

"Mary," he said when she turned to rinse the razor under a trickle of warm water.

"Yes?"

His grave gaze met hers. "Are you fussing now?"

The corners of her eyes crinkled as she looked down at him. When she drew the razor across his cheek, it felt like a caress. "I think we can say I'm officially fussing now."

WHILE HE WIPED his face with the washcloth, Mary found clean clothes for him and set them beside the tub. She had to step between his long, outstretched legs in order to move around the tiny bathroom.

A spark lightened his sober gaze. He took hold of her forearm, and she stopped moving. Watching her steadily, he stroked the callused ball of his thumb along the sensitive skin inside her elbow. Sexuality shimmered between them again. She gave him a crooked smile back, shook her head and slipped out of the room so he could bathe in private.

Linen, blankets and pillows were stored in tubs underneath the bed, packed with rings of cedar. She made the bed efficiently with old, soft cotton sheets, two cotton blankets, and a heavy, insulated green bedspread. With only the fireplace for heating, the cabin would get cold at night.

Then she tackled her neglected hair with the travel brush from her purse. The shoulder-length tangled mane was already partially dried, and she had a miserable fight with it. She had just managed to wrestle it into a simple braid when Michael strode out of the bathroom, his dark, wet hair slicked against his well-shaped head. He wore only black cotton pants that rode low at his hips, revealing a long washboard abdomen, and carried socks and a T-shirt in one hand.

She had known he was big, of course, but she hadn't realized how massive he was across his chest, arms and shoulders. He had the heavy, mature muscles of a man who had spent his life fighting.

She forgot what she was doing and stared at him with her mouth open. Her body forgot how much it had been kicked around, as her long-dormant sexuality came to singing life, not as a brief shimmer of possibility this time but as a searing bolt of urgency. Red heat settled into a sharp, throbbing ache between her legs.

Then she closed her mouth with a snap, spun around and turned down the bed, her hands lingering unnecessarily to twitch the bedspread into better alignment. Maybe while she was fussing at the bed, she could find a way to stuff this attraction under the mattress.

Of all the times for this to happen. Could it be any more inconvenient?

She couldn't remember when she had last been sexually attracted to someone. Had she ever been? After some experimentation, and her lackluster experience with Justin, she had shrugged, said no big deal and closed the door on the whole subject while she concentrated on getting through the rigors of her residency.

To tell the absolute truth, a part of her had been relieved and even eager to shut that door, for she couldn't regard sex as just a physical act and she wasn't able to handle the intimacy, the emotional involvement.

Michael gave her a long, deliberate look then walked over to the table and picked up his gun. He reached into the large black bag and removed a sword in a scabbard. "Do you know how to shoot a gun?" he asked.

Jolted out of her preoccupation, she lifted her head and stared at what he held. Then she sat down slowly on the edge of the bed.

She had been right earlier. That was an honest-to-goodness sword.

"I know how to point and pull a trigger," she said. "Theoretically. I mean it's pretty evident. Do I know how to aim, or where the safety catch is, or how to clean a gun or reload it? I do not. I've never held a gun before in my life, and I never want to either."

He raised his eyebrows. "I hope you never have to. But in case you do . . ."

"Oh no." She threw herself backward on the bed with a groan, flopping her arms flung over her head.

"Oh yes," he said.

He knelt on one knee on the bed, caught her wrist and yanked her upright. Then he sat beside her and proceeded to show her the sleek, black weapon he held in one hand. She sighed as she thought of the BabyMamas.

"This is a nine-millimeter," he said. "It's my smallest gun, and it's the only thing I have that's halfway suitable for the size of your grip. Here's the safety catch. This is when it is on safety, and this is how you turn it off. This is how you reload." He removed the clip and slapped it back into place. "If you ever have to fire this or any other gun, remember it has a kick. Try to anticipate that and brace yourself as you shoot. Squeeze the trigger, don't yank at it."

She endured the impromptu lesson as he made her hold the unloaded gun, heft its weight in her hands and practice holding it in a shooting posture. The gun was lighter than she expected. She stared at it in revulsion.

"That's it, I've had it," she said. She flopped back on the bed again, a Raggedy Ann doll of passive resistance. "I've had-it-ten-hours-ago had it. I don't want to see or do anything else."

"I guess that'll have to do for now. Just be sure to grab this one if you need to." He placed the nine-millimeter on the dresser and laid the sword on the floor beside the bed. Then he went to the black bag and pulled out another, much bigger gun. His large hand gripped it with casual effortlessness. "This is my gun."

She stared. "That's not a gun, it's a hand cannon."

"It's an assault rifle. It fires more than six hundred and fifty rounds per minute."

"Yeah, well," she muttered. "Like I said, hand cannon."

His well-shaped mouth quirked. "Whatever. Just don't grab this one, okay?"

"That is so not a problem," she told him as she stared at the ceiling.

Guns are not sexy. They're not.

Watching him, now, as he held a gun, checked the chamber for rounds, took it apart and reassembled it, his every movement economical and efficient, while his tough face remained thoughtful and calm—okay, that was sexy. That was very much sexy.

Damn it. She had never been a soldier-groupie, and she wasn't going to start being one now.

"Good." He placed it on the dresser alongside the other one. "Tomorrow I'm going to take you outside so you can practice firing at an actual target and reloading."

"Just for the record," she said to the ceiling, "I'd rather not."

"Duly noted," he said ruthlessly. "We're still going to do it."

She raised herself up on one elbow and glowered at him. Then she touched the edge of the sword's scabbard with a delicate toe. The scabbard was plain leather, ugly with scratches and scrapes, the hilt of the sword worn.

This wasn't a replica or a museum piece. This sword was used hard on a regular basis. No wonder his muscles were so built up across his chest and shoulders. She wondered where and how he practiced, and with whom. "Why a sword?"

"Sometimes it's the best weapon." He checked outside then bolted the door.

She brooded. "You know how to use a lot of different weapons," she said. It wasn't a question.

He sat on the bed beside her. "Yeah."

"It's what you do," she said. "I know."

He sat far too close. The mattress tilted down toward his greater weight. The pulse in her throat and wrists gave an erratic leap. Sitting upright, her gaze flew from him, to the fire dying in the fireplace, to the guns on the dresser like a trapped and panicked bird.

"Mary," he said in quiet voice. He touched her temple

and traced along the edge of her hairline. His callused fingers ghosted along her skin with remarkable sensitivity. She shivered. "We should sleep now."

She nodded. She gave the wall a ferocious frown, miserable with confusion and desire.

She said with grim determination, "Those creatures we once were. They belong in the past."

He said nothing. He stroked along the curve of her cheek and caressed the soft, sensitive skin of her lower lip.

The muscles of her thighs shook with fine, small tremors. She looked straight ahead then closed her eyes and said unsteadily, "We're nothing to each other anymore."

He curled his fingers around her ear. "Don't be ridiculous," he said. "We were what we were, and we'll always have a deep soul connection because of it."

"We might have known each other for forever, but crazy as it sounds, we also met less than two days ago," she insisted. Even to her own ears she sounded weak. "We're human now."

"We're more than human. We'll never be fully human. Look at me."

She opened her eyes and turned her head. When their gazes met, she felt a deep sense of falling. His lean, tough face was serious. He said, "You are looking at your best friend in the entire world right now."

She went still, both physically and mentally, everything going quiet and calm, as she realized she believed him. "I know."

"That would still be true if I was seventy-five years old and looked like Santa Claus," he said gently.

He surprised her into a small laugh. "Would it? What if I looked like one of Snow White's seven dwarves?"

"Of course." He cocked his head, considering her. "You do realize that we have been together in many lives, but we have not always been sex partners."

She blinked. "I . . . haven't had a chance to think about it."

"Of course you haven't. But the fact is, I am not Santa Claus, and you are not a bearded dwarf. We're also not siblings in this life, or parent and child, or grandparent and grandchild." He gave her a slow, male smile that creased his lean cheeks and lit up those pewter eyes. "Instead, you are a woman who is so beautiful and vibrant you take my breath away."

"No," she whispered. "Don't you dare."

His eyebrows rose, and his smile deepened. Who knew. The tough soldier guy had dimples. His fingers slipped under her chin and caressed the slender column of her throat. "Don't I dare what?"

Her eyelids lowered to half-mast. Her recalcitrant lips kept trying to droop into a soft sexy pout. She folded them tight and warned, "Don't you dare try to seduce me."

"I won't, I promise," he murmured. "I'll just kiss you instead."

He gave her plenty of time to pull away, she had to give him that. He twisted at the waist and tilted his head, and somehow she found herself leaning forward as she lost control over her renegade mouth. When his warm firm lips took hers she was already kissing him back. Her pulse ratcheted to a higher speed.

His hand moved up to cup the back of her head as he deepened the kiss. The texture and pressure of his firm lips, the penetration of his tongue, were intensely sensual.

Just sharing that one, light kiss with him was more arousing than any sexual encounter she'd ever had. She curled a hand over his thick wrist as she lost herself in shocked pleasure.

He pulled back with obvious reluctance. She forced her heavy eyelids open as he took in a breath that shuddered through his muscled frame. He cleared the back of his throat and said in a husky voice, "I know the timing sucks. And maybe we are more human now than we were, and maybe we don't know who the hell we are to each other any more. All I know is that we have a rare chance to find out."

"It's just all happened so fast," she whispered.

"I know. But it would be a damn shame if we didn't keep

an open mind about each other. You have been missing for so long, and he took all of your choices away from you for hundreds of years. Give us a chance to find out who we are to each other right now, in this life. Whatever that might be."

She touched her mouth as she stared at him. Her lips were still slick and moist from his. She whispered, "Yes, you're right. Of course I will."

He kissed her mouth again, more quickly, and then her nose, and the thin, tender skin at her temple. "And," he said, "we need to sleep. I'll warn you, I am horribly pragmatic."

"I *know*," she said.

Surprise bolted across his face. He burst out laughing.

She gave him a small grin and hurried on to say, "No, I mean, I *agree*. You're absolutely right. We've got to get some rest."

"All right," he said. "Scoot over. You get the wall side of the bed."

He was putting himself between her and the door, in reach of his weapons. She didn't argue with that logic. Instead she slid over and slipped under the blankets. He stretched out on top of the covers with a weary sigh, reached for her and pulled her down against his side. She curled against his long body. He kept one arm around her shoulders, passed the other hand over her hair and kissed her temple one more time before closing his eyes, while she rested her head on his warm bare shoulder.

His male energy surrounded her, warm and nourishing. She relaxed, basking, and something cramped and long-starved melted away.

Maybe that had nothing to do with her ancient, alien self. Maybe that was her human self, relishing the simple pleasure of being held in a strong man's arms, the exotic sensation of feeling safe and well. She blanketed him with her lighter, more delicate energy, and felt him ease into peace.

They seemed to fit together with such perfection. Contrast

and confluence, two interlocking pieces that balanced and sustained each other.

"I'm so glad you found me," she whispered.

His arms tightened. He murmured, "I am too. Rest."

She did. She slipped gently into a deep, dreamless sleep, as light and silent and drifting as snowfall.

Chapter Twenty

GRATEFUL FOR THE chance to let his tired body go lax, Michael fell into a heavy sleep.

If asked, he would have said he was so unconscious that he didn't know a thing, but there was a part of him that went deeper than unconsciousness, that was more buried than his bones. That part was aware of the warm slender body curled against his side, and the bright energy that lay over him like a silken blanket.

The sensations sent him on a strange journey. He crossed a border into an exotic country filled with comfort and easement, and for the first time in centuries, he enjoyed a nourishing peaceful rest.

When an entity began to probe at the corners of his mind with a subtle, delicate dexterity, he roused.

He met it head-on. When he recognized it, he managed to stay the daggerlike psychic lash he had almost flung in its direction.

He said, *Astra.*

Michael. Amusement colored Astra's words. *Always the stronghold.*

Naturally, he told her. *It's what I do.*

I've never once managed to get all the way inside your head, she mused. *Or touch your dream images, not even when you were a child.*

He said nothing. He remembered it well, how she had probed at him, trying to get in.

I wish I could figure out how you do that, she continued. *It's a hell of a talent. I can get into anyone else's dreams, human or otherwise, even the Deceiver's, although I do not like going there. But not you. You do dream, don't you?*

Of course I do. He pulled an image around him, the mental gesture like donning a cloak.

A great hall in an early Norman castle appeared, with a long scarred wooden table, a massive fireplace standing cold and empty and suits of armor displayed at various points around the room. The castle was from that first, strong memory he had recovered, their home in a previous life. The life that had taught him the simple, powerful lesson of happiness.

He had never let Astra see any other mental image but this public arena where he had once ruled as warlord. It served as both message and reminder to her.

After he had formed the great hall, he created the mental construct of his physical self. Soon afterward, Astra's small dark, feminine shape appeared. She never appeared as an old woman in dream or psychic sendings. Instead, she wore the appearance of the young woman she had once been so long ago.

She looked so delicate and innocent, in the first blush of her youth, and that, he knew, was one of the most dangerous illusions anywhere in the world.

"What do you want?" he said, his tone truculent. He stalked over to the head of the table and sat. "I'm busy."

"Are you? Busy doing what?" she asked. She studied him with large, expressive eyes. "I wouldn't have been able to reach you if you hadn't been sleeping. Why don't you want to visit with me?"

She still probed along the edges of his awareness with delicate little touches, rather like a cat lapping at a bowl of cream. He had lost count of how many times he had endured it before. He had always been faintly repelled by the sensation.

"I was *resting*," he snapped. "Which is entirely different from just sleep. Let's get this over with. What do you want?"

She ignored that. "How long will it take for you to reach me?"

"We've stopped, so it will be a couple of days." His foul temper prompted him to add, "If we come."

"What?" The single word hit him like a slap. Fury suffused her features. "You would never seriously consider such a thing. Why would you make such a threat?"

"Because you're pissing me off," he said. "Seriously. I am sick to death of your constant questioning and testing. Now quit screwing around with me, and tell me what you really want. Are you trying—again—to see if I've been corrupted?"

Anger vibrated through her. "I have seen it happen."

"I'm sure you have," he said, regarding her with weariness.

"You of all people should know why I do the things I do!"

"Should I?" His voice turned hard. "There's a huge difference between someone who refuses to be controlled by you, and someone who's been corrupted by the Deceiver. I know you've always been freaked out that you can't get inside my head. You think I'm not aware of how often you've wondered whether or not I might be too great a risk for you to handle? Get the fuck over it, Astra."

"You forget your place," she hissed. "How dare you speak that way TO ME."

"I haven't forgotten anything. My sense of autonomy doesn't mean I've been corrupted, and I don't want to play this game right now. Be straightforward for once in your life—if you can—or I swear Mary and I might just walk away, because I've earned better from you over the years, and I've had it."

Silence fell. Underneath the illusion of imagery, her

energy roiled with anger. He remained as still and obdurate as stone.

Finally her energy calmed, and she approached to sit at the table near his right hand. She asked, "I could sense when Mary stopped bleeding in the psychic realm. You don't have the skill to heal something like that, and she couldn't have healed herself. That wound was too severe. I want to know who healed her, and what happened to her."

He drew on his reserves of patience. "She summoned one of the Eastern dragons. It was a very old, powerful one. It remembered her from a former life and looked on her kindly."

Quick suspicion chilled her features. "She knew to call a dragon?"

He pinched his nose. "Mary is not faking. She's not twisted, and she's not controlled by anyone either. Once I found her, I haven't left her alone for any discernable length of time. I watched when the dragon breathed fire on her. It burned her clean." He paused then added slowly, "It was quite a miraculous sight, and I don't say that lightly, because I've seen a hell of a lot."

"Why have you stopped moving? You know he's going to redouble his efforts to find you."

He had to quell another upsurge of irritation. He told her what Mary had said earlier. "We made the best decision we could under the circumstances. We've had a complicated, dangerous and exhausting couple of days. Mary was attacked by two of his drones, and we've both had traumatic memories surface. Yes, stopping is a calculated risk, but it's a necessary one, and I've taken every precaution."

She searched his expression. "You're sure?"

He knew that the closer they came to confronting their old enemy, the more paranoid she had to feel about the possibility of being deceived, but he thought she was beginning to be mollified and reassured. He replied, "Of course I'm sure. You know as well as I do that there are no guarantees, but I've set sentinels in place. If he gets close, we'll be warned."

"I don't like it," she muttered, her delicate brows drawing into a frown. She spread her hands on the table, running her fingers along the scars on its surface.

"You don't have to like it," he said, crossing his arms and propping his feet on the edge of the table. "You just have to live with it."

Her mouth tightened briefly. "At least she's healed—she's really healed, and she knows who she is? That is so much more than we dared to hope."

He smiled. It creased his lean face and lit up his eyes, an expression proud and savage at once. In a soft voice, like velvet sheathing steel, he agreed, "Yes, it is."

Her glance lifted to his face and lingered on the smile as if it were a strange sight. "You said you both recovered traumatic memories. Do you know what happened to her, and how she got wounded? Were you there?"

The smile vanished, leaving only the savagery. "Yes."

Her gaze dropped to her hands. After a moment, she said, "I see. I'm sorry."

"Sorry for what—that you couldn't help me remember? Don't be," he told her. "We didn't recover anything of that lifetime because I couldn't stand to remember. Now I know, and I needed to know. But I also wish I didn't."

She took a deep breath. "What happened?"

"I'm not going to talk about it," he said. "I can't speak for Mary, so you'd have to ask her what she's willing to discuss. But my experience isn't relevant to the present. That's all you need to know."

She nodded and stood. The illusion of the young woman wavered and grew thin. "I will see what I can do pinpoint his location," she said. "Don't take too long to rest."

He said, "We will see you soon."

"Creator willing." She faded.

He did not echo the sentiment. He doubted there was a God, but if there was, Michael had no use for him.

He had no reason to linger after Astra left but he did anyway. He let his gaze roam over the scene. The only items that were anachronistic to the great hall were the suits of armor on display. At one time or another he had worn each one. He had added them to the hall image over the years, as he had recovered memories of different lifetimes throughout the ages.

He walked toward the oldest sets of armor and let the memories from those lives unfold. The armor was from one of his earliest lifetimes, soon after the group's arrival on earth. His earliest lives were also his most public. He had only fallen into the habit of stealth much later. This one; yes, he remembered this one well. It had been a time of almost constant war, but then so had most of his lives.

They'd had the Deceiver cornered and had laid siege to the city that sheltered him. The siege had been a long, filthy, brutal business. He remembered the blood and the dust and the sweltering, crowded life of the army.

Gabriel and Raphael had been there. In that lifetime some quirk of destiny had seen them born as identical twins, insepa-rable as always, vivid and reckless and brilliant as two fire-brands. They had loved to switch places and pretend to be each other, but they could never fool anybody from their group. Their birth mother had named them Castor and Pollux.

They had burst into his pavilion late one night, laughing drunkenly over some stupid escapade. Now he couldn't remember what they had done. He had met the twins just inside the flap, naked, with sword and knife in hand, while Mary had scowled from the pallet of furs where they had slept.

What had been her name? He frowned, unable to grasp it. Members of their group had fast become the stuff of legend, until the stories took on a life of their own. In that culture and time gods and demons mingled freely with kings and ordinary men. The group hadn't needed to cloak their abilities, which was refreshing in retrospect.

He had fast earned the reputation of being an invincible warrior, gifted by the gods. Whatever her name had been, he smiled to remember Mary's obstinacy. She had insisted on dogging his heel everywhere he went, no matter how many times he had shouted at her to stay behind in safety.

It became well known throughout both armies that she was his only point of vulnerability.

Astra had asked, in equal parts amusement and uncertainty, whether or not he dreamed, and he did. But what he dreamed was none of her business nor was it anyone else's, except perhaps for one other person. In all four realms, physically, psychically, spiritually and emotionally, he was a fortress. He might be destroyed but he would never be conquered.

Except, perhaps, by or through one other person.

The long-dead people from those days had said that to strike at his heel was to strike him down.

After all this time he supposed that it was still true.

Chapter Twenty-one

HUNGER WOKE MARY, an insistent, healthy ache.

She lay for a while, drifting sleepily through memory while she rested against Michael's warm, hard body. He was so much bigger than she was. Sprawling together gave her a simple, animal sense of comfort and safety.

Earlier in the bathroom, he had been trapped in the past and going into shock. Then she had done something. Something important. In that moment, without any time to really think anything through, she sank her awareness into his body and poured her energy into him, just as he had done to her when he had found her. She willed his heart to return back to its normal rhythm and opened constricted pathways, and his body had obeyed. Now, as she thought back to what had happened, part of her wanted to shout in astonished triumph.

What she had done felt right and true, and familiar, as if she had done such a thing many times before. The realization opened other possibilities in her mind, along with barely glimpsed images of different healings for other injuries and illnesses.

She felt as though she had discovered a hidden door inside of herself. Opening that door led to a secret, golden chamber filled with such wondrous treasure, she could wander within its halls for years.

All the pieces of her past that she had recovered thus far pointed the way to further discoveries. She had not only been a fine healer in her first life, but she had learned valuable lessons in successive lives too. She needed to work hard to reclaim those lost skills.

At last she went into a full body stretch. Bruises and contusions throbbed, and she bit back a groan. Her body had stiffened while she slept.

When she opened her eyes, she sensed that time had changed.

The fire that had been crackling in the fireplace had died down, and the shadows in the cabin had shifted places. She thought of those shadows moving throughout the days, not quite dancing the same dance every time, infinitesimally shifting their path throughout the seasons, yet still completing a circle.

Michael watched her with a serious, contemplative expression, lying on his side, with his head propped in one hand. His short, dark hair was tousled, and the harsh lines on his face had eased. He looked as though he had been awake for some time.

She had the impulse to smile or say something, and then her gaze connected with his.

The cabin disappeared.

Everything disappeared as she looked at her mate.

The stern, inhuman lines of his strong face, the piercing light in his fierce eyes—every detail was as familiar and as necessary to her as her own hands. His energy mantled his masculine form like a midnight blue cloak and followed the lines of his high cheekbones and lean jaw like a royal collar. He was one of the most graceful of their people, and also one of the strongest and most deadly, and he was utterly devoted to her.

As she was to him.

And when he touched her, with his hands and his body,

and all the passionate colors of his emotions, everything inside of her sang.

Then the cabin snapped back into place around her, and she stared at Michael in his human form. A few tiny flecks of white had begun to sprinkle the black hair at his temples, and crow's-feet etched the weathered skin at the corners of his eyes. Lines bracketed his mouth. If he wasn't forty, he was only a few years shy of it, and while physically he might appear to look like an ordinary man, for the first time, she truly saw the power sheathed inside his body.

His light-colored eyes regarded her, the expression on his lean face quizzical.

Her eyesight flickered from the physical to the psychic and back again, blending the two images.

Light-colored eyes like—moonstones set in a midnight blue cloak—his energy mantling him like a royal collar—etching his high, strong cheekbones and that thin, mobile mouth.

She jerked her gaze away, shaking, and stared in the direction of the table across the room.

He put a warm hand on her arm. "Are you all right?"

"Yes," she croaked, and cleared her throat. "I think I just saw who you were."

She heard the frown in his voice. "What do you mean?"

"I saw an image of you. Not you as you are, here in the present. Well, at least not at first." Vaguely aware that she was babbling, she made an effort to control herself. "I think I saw a vision of what you looked like in that first life."

But if that was real—and she was so far beyond questioning the reality of her own experiences, so it must be real—then it had been no vision at all, but a memory.

My God, what a magnificent creature he had been.

And still was.

His fingers tightened. She felt each individual one, pressing gently into her flesh. He controlled his own strength completely, not adding a single twinge of discomfort to her still healing body. Not only must he have absolute knowledge of his own capabilities, but she realized that he had studied and marked the position of every one of her bruises. He had to have, to avoid them so completely.

Then he let her go. As she turned her gaze back to him, he rolled away from her and onto his feet, moving lightly like a dancer. "Come on," he said. "We slept the day away, and we only have an hour or so of daylight left."

Thrown off balance, she fumbled her way out from under the covers. The scuffed hardwood floor felt like a sheet of ice, and her toes curled in protest. Trying to minimize the discomfort, she stood on one foot. "What are we doing?"

"We're going outside for target practice, remember?" He strode over to the table where he had left his T-shirt and socks, and he dressed swiftly, the bulky muscles of his arms and chest flexing as he drew the shirt over his head.

The cabin was too cold for half measures. Either she needed to get dressed or she needed to dive back under the covers. For a moment she wavered, but she knew that if she tried to go back to bed, he would only pull her out again bodily.

Shivering, she minced across the freezing floor to the dresser and dragged on a pair of socks. As predicted, they fit. Then she tried on the new jeans. They hung on her hips, but her other pair was still drying on the water heater, and these would do in a pinch. Finally she dove into the voluminous gray sweatshirt, hunting for the neck and armholes.

Her voice muffled by the thick material, she grumbled, "I would rather have some supper, you know."

"Target practice first," he told her. "Then I'll cook you supper."

That brightened her outlook on the near future considerably. She emerged from the depths of the sweatshirt with a smile. "You cook?"

"I cook." He sat in the one of the chairs and laced on his boots.

"Do you by any chance cook omelets?" She hopped into her shoes.

One corner of his mouth lifted. "I do cook omelets. I

cook other things too. It's not haute cuisine, but it's good enough."

Somehow that didn't surprise her. Autonomy would matter to him. He would be competent at a lot of things.

After only a brief hesitation, she walked over to put a hand on his wide shoulder. As he lifted his head in inquiry, she bent and kissed him on his hard, warm mouth. "I noticed that you bought asparagus, mushrooms and strawberries," she whispered. "I meant to thank you earlier but got sidetracked."

His expression relaxed, and he gave her a smile. "You're welcome." He stood, foraged in his weapons bag and pocketed a couple of spare clips. Then he strode to the dresser to pick up the nine-millimeter. "Come on."

Grimacing, she followed him outside and around to the back of the cabin, noting how he studied his surroundings, his gaze clear and sharp. The clearing hadn't been mowed in a while, and the long grass was tangled underfoot.

She muttered, "Have I mentioned recently that I don't want to do this?"

"Not since you woke up," he said. "In fact, I was just admiring your restraint, but I suppose that's all in the past now."

He held the gun out. She turned her back to him.

Circling her, he came back into view and held the gun out again, his expression implacable.

She scowled at him and snatched the gun out of his hand.

"Show me where the safety is," he said.

She pointed, her mouth folded tight.

"Good," he said. "Now, show me that you remember how to reload it."

She pulled the clip out and slammed it back in. Her hands were shaking so that she fumbled the move.

[flat, popping sounds . . . people falling like mown flowers . . .]

He put a hand over hers. His grip was sure and steady. "Are you thinking about what happened to those people?"

"Yes," she whispered.

He tilted her face up. "It's time to take your own advice,

Mary," he said. His voice was calm. "The memories are terrible, but what happened is in the past. Acknowledge that, and let it go. This is just a gun. It's a thing, like a scalpel, or a chair, or like any other thing. It's up to you what you do with it."

"There's something wrong with that argument." She pressed a fist to her forehead, trying to clear her head. "I can't think what it is right at the moment, but there is."

"You are in control of this gun," he told her, clearly unmoved by her shaky reaction. "It is not in control of you. If you are not in control of yourself, you might slip and kill or injure someone, but that is true of the scalpel as well. If you have the nerve to wield a scalpel, you can shoot this gun. Now, take the safety off. Hold it like I showed you."

His calm, relentless attitude was actually helping, not hurting. She slipped off the safety and held the gun two handed, like he had demonstrated earlier. The muscles in her arms and shoulders bunched with tension.

He walked behind her and pointed over her shoulder. She sighted along the length of his arm to where his finger pointed. "Aim for that low-hanging branch. Remember, pull the trigger. Don't yank at it."

She pulled the trigger. The gun spat a bullet. Startling wildly, she dropped it.

Silence. She dared to peek over her shoulder at him. He had raised his eyebrows, and his mouth was compressed in a suppressed smile. "You surprised me. I thought it would take at least another ten more minutes to talk you into doing that."

"I hate you," she grumbled.

He spun her around so fast she didn't even have time to squeak. Snaking an arm around her neck, he gave her a savage kiss that was so scorching, she felt as if all of her clothes might burn off of her body. Electricity sizzled through her nerves. By the time he was finished, she was shaking all over and unabashedly clinging to him, with her fingers tangled in his short, fine hair. His mouth left hers with obvious reluctance, and as she sagged limply in his hold, he studied her with a heavy-lidded, predatory look.

She licked her lips. Even her mouth was shaking. "Okay, you caught me. I was kidding. I don't hate you."

He circled her throat with one hand. It was such a barbaric gesture, and he did it so tenderly. She looked up into the dangerous face of her best friend in the entire world.

And she knew beyond a shadow of a doubt that he would never hurt her, would always defend her. Always.

Something invisible hovered in the air, some decision in his edged expression. He looked like a tiger might, as it walked up to a fence and considered whether or not it might be time to jump over to freedom. Then the tiger retreated, slowly, and he smiled again as he let her go.

Even when he was no longer touching her, the skin at her neck burned with the memory of the warmth from his hand.

He said, "Pick the gun up, and this time, really aim for that branch."

Flooded with sensation and blind with desire, she managed to pick the gun up again and not shoot herself in the foot.

After a half an hour, he called a halt to the lesson. Not, she thought, because he had any pity on her, but because the shadows were lengthening too much on the branches to use them for proper target practice.

And not that she had managed to hit any of the branches, anyway. As wrung out as if they had been boxing the entire time, she clicked on the safety and tried to hand the gun to him, but he wouldn't take it.

"I did good, didn't I?" she said brightly.

The tiger that lived behind his face laughed. "Come on," he said. "I promised you supper."

Back inside, the cabin was almost as cold as it was outside. Teeth chattering, she went to build a new fire in the fireplace while he pulled out various ingredients from the fridge and set to work.

While she waited for the flames to take hold, she wandered into the bathroom and checked her clothes that were still draped on the hot water heater. They were dry, and the material felt stiff and rough. She shook them out and folded them, then set them on the dresser. Then she went back to squat in front of the bright new fire, holding her chilled fingers to the growing warmth.

With his dark head bent to the prosaic task of chopping vegetables, he said, "Tell me your long, stupid story."

It took her a few heartbeats to connect to what he meant. When she remembered, she said, "Justin and I both went to Notre Dame. I wasn't very good at making friends, but he has—had—a knack for it. It's a big university, but he still seemed to know everybody on campus. One of his friends was a roommate of mine, and she introduced us. We really liked each other, you know. We made each other laugh." She paused, but he remained silent. She bit her lip. "The truth of the matter is, he was gay and couldn't admit to it, and I wasn't interested in anybody. We each pretended to be something we weren't, and we tried to create a life that would look right. Look normal. I thought if I acted normal for long enough, I might eventually start feeling normal. You know, fake it till you make it."

She looked over her shoulder. Michael's expression revealed nothing but calm interest. He asked, "How long were you married?"

"Just under two years. It was a relief when we called it quits." What was he thinking? His reaction, or rather the lack of one, threw her off balance. Did he . . . care? She asked hesitantly, "Have you had a serious relationship?"

His gaze lifted from his task briefly. "No."

Unsure about the undertones in his too-brief reply or in that clear, wry look, and not confident about asking him anything further, she stood and walked over to the table. He had blanched the asparagus and sautéed the mushrooms. Now, he beat several eggs in a large metal bowl while butter melted in a skillet over low heat.

The package of strawberries remained on the table, as of yet still untouched. It was too early in the year for local, seasonal strawberries, and the price on the packet was exorbitant. She carried it to the sink to clean and slice the fruit into plain bowls.

"Your ally in the Secret Service," she said, watching the knife in her hands. She was good with a knife, and confident. "The one that was killed yesterday morning. How did he die?"

"He didn't tell me the details," Michael replied quietly.

She lowered her hands, resting them on the edge of the kitchen sink. "Excuse me?"

He poured the beaten contents of the bowl into the warm skillet, and the fragrant smell of cooking eggs filled the room. "His ghost came to tell me that he had been killed. That's all I know."

Well, hell. She rubbed her face with the back of one damp hand, surprised that she was still capable of surprise. After all, she did live in a world with hawk allies, talking wolves and dragons, wind spirits and possibly a Virgin Mary.

Gretchen had mentioned the spirit of the girl that had died in Mary's ER, but if Mary had thought about it at all, she had imagined BabyMama Two like the popular, modern view of ghosts. All mystery and woo-woo, but not a lot of practical sense or communication.

She muttered, "I didn't know ghosts could carry on a conversation. Actually, I guess before yesterday, I didn't know there was such a thing as ghosts."

"Most ghosts are not very coherent," he said. He added the mushrooms and asparagus to the skillet, along with a sprinkle of cheddar cheese. "In fact, most people aren't ghosts at all. It takes an especially strong-minded, passionate individual to become a ghost, let alone one as . . . complete as Nicholas."

"That's your friend's name, Nicholas?"

"Yes. He was strong in a lot of things. Not only was he a good warrior, but he was also an adept in spiritual matters and the psychic realm. He was a unique human being, and his death was a serious blow." He shook his head. "For him to have become a target, he had to have given himself away somehow. Maybe he reacted to one of the Deceiver's creatures, when a normal human wouldn't have sensed anything. I only hope that the Deceiver doesn't target his family because of it."

Sadness swept through her. So many people lost in just a few days.

Then a chill followed on that thought: at least, those were the deaths that she knew about.

She said softly, "I'm sorry for your loss."

He picked up the skillet and flipped the omelet, then stood frowning down at the contents. Sounding almost surprised, he said, "I'm sorry too."

They fell silent for a while, as they served up the simple meal. Michael cleared his weapons and tools from the table, and she found the silverware. Then they sat and ate. The food was delicious. The earthy mushrooms and asparagus contrasted nicely with the sharp tang of cheddar cheese, and the rich butter complemented the browned, golden egg. The dish was offset with the sweet tartness of the strawberries. She didn't truly take another deep breath until after she had cleaned her plate.

In the fireplace, the fire had taken hold and blazed bright and hot, chasing the last of the chill away until she was so warm, she had to pull off the sweatshirt. She hung it on the back of her chair.

Outside, she realized, the sun had set and full night blanketed the scene. Quiet surrounded the cabin, but she didn't find the silence desolate or too isolated. Rather, it was replete with a sense of green plant life that was burgeoning with the return of warmth and sunlight. In full summer, the place would be aggressively lavish with weeds and vines.

Her thoughts turned whimsical. Michael could trim back all the foliage and keep the clearing mown, and she could plant a small garden in the back. Some tomato plants, and zucchini, maybe some green beans, lettuce and green onions. The Wolf Lake country store seemed like the kind of place that stocked a little of everything. It would probably sell packets of garden seeds in the spring.

Michael could go fishing. They could eat rainbow trout or perhaps bluegill for supper, along with the garden vegetables. She could sit in the sun and let the light wash her clean and new, as she explored the internal halls of her treasure chamber and relearned its secrets.

As quickly as the fantasy bloomed, it died again.

They wouldn't be here past tomorrow, let alone for an entire summer.

"What are you thinking?" Michael asked. He had also finished his meal and sat with his plate pushed back, elbows on the table as he angled his head toward her.

She just shook her head.

"Tell me," he insisted.

He took her hand and squeezed her fingers, and she could still see him with both her psychic and physical eyes, that royal, midnight mantle cloaking his all too human figure, and he was neither and both all at once, and yet the sum of him had become much more than each creature alone. And instead of feeling proud, enriched and replete with the sure knowledge that he was her mate, she was filled with the sharp, anguished spike of wanting, wanting.

She gave him a small twisted smile. "I'm just still trying to figure out how I can learn to milk a cow, I guess."

He lifted her hand and, head bowed, pressed his lips to it. His eyes closed, he held her fingers against his mouth. She sat still, watching him, and felt pierced to the core.

When his grip loosened, she pulled away and stacked their supper dishes together at random. Pushing her chair back, she carried the dishes to the sink. The air in the cabin felt thick and intimate on her overly sensitized skin, and her body seemed too heavy to hold upright. Hardly aware of what she did, she leaned against the sink, squirted soap over the dishes and turned the faucet on.

Even though he moved so lightly that he made no noise, she felt him come up behind her, so close that she felt his body heat at her back.

Her hair was still bound back in the simple braid. He stroked the edge of her hairline, from her temple, around the delicate shell of her ear, to the nape of her neck. His light touch reverberated through her body and she shivered.

"I would love to see your hair loose, if I may."

He sounded strange, unlike his usual self. He sounded wistful, and somehow that hurt, twisting the spike deeper. She raised her shaking hands to the back of her head to pull out the elastic band, as she whispered, "It's a crazy mess at the best of times, you know. It's even crazier without conditioner."

He pulled his fingers through the loosened braid, and her hair sprang free. His quiet intake of breath sounded loud in the silent cabin. He sank both hands into the wild abundance and gently spread out the curls until they lay loose around her shoulders.

The sensation of his fingers moving through her hair was exotic, sensual, not just physically arousing but emotionally moving. Closing her eyes, she turned her head slightly toward him. He took such extraordinary care with her. She realized that he had not bruised her once, not even during the most violent part of their initial meeting.

"Thank you," he said. His voice was a rough, bare thread of sound. "It's beautiful."

The physician in her realized something else, and she felt stricken. "We don't have any condoms, do we? At least I don't." Carrying a condom in her purse. Taking birth control pills. What a ridiculously foreign concept to someone who once had no interest in sex.

He put his hands on her shoulders and turned her around. His expression was flushed with heat yet filled with a kind of settled, mature patience that both astonished and moved her even more. "I took a chance and bought a pack of condoms at the store," he said. "We can do anything we want, or nothing at all."

She took a step forward. As his arms folded around her, she tucked her head into the crook of his neck. He stroked her hair and the sensitive skin along the side of her face, all with that light, gentle touch. He was bigger than she was everywhere, from the length and breadth of his chest and flat abdomen, to the muscled biceps that were so thick she couldn't span them with both hands if she tried.

Sensual awareness had been a perpetual backdrop to all of their interactions with each other. It welled now inside of her, a dark, rich energy that was as life-giving as the earth. She rested against the strength of his body, inhaled his scent and savored the texture of his warm skin as she nuzzled into him. He murmured something and pressed his lips against her temple then simply held her, his mouth resting against her skin.

To experience desire now, after going a lifetime without it, seemed like a gorgeous and unearthly gift. How strange that it came at such a time. What did someone say in a situation like this? Honey, I'm going to war and I would like to spend the night with you?

She licked her lips and whispered, "I haven't been with anybody in a long time. Justin was my last attempt at any real intimacy."

His hand came under her chin. He tilted her face up and looked into her eyes. His gaze was somber, the lean, tough lines of his face filled with tenderness. "I don't remember what making love is like. I would love to be with you, but only when you're ready."

Shock tightened her face. He was so masculine. He was at least thirty-five years old, and he had been that controlled, that cut off, his entire life? "You've never been with anyone? Ever?"

He shook his head, his gaze lowered as he watched his thumb stroke her lower lip. "My memory of you was so much stronger and brighter than anyone I met. Other women were pale shadows by comparison."

Her eyes filled. Her mouth trembled, and so did her hands as she stroked his back, his cheek. "I didn't know to wait," she whispered. "I didn't remember."

"Of course you didn't," he murmured.

"I wish I had. None of them meant anything. Afterward, I always felt empty and more disconnected than ever, and I could never understand why."

"Hush. Whoever you were with before—Justin or anyone else, it doesn't matter." He bent his head to lick the path along her lip that his thumb had taken. "This is what is real, not what happened in the past. This, right here and now."

She stood on tiptoe, cupped his face and kissed him with everything she had. His arms clenched, his lips warm and responsive on hers. Urgency flared hot and bright between them, and he turned the kiss aggressive as his powerful body tightened.

They were flush against each other, torso to torso. She felt a heavy, thick length growing against her hip bone. Instead of feeling the usual revulsion that she'd always had to mask before, her body moistened in a sharp pulse of arousal.

As he grew harder, she softened, inviting him with her mouth and her body while she wrapped him in her energy. He slanted his lips over hers, driving his tongue deep into her mouth while he sank both fists into her hair. His breathing came hard, as if he had been running for miles. For uncounted years.

She slipped her hands under his shirt. They both groaned as her palms connected with his warm skin, and he arched with a gasp as she stroked the long, muscled length of his broad back.

She caught a glimpse of his expression. The bones and contours were the same, but he looked radically different, unleashed. The tiger that lived behind his face had finally escaped its confinement and leaped to freedom, and there was nothing at all human in those glittering, moonstone eyes.

The sight should have frightened her. If she had been sensible, sane or fully human herself, it might have.

Instead, she, who had shrank from every caress or gesture of affection from her gentle human partners, raked her fingernails down that tiger's back and egged him on.

Something extreme flashed in his expression.

He tore her clothes off her body. Just ripped them to pieces, even the tough material of her new denim jeans, shredding it as if it were as thin and fragile as paper.

That he had that kind of inhuman strength shocked a sound out of her, the noise filled with incoherent amazement and need.

After she was naked, he tore his T-shirt off too. The heavy muscles of his chest and arms clenched and flexed as he flung the shreds of material aside. A scatter of dark hair sprinkled his chest from his flat, male nipples to the length of his taut, washboard abdomen.

She couldn't take her eyes off him, even as she reached for the fastening of his own pair of jeans. She jerked open the top button and yanked down the zipper, and his large, erect penis spilled out of the opening, into her hands.

At last her gaze fell from his face. She looked down, from the broad head to the thick, veined shaft. Discovering such a private part of him made her feel delirious, intoxicated. The stretched skin over the hard, swollen flesh of his erection was soft as silk and hot to the touch. She stroked the length of him and rubbed the ball of her thumb over the thin slit at the tip.

He hissed and shuddered all over. He gripped her wrists, shackling her. Then he pulled her hands away from his erection. Before she had time to grow disappointed, he swung her into his arms. Moving swiftly, he carried her to the bed. The bicep muscles in his arms bunched as he threw her onto the bed.

Even as she hit the mattress, she was already twisting up to reach for him again. Urgency gripped her, and a kind of crazed greed. She could not remember having ever felt this way before . . .

. . . and then her mind opened again, and she could.

Snatches of images filled with the same need, echoing back and back throughout millennia, time out of mind.

The tangle of naked limbs. His fist in her hair. Screaming as she climaxed, as he took her again and again. He took her so far out of her body, she knew ecstasy like a pure, soaring note.

She knew *him*.

All the pieces, fitting together with such perfection.

Journeying through life together. Not quite dancing the same dance every time. Infinitesimally shifting their path through the seasons, yet still completing a circle. Making a pattern.

Two interlocking pieces that sustained and balanced each other.

While she knelt frozen on the bed, he turned off the overhead light and yanked off his pants. The flames from the fire threw long, flickering strands of golden light across the room. The gold danced along his tall, nude body as he opened a foil packet and rolled a condom over his erect penis. When he turned to her, she opened her arms. He came over her as she lay back on the bed, and they settled their bodies together.

Stricken, she stared up at him, and this time she accepted the duality of her experience. They had never lain naked together, yet it was the most familiar, most necessary thing she had ever done. She stroked his cheek. He kissed her palm. And it was the same dance all over again, a very old dance, the oldest of all, yet now it was made new again.

He stroked and explored her, kissed her breasts and suckled at her nipples, while she explored and kissed him too. It all happened too fast, as urgency built into a cascade of need.

She ran her mouth along the heated skin of his chest, feeling the bulge and shift of iron muscle underneath his silken skin, while the sprinkle of hair on his legs rasped against her inner thighs. The urgency would not let her settle or slow down. She raged mutely against the condom, hating the necessity for even that small barrier, and soon at her urging he brought the tip of his erection to her moist, fluted opening, holding her gaze as he settled into place between her legs.

His eyes were a darkened stormy gray, stricken with vulnerability. Riveted by the expression, she cupped his face, nuzzling and murmuring at him as he eased his rigid thick length inside her softened, slick entrance. He was shaking. The long, hard shudders rippled through his tough frame. Her breath caught as he seated himself fully inside. He froze, leaning on his elbows so that he could search her face.

"It's beautiful," she whispered, answering his unspoken question. "You're the most beautiful thing I've ever seen."

The anxiety eased from his face, and pleasure transformed him. "You're a miracle," he said. "I didn't think I knew how to feel anymore. I thought I was half dead." He covered her mouth with his and whispered against her lips, "My miracle. My home."

The words pierced through her as he began to move. He watched her as her eyelids grew heavy and her plump moistened mouth grew soft, and he was clever, so clever. He learned quickly the language of what pleased her through the catch of a sigh, a murmur of need.

He framed her face with his big hands as their bodies flexed and interlocked. She arched her torso up to him and worked her inner muscles, clasping him tightly as he slid in, and in, and in.

When he climaxed she looked deeply into his unshielded gaze. It brought her to climax along with him. She lost herself as her body shook, and once again, ecstasy sang that pure, soaring note. And she knew it didn't matter where they traveled next, who they had to fight or what world they had left behind. She had come home.

Tears spilled out of the corners of her eyes. He held her tight against him with an arm hooked around the back of her neck. It was his turn to murmur as he kissed the tears away. She offered him her mouth. As he covered it with his, her lips shaped the words.

Home.

He went still, all breathing suspended, and she knew that he focused everything on the movement of her mouth. Then he crushed her to him, kissing her so hard, she knew he had understood, although she had said no word out loud, nor had she made any sound.

Chapter Twenty-two

THE LITTLE DARK spirit outside the cabin was wretchedly disappointed and growing desperately hungry.

At first the pair inside had shown such rich, bountiful promise, but as time progressed they were actually healing and comforting each other. Raw, deep spiritual wounds closed, and they grew stronger and brighter.

In the meantime, the spirit had trapped itself with its own greed by following them to such a secluded place. It couldn't sense any other prey around for miles. So it lingered in the deepest shadows of the clearing, hoping against hope to catch one or the other of the pair alone, vulnerable and in pain again. Whenever they came outside together, or the man stepped out by himself, it hid in the recesses of the car's engine.

Then something else snagged its attention.

A call reverberated through the psychic realm. The voice was a familiar one, dark and seductive as a siren. The spirit wavered in indecision but, while the people in the cabin had been luscious and tempting in the midst of their struggle, they had grown into too robust a force for it to feed on unless they became injured to the point of dying.

Whereas the voice that called came from someone that led a life rich in all the dark paths. He birthed a fertile feeding ground of pain and suffering wherever he went, and he rewarded those that pleased him.

Detaching from the cabin window, the spirit drifted upward like a feather on the wind. It began to travel in lazy swirls in the direction of the voice.

Chapter Twenty-three

"WHEN DO WE have to leave?" Mary asked.

The sound of her soft voice vibrated in his ear as he rested his head on her flat stomach. He turned to press his lips against her skin.

She was unutterably gorgeous to him, her slender body perfect in every way. Small, high breasts, a narrow waist, the lightly rounded hips and calves and those long, delicately muscled thighs that could grip him with such surprising strength. Her wild, corkscrew curls spilled across the pillow, the tawny color glinting with threads of gold.

The physical details were delightful, but absolutely the most important thing was that she was here with him now after so very long, and her body was healthy and strong, a temple that housed her unique spirit.

He did not want to answer her question, but in spite of himself, his mind, ever pragmatic, turned to the subject. He calculated the hours they had taken against the risk of remaining in place.

The cabin was secluded, and he had walked the perimeter of the clearing several times. They had rested, stabilized and eaten good, nutritious food. Their survival needs had been met. And, as he had mentioned to Astra, he had also set sentinels to keep watch along the gravel roads that led to his property.

But information could be gleaned from the slightest of things. The fact was, the longer they stayed the greater the risk grew.

What if Mary's picture had been circulated in the press? What if the attendant from the gas station saw it and recognized her? Or the server at the drive-thru where he had bought breakfast and coffee? Mary had been asleep but clearly visible. And when they had stopped at the Wolf Lake store, even though she had remained in the car, he could not guarantee that she hadn't been seen.

They had so much they still needed to do. Her aptitude with a gun was almost nonexistent. She needed more target practice. He needed to show her basic defensive moves, and to see if he could coax her into learning knife work. Coupled with the element of surprise, just one or two moves could save her life.

He needed to pin her down and cover her so that nothing so cruel could ever happen to her again.

Finally he gave her the only reply that he could. "We need to go soon."

They lay tumbled across the tangled bedcovers where they had last fallen. In the fireplace, the fire had begun to die down again. Darkness was rising, and the dancing golden illumination that had crowned them at the peak of their joining had now begun to fade into a pulsing red.

But the darkness had not yet taken them. The time that they had stolen for themselves was not yet done.

His mind drifted. As part of his wider education, Astra had set him to study many of the most ancient texts. A verse from Psalms came to him:

Let the morning bring me word of your unfailing love, for I have put my trust in you. Show me the way I should go, for to you I lift up my soul.

In the shadowed light, her skin looked like honey, and she tasted like manna from heaven. He had wandered through a godforsaken desert, starving for uncounted years. Now, even though they had flung all the passion they had at each other, and even though their bodies were replete, he could not stop kissing or tasting her.

Slender fingers stroked through his hair. Her torso moved as she heaved a resigned sigh, but she didn't try to argue with him. She must feel it too, this gut instinct that said they could not stop moving for too long.

"So we leave in the morning?"

"Yes, first thing."

He wanted so desperately to say no. To say that they could have more than a single day together. That they could have years of leisure and safety together.

But that old bastard time was winging away from them again. With every ounce of passion inside of him, he willed that everything would be different this time. But as much as he wished it to be otherwise, he could not lunge after the fleeting moment and capture it in both hands.

Her fingers trailed along his collarbone. She touched his cheek and tilted up his head. Even in the growing shadows, her gaze was brilliant, glittering like precious aquamarines.

"Oh good," she said. "We still have hours and hours."

"A veritable wealth of minutes," he said.

She lifted her eyebrows and smiled. "A staggering fortune in seconds."

The sound of his own laugh shocked him. He was still not used to hearing it. He reached for her hand and laced his fingers through hers.

Her expression turned vulnerable. "Do you have memories of us being together in other lives?"

"Some," he said. "Do you?"

"Just flashes." Her fingers tightened on his. "They keep hitting at random. So many memories. It's like a floodgate has opened."

"You've only just healed," he said. "Maybe the images are like aftershocks. I went through a period when images would bubble up unexpectedly, but after a while it calmed down. I think it will for you too, after things have had a chance to settle into place."

She was silent for a moment. Then she said, "They're disconcerting, but I like them. Of course, it helps to know what they actually are."

He thought about telling her of his first, best memory, of that time they had lived together in England just after the Norman Conquest.

See what I know? he wanted to say. Have you had memories of this time too? Are they the same for you?

Were you happy?

But he didn't want to prompt her into any false memories. When he had been younger, Astra had been very careful to avoid prompting him too much, and he thought it best to emulate that example.

Besides, his memories of that lifetime meant too much to him to risk corrupting them. It would mean so much more if Mary recovered images from that time independently of him. If she could say, as he thought and hoped she might, that she had been as happy during that time as he had been.

Even though they had just made love twice, the hunger for her came back. It rode him hard and he succumbed to it. He slid down her body, coaxing her legs apart.

Her breath catching audibly, she opened readily to him. He nuzzled the soft tuft of private hair at the graceful arch of her pelvis, breathing her in. Her scent mingled with his, musky, rich and evocative. While she stroked the back of his head, he fingered the plump, moisture-slick petals of her sex. Her breathing deepened and turned ragged, and her arousal drenched his fingers.

He was enchanted with every sensual detail.

As he had grown into maturity, abstinence had become just another part of his discipline. His knowledge and understanding about the sexual act, while detailed, remained purely clinical. Not only had every woman he met been a pale shadow in comparison to his memories, but in the end he had always found it so much easier and quicker to find his own release when his body had craved it. Being alone had been so much more preferable than looking with irritation into the uncomprehending expression of a strange woman he would never grow to care for, and would end up leaving soon enough.

Everything about this intimacy with Mary transcended both his memory and imagination. It enveloped him utterly.

The warmth of her body, the touch of her hands. The light, feminine scent rising off her soft skin.

His own powerful response to her. The primitive urges that overwhelmed him, to cover and take, and to penetrate, to discover a rhythm that his body already knew.

The rich texture of experience highlighted all over again how starved and sharp he had become.

He had already known that he was only half alive without her. Now he realized something else. Being with her brought him fully into the present, and fully immersed him in the experience of being human.

Gently he parted the exquisitely shaped folds of her sex, bent his head farther and licked her. Even against his sensitive tongue her private flesh felt incredibly soft, like velvet. Her pelvis arched up to him as she gasped.

Her response electrified him. Pausing for a moment to savor it, determination hardened in him. Those other lovers she had taken had meant nothing to her, and therefore they meant nothing to him. The decision to set all of that aside was an easy one for him to make, much easier, he suspected, than it was for her. After all, she was the one who had to live with the memory of those empty experiences.

But she would never have another lover. Only him. They did not have to say it to each other. He already knew.

He parted her farther and found the delicate, stiff little nubbin of flesh seated at the heart of her pleasure, and he put his mouth to it.

A small scream broke out of her, and her torso lifted off the bed, and the intensity of his own reaction astonished him. He grew hard again as he licked and suckled her and listened to the incoherent, uncontrolled sounds of her pleasure.

When the urge to penetrate became too much to ignore, he slid first one finger into her, then another. Her inner muscles tightened on him. He lost himself in the sumptuousness of it, fucking her tenderly, his fingers gliding in and out of her wet, hidden sheath as he massaged her clitoris with his tongue.

He could feel her climax. Her inner muscles clenched on his fingers. Then the rippling began, and she shook as though she would fly apart at the seams. She cupped the back of his head, holding him to her, and he complied, licking at her rhythmically until she screamed and climaxed again.

Then he could not stand it any longer. He rose up and reached for another condom, rolling it over his erection with hands that shook with urgency. As he came down to her, she was already reaching for him to guide him into place.

Gentleness fled, along with his control. He thrust hard and impaled her. She tilted her head back and cried out again, wrapping her legs around his hips. Elbows planted on either side of her head, he succumbed to barbarity and sank his fists into her fabulous, wild hair, pinning her down as he moved inside of her, harder and faster, until his own climax twisted him up. The pleasure was excruciating, necessary.

All the while he watched her face, her beautiful face. Her lips were parted, her gaze blind, as she stared inward, focused on what he was doing to her.

I am the only one, he thought. The only one who has driven you to this extremity. The only one who has given you this kind of pleasure, this completion.

And by God, I am going to be the last lover you will ever take.

The very last, and only one.

Chapter Twenty-four

THEY SQUANDERED THEIR veritable wealth in minutes, their staggering fortune in seconds, on pleasuring each other. Then, as the last of the coals in the fireplace faded and the darkness was complete, they fell asleep. The last thing Mary knew was Michael resting his head on her shoulder, his big body sprawled over hers, a heavy, reassuring weight.

She woke suddenly with a hand clamped over her mouth. Predawn filtered into the cabin, turning everything bleak and gray. Michael leaned over her, his broad, naked shoulders and head in silhouette. Her heart kicked. Staring up at him, she gripped his thick, strong wrist with both hands.

His shadowed gaze was the polished steel of a drawn sword.

"Get dressed," he said. "Hurry."

She nodded. He rolled out of bed in one smooth, lithe motion. When she scrambled across the bed and would have risen, he gripped her shoulder. "Be careful. I kept the trees tall around the cabin on purpose, but long-range rifles can be remarkably accurate. Don't take a chance and stand in front of the windows."

She nodded again, slid to the floor and scurried in a

crouch toward the dresser where she had left her clean, dried clothes. As she went she saw Michael out of the corner of her eye. He stood at the table and had already slipped on a T-shirt and his shoes. He strapped the sheath of a long knife to his thigh. The assault rifle lay within his reach.

She tore into her clothes, cursing her slow shaking fingers, and wriggled into her sweatshirt. As she yanked her shoes on and tied them, she heard a hawk scream outside. Her head lifted. When she had been attacked, she had heard that same sound coming from a countless number of hawks. There was no time to braid back her hair. She yanked it into a ponytail.

Michael strapped the sword to his back. Then he settled two belts of magazine clips across his shoulders. His expression was calm, even peaceful. She took one look at him and a fresh wave of dread threatened to buckle her knees. What did he know that would make him arm himself like that?

He pivoted toward her. "All right," he said. "Now it's your turn."

He grabbed her with one hand. With the other he reached for the vest hanging on the back of a chair. "What are you doing?" she said. With an effort she kept her voice as quiet as his. "What's going on? What do you know?"

"Meet Kevlar. It's your new best friend," he said. He didn't wait for her to do it herself. He began to stuff her into the vest. It was far too big for her and felt strange, thick and stiff and heavy. "We have problems coming our way. Right now they think they're being sneaky. You're going to take your gun and slip out the back bathroom window. That path I told you about, the one that leads north to the lake—there's an opening in the back clearing. It's not very noticeable. I've kept that overgrown too. You're going to take the path, skirt the lake and keep going north. I'll catch up with you in a bit."

"No," she said. She gripped his forearm. The corded muscle felt as hard as marble under her fingers. "We'll both go. Michael, let's just run."

"They would follow," he said. "Then we would have to fight them a quarter of a mile from here, or a half a mile from here, and I wouldn't have the advantage of the cabin or familiar ground for cover." He grabbed her other arm and tried to force it through the second armhole. "You need to go. I need to stay."

"Stop it," she said. She twisted away from him and slipped out of the vest. "I'm not going."

He took her by the shoulders and jerked her toward him. "Don't do this," he growled in her face. "We don't have time to argue. They haven't circled around the cabin yet but they will. You are getting out of here."

"I can't just leave you!" she snapped. "I need to help."

He said with rapid force, point-blank in her face, "If you need to help then you will leave. *Now.* You're a liability if you stay." He grabbed the vest from the floor and began to stuff her back into it. "You're a doctor, not a soldier. You don't know how to fight, and we've had no chance to really train together. You're vulnerable, and you're a target. I need you to protect yourself so I can be free to do what I need to do. Otherwise I'm expending all my energy trying to protect you. Do you understand?"

"Yes," she said. She foiled his efforts by going limp, slithered out of the vest and sat down hard on the floor. He glared at her. She pointed to the vest. "I'm not wearing that. It's too big. You make sense. I'll go. But only if you wear the vest. Don't argue with me about this. It's a waste of time."

Looking furious, he dropped the vest and hauled her to her feet, scooped up two spare clips and slapped them in her hand. As she stuffed them into her pocket, he grabbed the nine-millimeter, marched her to the bathroom, unlatched the high window above the bathtub and opened it wide. He dropped the gun outside and swung her into his arms.

Her gaze swam with unshed tears. She ordered, "You put the vest on when I'm gone, do you hear?"

"You're quite the tyrant, aren't you?" he said, his face grim.

"Yes." Her fingers twisted in his T-shirt. "I mean it, Michael. Put the vest on."

"Fine." He gave her a brief, hard kiss then he raised her to the window feet first.

She wiggled through the space as he pushed her, turning so that she rested on her stomach as she hung halfway out of the window. She grabbed his muscled forearms.

"I'm going to be really pissed at you if you get yourself killed," she warned. "Don't think I won't find a way to hunt your ghost down and kick your ass."

He kissed her again and stared hard into her eyes. "I'll see you soon. GO."

He grasped her by the upper arms and helped to control her descent to the ground. As soon as she gained her footing, she searched for the gun and found it, and looked at the window as she straightened.

He lingered long enough to point in the direction of the path. She saw the subtle break in the bushes and nodded. During target practice yesterday, she hadn't even noticed it. He passed a hand over her hair in one last caress and disappeared inside.

She looked at the tangled greenery and took a deep breath.

That was an awfully big, strange forest. Whatever was sneaking toward the cabin would be crawling right through it. She could be intercepted on the path to the lake.

Despite all promises or common sense she nearly tried to crawl back through the window. Then she saw a speckled kestrel perched in a maple tree by the path. It tilted its head, focused a huge amber eye on her and mantled its wings. It was such a fierce little thing that, in spite of everything, she almost smiled.

"Okay," she whispered. "I guess it's just you and me for a while, kid."

She stepped onto the path, such as it was. It was narrow and as overgrown as the clearing. From a few feet away, she wouldn't be able to see it. The kestrel took wing and followed.

When she rounded a curve, a transparent, shimmering form of a man stood in front of her. She jerked to a halt in dismay, for she had already been caught.

The form held out a hand in greeting. *Peace. I'm here to help.*

She stared. The figure bore none of the malevolence of any of the dark creatures she had encountered. It seemed to wait patiently until she recovered her composure.

She squinted as she tried to see the man more clearly. He was much taller than she was, as tall as Michael. She received an impression of black military-short hair, hawkish features and the glitter of intelligent, dark eyes, but no matter how she tried, she could not bring him into the kind of sharp focus with which she had seen Astra in the Grotto or other creatures from the psychic realm. He was different in some fundamental way.

Who are you? she asked.

I am a compatriot of Michael's, the man said. *My name is Nicholas Crow. After I was killed, I stayed to watch at my post, but the Dark One is not there. He's here.*

This was Nicholas? Her astonishment at meeting the ghost was outmatched by an upsurge of panic.

The Dark One. Nicholas meant the Deceiver. Somehow he had found them. Despite their best efforts, someone had noticed something, or in their preoccupation with their own internal crises, they had let some small thing slip.

He was here.

Come, said Nicholas. He turned and appeared to run down the path.

The kestrel swooped in front of her, eyed her fiercely and flew after the ghost.

Clutching the gun in one hand, she shook her head and ran after both of them.

WITH A FEROCIOUS sense of relief, Michael watched as Mary disappeared down the path to the lake. Once he was alone he almost didn't take the time to put on the vest, but then he hesitated. He had known how hard it was for her to leave him, but she had kept her word. He didn't want her to find out later that he hadn't kept his.

Moving fast, he stripped off the ammunition and the sword, shrugged on the vest and yanked the Velcro edges into place. The weight of the vest was so familiar to him that he barely noticed it.

He slung the sword in its scabbard onto his back and adjusted the ammunition belts across his chest again. Finally he reached into his weapons bag and pulled out his throwing stars, which were stored in protective leather wrist guards. He fastened those onto each thick muscled wrist.

He could have armed himself in his sleep. All his preparations were automatic. He focused most of his attention somewhere else.

He had set three guardians to watch while they had slept. One now traveled with Mary. It took only a moment to connect mentally with the kestrel and to confirm they were safely on the path and moving away from the area.

They traveled with someone else.

He narrowed his eyes. The kestrel was fast moving out of contact range, and he could not make sense of what it saw. The only things he could tell was that whoever was with them was not embodied and meant to help, not harm.

They were no longer in physical contact with each other, as they had been in the car, and unlike their encounter with the dragon at the gas station, they were both embodied, but they could still speak to each other.

He said, *Mary.*

He could sense her astonishment at yet another new concept, but she overcame it quickly. *Yes?*

I know someone has joined you, but I can't tell who it is.

It's Nicholas. He said he came to help.

Good, he said. *That's very good.*

Despite their situation, he found room for a wry smile. Nicholas was far more generous than he. If their roles were reversed, Michael would not risk himself for the other man. Too much depended on him.

He turned his attention to the other two hawks circling overhead. Hawks did not count like humans. With some effort and a few educated questions, he was able to translate their responses into a rough head count.

They responded twenty times when he asked them to

identify a new enemy. So he had twenty problems approaching on foot, along with a black vehicle that held an unknown number of occupants as it quietly purred down the gravel road toward the cabin.

Three problems were thirty yards away and closing fast.

He closed his eyes and took a deep breath. As he exhaled he put himself in his meditative state of mindfulness. He acknowledged all sensory input then let it pass through him, neither clinging to details nor ignoring them.

From that still quiet place, he expanded and heightened his awareness to include the cabin and the surrounding area. As his awareness expanded, his center remained calm and detached, a pool filled with infinite peace. It was the eye of a hurricane.

There—and there—and there were his three nearest problems.

Two problems crept close on either side of the cabin's gravel driveway. The third moved through the woods to get behind the cabin. That one might discover the path to the lake.

As if he would let that happen.

He took another deep unhurried breath.

Then he became the hurricane.

Sprinting out the cabin door, he pivoted on one heel, leaped for the roof of the porch and landed in a half crouch on the balls of his feet. He scanned the nearby forest in the direction of the third problem. There was a tree twenty feet away that was large and sturdy enough to bear his weight. He raced across the cabin roof and leaped to the nearest heavy branch, ignoring the leaves and smaller branches that whipped across his face and arms.

The problem closest to the path lifted his head and his gun at the sudden, heavy rustling overhead. He searched with calm efficiency among the nearby trees. One of Michael's throwing stars sliced the air and embedded in his forehead, and he died.

The other two heard nothing unusual, except perhaps for a sudden gust of wind rustling through the trees.

Agile as a cat, Michael leaped to the ground. All his physical movements were enhanced and strengthened beyond the capacity of a normal human, directed by the powerful spirit housed in his body. He took three running steps and vaulted high into the boughs of the large pine tree by the drive. In his mind's eye, he tracked the energy signature of the man closest to him. He took aim and launched his second throwing star without ever physically laying eyes on the man.

The star took the second problem in the throat, who died almost instantly.

Almost was not quite fast enough. The man's grip convulsed. Gunfire sprayed the forest as he fell. That was unfortunate, Michael thought, but inevitable. Sooner or later the fight had to get noisy.

The third man spoke into his headset in an urgent rapid undertone.

Mary said in his head, *Michael?*

Yes? His reply was as calm as hers was shaken.

The third man twisted to dive for cover in thick underbrush. He spun around and shot the man in the temple before he'd taken two steps.

Mary said, *I heard shots. Are you all right? I'm sorry. I know you must be busy. I shouldn't be bothering you, but—*

Her fear beat at him through the telepathic contact. He kept his mental voice unhurried and soothing. *I'm quite fine. We can be overheard. Don't say anything telepathic that should be confidential. Just keep doing what you're doing.*

Okay. I'm sorry. God. Her stress strained their connection.

Mary, he said. He scanned the area for signs of the other problems. *I haven't even broken into a sweat.*

Yet.

Yes. I'll go now.

She sounded so perfectly wretched he pitied her. He would be in as bad or worse shape if he were in her shoes, hearing gunfire in her vicinity and unable to do anything. But she was going to have to deal with it. He didn't have any more time to spare for her, because something was amassing from the direction of the black vehicle.

It was an amalgamation of power, like the towering buildup of a funnel cloud.

He put one hand on the trunk of a nearby tree and leaned on it. Neither side had yet been surprised except, perhaps, for the three dead men and Mary. The black vehicle held his real problem. His real problem had thrown those first men at him as cannon fodder, just to tickle him to see if he was paying attention.

The form of a young, dark-haired woman shimmered into place beside him.

He turned his head and looked at Astra's crystalline form. She looked both furious and terrified.

They stared at each other. He gave her a resigned shrug.

She snapped, *I told you that you shouldn't have stopped moving!*

He could have said a lot of things in reply.

He could have said that he had been tired and the sexy blonde had flirted with him and had said pretty please.

Or he could also have said that even if they hadn't stopped, their enemy still might have found them. Michael had found Mary so late in the game, while the Deceiver had been so close behind them.

Each statement contained a facet of the truth, and none of it mattered anymore.

And, really, there wasn't any point in arguing with Astra or kicking himself since somebody else already wanted to do it so badly.

I'll do what I can to help, Astra said grimly.

Of course you will, he said.

He knew exactly just how much stock to put into that. Astral projection from such a long distance was a massive drain on her reserves, and here, while she might join in the fight, as disembodied as she was, she could only wield a fraction of her strength.

Then, when the fight got too dangerous, she would vanish. She would have to. Just as Michael was too valuable to risk in helping Nicholas, Astra was too valuable to risk helping Michael or Mary.

The funnel cloud of power built and built until the land itself seemed to skew out of balance from the compressed force.

" 'By the pricking of my thumbs . . .' " Michael muttered. He sighed and rubbed his eyes with thumb and forefinger. Beside him, Astra visibly braced herself.

Something wicked this way comes.

It approached with a confident and unhurried pace.

The dark cloud was aimed at them, and released.

Chapter Twenty-five

MARY WAS GOING to remember that damn forest path for the rest of her life. Her lives. However long any of them might last.

Her body couldn't keep up with her adrenaline-spiked mind. Every step she took felt leaden and slow, as though she ran through waist-deep mud. In contrast, the ghost of Nicholas floated effortlessly in front of her, while her kestrel flitted at an almost leisurely pace from branch to branch.

When she heard that first staccato percussion of gunfire, she stumbled to a halt.

Nicholas swung around to face her. *Don't stop.*

She shook her head at him. Terror made her leg muscles go watery.

Terror not just for Michael, but for whatever abomination might be sent after her, like Sport Coat and Spring Jacket with their dark, smudged auras. The dinginess clung to them like pollution belched from a coal-burning plant, telling a tale of spirits that had become skewed or perhaps had died. Those bizarre smiles had never left their faces even as the hawks had torn them to shreds.

One ghost and a small, fierce bird would not be able to stop a creature like those two men.

She shuddered even as she called Michael, frantic to know if he was all right. He was. His calm reply soothed and chastised her.

So she started running again. The hand that clutched the gun hung at her side. The other pressed at a stitch that gnawed just under her ribs.

Follow the path. Skirt around the lake then go north again. It was afternoon, so she should keep the sun to her left. None of this was rocket science either. Even someone who was directionally challenged couldn't screw that up, right?

Michael probably came with an internal GPS system already installed. He would find her. She just had to have faith and follow orders. She had to trust his expertise, because, surely to God, she didn't have a clue what to do next.

He had trained his whole life for this conflict, whereas so far she had managed to avoid bleeding to death. Not that she wasn't glad of the result. She was, but let's face it. She had only achieved that much by asking for someone else's help.

She had life-altering realizations to ponder, and a powerful deadly danger to avoid, and Michael to fret about. But in her panic, she had managed to yank on her old socks, the ones she had washed in the bathroom sink and dried on the water heater. They felt stiff and rough, and blisters were forming on her heels. Soon the raw pain consumed her attention until each step felt like a jolt from an electric socket that shot up her calves.

She hated this path. She hated these woods. She hated this gun.

As soon as she could, she was going to shoot her socks.

She was so consumed with her own internal misery, the rest of the world slipped out of focus for a heartbeat.

Nicholas rushed at her. Her attention snapped to him. Even though he was not corporeal, instinctively she jerked out of his way.

Get down! he hissed at her.

Far be it from her to question him. She dropped like a stone, cheek to the ground and gun hand protectively covering the back of her head.

He rushed away. A few moments later, she felt a nearby snarl of violent energy. Still a step behind events, she switched her focus from her physical surroundings to the psychic and tried to glean details of what was happening just a few feet away.

Nicholas had tangled with a transparent darkness that seemed to have no form at all, yet it wrapped around the ghost's brighter form and flexed, as if squeezing him like a boa constrictor. His presence blazed with a savage fury and dislodged the dark form. He took hold of it and ripped it apart.

Then he came and knelt beside her. Cautiously she lifted her head and stared at him. *What the hell was that?*

One of his spies, he said. *A greedy little bastard. If I'd been weaker, it could have drained me completely. Watch out for creatures like that. They could drain you too, if you become injured badly enough.*

Thank you, she said.

He tried to put a hand on her shoulder then seemed frustrated. *Keep your senses sharp for any more of those. We can't let any of them take word of our position back to the Dark One. Come on.*

She pushed to her feet. There seemed to be a lesson every minute these days. If she could be affected by creatures in the psychic realm, like the dragon or this formless, dark creature, then she could affect them too. Maybe she could tear them apart like Nicholas did. She had to remember that, in case it ever became necessary.

Then she sensed something in the distance behind her, something so strange and wrong she stumbled over a tree root and would have shot a sock while it was still on her foot if she hadn't kept the gun on safety.

She stopped, turned and scented the air like a bloodhound. Her kestrel flew around her, dive-bombing her head as it tried to shepherd her into moving in the right direction. She ignored it.

A massive black mass teemed and buzzed in the distance. She fumbled with her rediscovered abilities. She had none of Michael's prowess. She swiped at her sweating forehead as if it would help her to see, but the mass wasn't a physical one. It existed in the psychic realm, like the dragon or the dark creature, and it seemed to be coming from the direction of the gravel road.

What could it be?

She longed to be with Michael, or to at least feel able to contact him telepathically. But she didn't dare to interrupt him a second time.

What IS that? she whispered to Nicholas.

That is a lot of creatures like the one I just killed, he said. He sounded grim. *Thousands of them. Come on. We've got to go.*

At a loss for anything else she could sensibly do, she turned to start running again after the ghost.

Behind her, the black cloud reached critical mass. It shot toward the cabin.

She jerked to a halt, made a noise and pressed the back of her hand against her mouth. If that many creatures attacked Michael, could they do any damage? He was whole and strong, and he shone like a tower in the backdrop of the psychic realm.

But according to Nicholas, if he were injured, those creatures could feed on him. That would weaken him further and expose him to greater injury, which would then in turn make him more vulnerable to their attack. Sometimes battles were not won in any dramatic, decisive move, but through the force of sheer numbers grinding the opposition into dust.

"Do as you're told," she whispered. Her voice was a ragged mess, but she was so scared and lonesome she said it out loud just to hear the sound of someone's voice. "Don't do something stupid. Don't be a TV heroine and go in the basement where you know the vampires are."

Nicholas seemed to look back at her, but he didn't say anything.

She turned the statement into a marching rhythm and trudged, not ran, away.

Do as you're told.

Do as you're fucking told.

Would she know if he died? Were they attuned enough to each other so she would sense his passing? If she did, how would she bear it? They had just found each other. She'd barely had one day of feeling whole and sensual. One day of feeling the most astonishing and necessary passion.

One day of feeling real, not like a shadow of a person.

Give us a chance, he had said. But what if their chance was taken from them?

She remembered the final images from her last life. After an immeasurable endurance of pain, she had opened her eyes to find him bending over her. He had looked different, of course, but all she'd had to do was look into his gaze, and she had known him. They had only had time to exchange those few precious sentences, their only contact in almost a thousand years. Her chest felt constricted with something hot and hurting.

Just in case there was a God, and he had some time to spare, she whispered, "Why did you do this to us? How are we supposed to bear it? Or did we do it to ourselves? Is all of this our fault? It's not my fault and it's never been Michael's. We've only tried to help."

A sickening, vertiginous lurch clutched at her. She felt as if she were falling, followed by a sharp shock of impact. Gasping, she went down on one knee and struggled with disorientation.

Nicholas knelt in front of her. *What happened?*

She held up a hand and managed to articulate one word. *Hush.*

The ghost fell silent, watching her.

The feelings disappeared as quickly as they had come. She whispered, "Michael's taken a bad fall."

Even as she said it the spray of gunfire sounded again, several staccatos at once.

That was when she gave up all pretense of trying to reach the lake. She turned around to face the direction of the cabin and sent all her desperate attention toward him. The physical world dimmed as she concentrated on what she could sense in the psychic realm.

Images slammed into her. The air was thick and black with innumerable dark spirits. They swirled and swooped on two figures that blazed with light. One of them was tall and masculine. Michael had already regained his footing from the fall. The other was smaller and feminine. Even from that distance, Mary recognized Astra in her astral form.

Astra's figure never appeared to move, but the dark spirits that swirled to attack her sizzled away to nothing, like moths encompassed by a pure, lethal flame.

Michael's blazing figure wielded a bright spear of light that slashed through attacking dark spirits even as, in the physical realm, he killed the men that rushed him.

Pride and fear for him locked her throat. To fight like that in multiple realms at once . . . he was incomparable. But there were too many spirits, and too many men who were suicidal with recklessness.

As she watched, Astra's bright figure flickered. Mary thought she heard the other woman call, *I cannot stay any longer.*

Then Astra disappeared from the scene. She blinked out of the scene as abruptly as if she had never been present.

Her departure left Michael all alone.

They battered him to the ground by sheer force of numbers.

Approaching the battlefield at a stroll was a black diamond man. Mary wanted to vomit out this reality but she was helpless to stop what she witnessed.

Then the black diamond man bent over the radiant one, and Michael was taken.

Chapter Twenty-six

SHE LEAPED UPRIGHT. Her bleeding feet grew wings as she raced back toward the cabin. The decision was no longer based on a question of intelligence versus stupidity, or doing what she was told, or even based on some fragile hope for survival. She knew she was running back to her death, or something much worse. But she ran anyway, because she couldn't do anything else.

The kestrel dove at her head, shrieking, and Nicholas stood in the path as if he would bar her way. She waved an arm at the bird and ran through Nicholas's insubstantial form.

As she passed through him, for a moment she felt intense warmth. A knife flashed at the edge of her/his vision, quick as a striking snake. It sliced across her/his throat. Blood spilled down her/his front, and she/he fell to the ground.

Then she stumbled out the other side, gasping, and left both the ghost and the vision of his death behind her.

She didn't have time to marvel at another weird experience, or mourn what had happened. Regaining her balance, she raced down the path.

Before she could make it halfway back to the clearing, the

black diamond man began to emit a strange humming noise, a harsh discordant vibration that made her want to claw at her ears. The noise grew louder and intensified. It tore a rent through the psychic realm, and Michael's vibrant, powerful energy began to keen with strain, like crystal about to shatter.

Her existence narrowed to a screaming denial.

WAIT! She hurled the word with the full force of her terror.

It was a horror. It was a miracle. The black diamond man hesitated before destroying Michael utterly.

There you are, Mary. The man's voice was creamy with satisfaction. *Didn't I say you might have been happier to leave all of this alone?*

Demented with fear, she said, *You wanted me once. Do you still want me?*

The black diamond man laughed. *How do you know I won't have you after Michael's been destroyed?*

You won't get me again that easily, you son of a bitch, she said. *Let him go and I'll walk back. I swear it.*

And if I don't?

Panic had her scrambling for scraps of supposition and guesswork that were so insubstantial it felt like she tried to clutch at dust motes dancing in the air. *Make no mistake, together Astra and I are more than strong enough to bring you down.*

That's assuming you can get free to join her.

She lifted her gun and clawed at the safety catch, transmitting everything she did down the telepathic link. Then she put the muzzle to her mouth. *I can stay free of you, one way or another. I'm going to count to three. Then I'm pulling the trigger, and you know I'll be back.*

Years from now? His chuckle was a darkness that crawled around in her brain. *I think I'll concern myself with that when it happens. Right now I'm going to enjoy destroying your twin. He's been such a pain in my ass. This is the first time I have EVER had him pinned to the mat. I'll deal with you after he's gone.*

She flung everything she had into one insane bluff. *I'm*

healed, and I have all my memories back. And I remember how much I loathe you. Destroying you will be the only reason for me to continue existing.

Funny, he said. *We haven't answered one vital question. Are you sure you CAN exist when Michael's gone?*

He and I have existed without each other for nine centuries, remember? Bitterness burned at the back of her throat.

No, Mary. You and he haven't SEEN each other in nine centuries. Existing in the universe without his energy to complement and balance yours is something I don't think you've learned how to do. Ariel and Uriel hadn't learned it. Neither had Gabriel and Raphael. I would destroy one twin, and the other just . . . unraveled. Both times it was kind of like pulling a snag in a knitted sweater.

Destroying Michael won't unravel me. You saw to that. She projected as much conviction as she could. *You altered my spirit. You changed me.*

I didn't change you enough, he said slowly. *I didn't have enough time to completely break your spirit and reform you. If I had, you would have been totally bent to my will.*

She shuddered. Was that a touch of doubt she heard in his mental voice? *No, you failed at that. I may not be what I once was, but I am stronger than I've ever been. I'm starting to count. One.*

Okay, I won't destroy him, he said. *Not yet. I'll hold on to him until you walk into the clearing.*

Her laugh was raw and animalistic, more like a snarl. The gun's metallic muzzle rattled against her teeth. *Let him go or it's no deal. Two.*

Slow down. You're counting too fast. There are things to consider here. How do I know you'll keep your word? His mental voice was a silken obscenity. *After all, right now I do have such a pretty bird in the hand.*

Can he walk on his own if you let him go? Her shaking legs wouldn't support her any longer, and she sank to her knees.

There was a thoughtful pause. *I don't think so. I'm not sure. I don't want to loosen my hold on him to find out until you and I have a deal.*

Her eyes stung with sweat. She pulled the muzzle away from her mouth and mopped at them. *Have two of your men help him. I'll walk in as they walk him out. When you see me, you'll tell them to leave him and come back to you. I'll know if you do.*

Hmm, he murmured. *Thinking, thinking.*

Despair threatened to drown her. What was she doing, buying them minutes at most?

If Michael couldn't walk, the Deceiver would only take her and then take him again. She wouldn't even have the brief peace of death.

But she knew that, even if all she gained were minutes, she would do anything to keep from hearing that strained-crystal keening from Michael's spirit again. Anything.

Her mental voice had turned to rags. *Make up your mind. Yes or no.*

Silence, both psychic and physical.

She waited another heartbeat then put the muzzle to her mouth again. Michael was right. It did have a kick. She bent over until she was in a ball, bracing both her hands and the butt of the gun against her knees, and angled the gun with care. If she pulled the trigger, she wanted to suicide successfully, not end up brain damaged and trapped in her body.

When the bullet tore through her head, would she know? The brain has no pain receptors, but all around the brain were nerve endings located in the head.

Her breath shook. She said, *Three.*

All right, the black diamond man said. *Congratulations, you have a deal.* He showed her a mental image of Michael's body sagging between two men. She could see both the psychic and the fleshly wounds that scored him. His face was covered in blood. The two men carried him away. She caught sight of his legs moving weakly before the image cut off. *They're leaving with him now, so start walking back.*

She pulled the gun out of her mouth and retched. All she brought up was bile. She shuddered and spat, wiping her mouth with the back of a trembling hand.

There, there, cookie, the black diamond man told her. He sounded cheerful. *Pull yourself together and get moving, or I'll tell my men to bring him back.*

"I'm coming," she said out loud, her voice hoarse. She climbed to her feet stiffly, like an old woman. "Keep your goddamn shirt on."

Edging down the path, still sick with tension, she darted her gaze everywhere in an effort to keep from being surprised by any of the Deceiver's creatures. The kestrel had disappeared, but Nicholas kept pace with her. When she glanced at him, the ghost shook his head, but he no longer tried to stop her.

She fought to keep in contact with Michael's energy. Her success was patchy at best, but at least it was enough to confirm that he moved away from the clearing.

The black diamond man wanted her badly enough to gamble on letting Michael go, and that frightened her more than anything. She flashed back to her last life, and the memory of him sprinkling some kind of powder into the crevices of her wound. Dread flooded her body again.

She whispered, "Okay God, if you're bored and you have a few minutes, now would be a good time to lend us a hand. At least until Michael has a chance to get away."

She hoped Michael would forgive her. She had done her best to rescue him. Once the Deceiver got hold of her, Michael would have to figure out the next move and rescue her. She knew this was a trap. She knew that the Deceiver wouldn't let Michael go if he could help it. If they lost this crazy gamble, she was very sorry, but selfishly she hoped she would get to die first.

Up ahead, the cabin appeared through a break in the trees. When she reached the edge of the foliage, she paused to peek into the clearing. Her gaze skittered around, taking in details.

Several bodies littered the ground. Several more guards were alert and positioned at various places through the open area. They all had that queer, smudged quality in their auras. A black limousine parked at a slant across the gravel drive, blocking the way.

A handsome young man leaned back against the limousine, one foot crossed over the other. He was dark-haired with a clever, narrow face and dressed in a tasteful navy blue business suit. He held a handgun in a relaxed grip at his side, the muzzle pointing to the ground.

For a startled moment she felt a happy, relieved incredulity. Justin hadn't died in the fire. He was alive.

Then she saw it. The aura surrounding Justin's body was so black that it shimmered, diamondlike, created from the pressure of an existence that had spanned the ages.

Her world crashed around her, and she clutched at a tree trunk to keep from falling. Horror sank razor-edged teeth into her.

No. No. No.

Oh God. Not Justin.

Justin was truly dead.

She didn't know she had any more tears left until they poured in burning streaks down her face.

Dark spirits clung to trees, bushes and to some of the men. They rustled and whispered, the oily sound like a toxic sludge pouring along the edges of her mind.

Two men crept toward her through the woods.

She held the gun to her temple and took a step into the clearing. By then she had gone so hoarse she didn't recognize her own voice. She said, "Two of your assholes are trying to come at me from behind. Call them off. Order the men with Michael to come back. Do it now."

Not-Justin turned toward her. He gave her a delighted smile, and he looked so like Justin's roguish, unrepentant charm she gagged.

He said in Justin's pleasant, familiar voice, "There's our princess. Hold on a moment."

She waited. Her stalkers withdrew. Her mind jumped from the men in the woods to the two transporting Michael. They dropped him and began jogging back.

She reached for Michael telepathically. *This was the best I can do. I'm so sorry.*

She thought she caught a thread of whisper in reply just before an invisible wall slammed down between them, blocking out all communication.

"Now, cookie," said not-Justin. "I'm a rather jealous sort. Right now I want all of your attention on me. I've kept my part of the bargain. It's time for you to keep yours."

She hesitated, remembering Michael's promise to kill her before he let the Deceiver take her. Her hand clenched on the gun's grip.

Not-Justin cocked his head. "You know," he said. "Much as I love Mel Brooks's sense of humor and his satire on racism, this is not nearly as amusing as that 'shoot-the-nigger' scene in *Blazing Saddles*, when the black man holds himself hostage. Put the gun down or my men go back to Michael. I'll have them cut off his hands and feet. If he doesn't bleed to death while I deal with you I can finish him later. I do promise you, cookie, if it comes to that I will be delighted to take my time with him."

The gun dropped from her nerveless fingers. It hit the ground.

"Excellent," he said, smiling. He pushed from the limousine and strolled through the bodies toward her. "I guess I've made it rather obvious how much I want you."

"Well, yes. . . ."

He lifted his gun and shot her.

She felt it punch her left shoulder. Her body arced backward as the clearing whirled. Then the ground came up and slammed into her. She thought she heard someone roaring.

Distantly, she got the impression of several men running out of the clearing. The dark spirits lifted from the trees and flapped away.

Two wingtip shoes came sideways into her vision. The Deceiver said, "As you might have gathered from your last life, I might want you alive, but I'm not averse to a little judicious maiming."

Her mouth opened. She tried to take a breath. One of her hands scrabbled at the grass. Then she spiraled inward in an agonized epiphany.

Red was important to her.

Red filled her mind, a warm, glowing vibrancy like live coals except for one dark torn place. Her awareness flew in that direction, past the pumping heart and the working bellows of her lungs, to the jagged hole that ripped through her body.

The bullet had entered just below her collarbone. It had flattened as it moved through muscle and tissue, creating more damage where it exited than where it had entered. As she followed the damage to the back of her shoulder, she sent commands to her body that would stop the worst of the bleeding.

And just like Michael's body had when she had commanded it, her body obeyed.

The abused flesh began to knit back together at the microscopic level.

She felt herself lifted and turned. The Deceiver probed curiously at her wound. As she tried to push the hard fingers away, she flashed back to that ancient horror when he had reached into her body and handled organs that were never meant to endure such exposure.

"The bleeding has already starting to slow." He sounded thrilled. "You are remembering. How delicious."

Inside, the door to her secret, golden treasure chamber opened, and precious knowledge scrolled out.

She staved off the lethargy of shock and kept her temperature controlled. White blood cells started to locate and destroy foreign bacteria.

Of course. How could she have forgotten?

She had always known she was a healer. This was how she healed.

The Deceiver picked her up and carried her toward the limousine. "You know, in that life when I found you, your family had sheltered you so much you never had a clue how famous you had become," he said, his tone conversational. "I wanted you from the first moment I'd heard of you. I was sure that you were one of us."

She only gave him part of her attention. Most of her awareness focused on her internal reality.

This was how she knew how close Michael had come to cardiac arrest, yesterday in the bathroom.

This was why she had poured so much energy into him, how she had calmed his heart. He had sunk so deeply into the memories of his own death he had almost killed himself again.

His heart. The blood, the arteries, and the rhythmic pumping of his heart, all normally so strong.

"You should have heard the names they called you in the city." The Deceiver jerked his head at one of his soldiers, who sprang forward to open the back door. "Blessed of Allah, Daughter of Heaven. You were a legend before you were twenty. They said you had a face like an angel and a touch like Jesus. It looks like you still do, Mary, Mary."

Quite contrary.

Before the intention had formed properly in her mind, she slapped a hand flat on his breastbone. She sent her awareness through that touch, thrusting into him like a scalpel.

And if she had the nerve to wield a scalpel, she could shoot this gun.

Justin's heart was wonderfully healthy, thirty years old and strong as an ox. He should have lived to be a wisecracking, mischievous old man.

She tangled her awareness in veins and arteries. She gripped the rhythmic pumping muscle with her mind like a fist then she—

Yanked.

Shock bolted across his face. His arms loosened. She fell hard and awkwardly. She cried out as the impact shot burning pain through her left shoulder and lung. Pushing against the ground, she managed to turn onto her back. She looked up.

He hunched over, clutching at his chest. The normal

healthy tan of Justin's complexion turned purplish. His features contorted with astonishment, pain and rage.

DAMN YOU! he roared in her head like a cyclone. *GODDAMN YOU!*

Wheezing, he fell to one knee. His eyes turned toward her, and they were black diamond eyes, as vast as twin black holes, and they were filled with her destruction. He reached an unsteady hand toward her.

Oh God. She couldn't let him touch her.

She rolled away and kept rolling as he lunged after her. How long before his hemorrhaging heart brought him to immobility, unconsciousness? Would it be soon enough?

He sprawled full length, his grasping fingers scant inches from her ankle. She glanced back at him. He fought to get his knees underneath him again.

Gunfire exploded nearby. She realized she'd been hearing gunfire in the background for a few minutes now.

The Deceiver grabbed for her ankle again. His fingers brushed the cuff of her jeans and hooked underneath the hem.

"*WHY DON'T YOU JUST DIE!*" she screamed at him.

She kicked him in the face. His head snapped back, and blood sprayed from his nose. Jackknifing away, she got to her hands and knees. The weight made her injured shoulder pulse with agony. She curled her left arm around her torso and scuttled away like a wounded crab.

After five feet, she sent a terrified glance over her shoulder.

He had to be close to death. He had to be.

He had abandoned his pursuit of her. He lay curled on his side, his psychic presence as malignant and as powerful as ever. The soldier that had opened the limousine door for him walked toward him. The man's aura was smudged and dark, his expression blank.

The soldier bent over the dying man with the stiff disjointedness of a marionette puppet. Not-Justin grabbed the soldier's hand. The soldier convulsed then collapsed on top of him.

She didn't dare wait to see any more. Instead she pushed

to her feet and lurched down the gravel driveway in a stumbling run, supporting her injured arm with the other.

Ahead of her, Michael lunged around the bend in the gravel drive. He was limping badly, sweating profusely and bleeding from several wounds. In one hand, he held an automatic weapon. In the other, he gripped a foot-long knife that dripped ruby liquid. The savage expression on his hard face made her sob.

She tripped and almost went down. He limped up to her, slung the gun onto his shoulder and sheathed the knife. Then, with as much care as if she were made of spun glass, he put his arms around her. She dropped her forehead to his collarbone. Heat poured off of him in waves.

"Thank you, God," she whispered.

"Where is he?" His voice was gravel. His chest heaved.

"Back there." She pointed with her good hand toward the clearing as she leaned against him, hungrily soaking in the sensation of his strong body next to hers.

He held her away from him. "Christ, you're covered with blood." His voice shook. "How bad is it?"

She shook her head and forced herself to take a deep breath. "It hurts, but I've slowed the bleeding. Michael, somehow he was in my ex-husband's body. I induced a cardiac arrest. He went down, but it doesn't feel like he's gone. One of his soldiers collapsed when he touched him."

"All right." Michael turned an executioner's expression toward the clearing. He asked, "Can you keep running?"

Words exploded out of her with violent force. "I'm not leaving you again!"

Sword gray eyes met hers in brief, perfect understanding. He let go of her, took his gun in one hand and started down the drive. "Come on then."

A car revved to life near the cabin. Michael spun, grabbed her good arm and dragged her into the tangled brush. Her aching body whimpered at the headlong pace. One of his hard hands clamped on to the back of her neck and pushed her to the ground.

"Stay down," he hissed.

She ducked her head and stayed down.

Gleaming black metal flashed between gaps in the foliage as the limousine roared past them. Michael stood and sprayed it with gunfire, but the car was armored. It disappeared. The Deceiver's raging presence faded.

Silence descended. No birds called. No wind rustled the trees. The mass of dark spirits had scattered. The scene seemed as peaceful as it had been before the intruders had arrived.

She sensed Michael scanning the area before he shouldered his gun again and knelt beside her. That was when her body exerted control, and she started to shake so hard her teeth clattered.

He eased an arm under her shoulders and lifted her to a sitting position. Then he wrapped his arms around her so tightly she thought he might break one of her ribs.

"Easy," she gasped as her gunshot wound gave a warning throb, and his hold loosened. She could feel tremors shuddering through his long hard body. He pressed his hot face into her neck.

She managed to get her good arm around his waist.

"Shoulder wound?" he asked. His hands passed compulsively down her back.

She nodded. "I'm okay," she gritted. "If I get enough quiet time, I think I can heal it. You?"

"I'll be okay."

Pulling back, she glanced down his body, noting the tears in his clothing that indicated injuries underneath. No matter what he said, those wounds needed attention. They needed to get back to the cabin. She needed her first aid kit.

She looked up and their eyes met. He said between his teeth, "What the hell were you doing?"

She struggled to speak coherently. "I did what I had to. I thought—I felt him start to tear you apart somehow. I didn't know there could be anything so horrifying. And there isn't anything I wouldn't do to keep from feeling that again."

He rocked her. His voice vibrated in her ear. "I'm so pissed at you I can't see straight. And grateful too. We're both alive and that's what counts. Come on. We don't have time to dissect what happened."

He raised her to her feet and kept a supporting arm around her. She put her good arm around his waist as they limped back to the cabin. "I was so sure I had him," she said. "He was dying, but then he drove away. Can he heal himself?"

"We all can heal ourselves to a certain degree," Michael said. "But not to the level of your abilities. In any case I doubt he healed himself. He takes life, he doesn't repair it."

If Michael believed Astra could have healed Mary's old psychic wound, apparently, Astra had more aptitude for healing than most of the group. "I saw Astra fighting with you," she said. "Then she disappeared. She wasn't injured too, was she?"

"No, but she is weakened." His mouth tightened. "She used all her strength in the fight. We can't expect any more help from her for a while."

It was illogical to take that news as a blow, since any anything Astra could offer was so limited by distance anyway, but still her shoulders sagged. She felt that they were more cut off than ever, and very alone.

They reached the edge of the clearing. Michael glanced at the bodies on the ground. He said, "Go straight into the cabin. I'll be there in a minute."

She ignored the order, refusing to turn away from the carnage. Instead, she stared at the body of the handsome man that lay curled on the ground. "That's my ex-husband," she whispered. "Did you see him earlier? That's Justin's body."

She walked over to Justin, and he followed. Remembering the black diamond aura that had surrounded him, she cautiously paused to study the edges of his curled figure. Just as she had suspected, the aura was gone.

Awkwardly, she went down on her knees beside Justin and touched the fingers of her right hand to the carotid artery, just below his jaw. There was no pulse. Gently she stroked his hair back from his forehead while tears swam in her eyes.

I loved you, she thought. Not the way either of us hoped

we would when we got married, but I did love you. If I could take that day back again, I would. And I would do something else, something wiser and better. I would have been patient with you, and I would have gone to see Tony. Or I would have stayed home to send you away. Justin, I am so sorry.

Michael stood beside her and waited until she looked up, even though he favored one leg. His expression somber, he said quietly, "He's dead."

He didn't phrase it as a question, but still, she nodded. Passing her hand one last time over Justin's hair, she struggled to her feet.

Michael put a hand underneath her elbow to help her. He said, "We both felt the Deceiver's presence leave with the limo. He's migrating from body to body without dying and being reborn."

Killing people and taking over their bodies. Michael's harsh voice sounded matter-of-fact, yet her mind whirled. "That soldier was one of his drones. Do you think he migrated over to that body?"

"Yes. He kills people's spirits, and either controls them or he takes over their bodies. That way he always remains at full strength as an adult, and he never forgets who he is or where he came from."

She shook her head. "How?

"I don't know. None of the rest of us would do such a thing. We haven't developed the knowledge or the skill for it. All I know is he's created a lot of drones." Michael's chest heaved as he looked around at the bodies in the clearing. His bloody face was set in grim lines as he turned to her. "I really want you to go inside now."

She stood her ground, staring up into his gaze. "What are you going to do?"

"If any of these survived, I need to put them down."

It was her turn to stare at the bodies scattered across the clearing. The physician in her rebelled against Michael's implacable words. It was one thing to fight and kill in self-defense, but to slit a man's throat while he lay helpless, unable to defend himself?

"These are people," she whispered. Or at least they used to be.

"They're *drones*." He emphasized the last word. "They're just like the men who attacked you. The Deceiver can control them. They will continue to act out the last orders they received from him. That means if any of them are still breathing and they get to their feet, they will attack us again."

"They're his victims too. If any of them are alive, I need to see if I can help them." She straightened her spine and said in a soft voice, "You already know this, Michael. That's what *I* do."

He raked a hand through his hair and swore savagely under his breath.

A shimmering presence formed beside them, appearing to focus all of its attention on her. It was Nicholas. He said, *Two have survived.*

She sucked in a breath. There was her answer. "I need my first aid kit out of the car." She looked at Nicholas. "Will you keep watch over the survivors and let us know if they start to stir?"

Yes, said the ghost. *What will you be doing?*

She turned her attention back to Michael. "I'm going to do triage."

Chapter Twenty-seven

TRIAGE.

Allocating treatment to patients according to a system of priorities. Usually triage was designed to maximize the number of survivors, especially in disaster situations.

This time, she was going to allocate treatment according to the value of the injured. She eyed Michael's wounds. "You first."

A complex expression passed over his grim face, acceptance and understanding, even, oddly, compassion. "We don't have much time," he said. "We have to leave here as soon as we can. You might have forced the Deceiver into retreating, but he can still send others after us with a single phone call."

"Then we'd better get to it," she said crisply. "I haven't even examined you closely yet, but I'm still fairly certain you're going to need stitches. I need my bag."

"I'll get it." Gripping his upper right thigh, Michael made his way to the car.

She put a hand to her injured shoulder. As her adrenaline faded, she felt too hot and cold at the same time. The skin around her shoulder felt raw and painful to the touch. She had slowed her own bleeding and cleansed the wound, but she still needed to be bandaged. She could use some pain medication too. Ideally she should get a blood transfusion, but there was nothing ideal about any of this situation. They should both be in a hospital, and that simply wasn't going to happen.

Sending a look of silent gratitude to Nicholas's straight figure, she went into the cabin. Everything inside looked just as it had when they had left it. Items from Michael's weapons bag lay scattered across the table. The sheets and blankets lay in a rumpled heap on the bed.

Then she saw the bullet holes that scored the cabin walls. Not everything was quite the same. First things first. She couldn't help anybody else if she was too bad off herself. She rummaged in her purse for a small bottle of Tylenol and dry swallowed two tablets. Then, because she had lost a lot of fluids, she hobbled to the sink and drank as many cups of water as she could. She sprinkled sugar into one cup and gulped it down. Then she sprinkled salt into another cup and drank that down too.

Then she sagged against the sink as the world went gray and formless.

A hand gripped her good shoulder, and she jerked back alert. Michael stood beside her, his eyes dark with worry.

"I'm okay," she muttered. Her mouth felt filled with cotton.

"Sure you are," he said. His voice was rough, his face clenched like a fist.

He took a knife and cut through the layers of her sweatshirt and T-shirt. She hadn't taken the time to put on a bra, so when the pieces of material parted, her torso was bared to view.

They both looked at the wound where a blackened bruise the size of Michael's spread hand covered her shoulder. She patted the area gingerly with a handful of the ruined T-shirt, until the point of entry was exposed. The merest trickle of blood seeped from the opening. It hurt. It hurt a lot, but she kept the expression on her face stoic.

"See?" she said. "I told you I slowed the bleeding. I remembered how. You can dress it for me, but after I see to the worst of your wounds."

The tension in his features eased. "Okay."

All those years she spent in med school. All that money spent on her expensive education, and in some ways, she had been a more powerful healer nine hundred years ago. She sucked on her lower lip, thinking. What would she be able to do, now that she had a modern education and she was recovering her memories?

Shaking two more Tylenol out of the bottle, she gave the pills to him to take, then with her good hand, she helped him to strip off his weapons, armor and clothing. When she found several marks on the chest plate of the Kevlar vest, she bit her lip hard but set it aside without comment. He leaned back against the table while she examined the wounds. He had been shot too, several times, but the wounds were very shallow, just glancing scores along the skin of his arms and legs, and one along the side of his neck. They had to hurt like a son of a bitch, but they weren't serious.

The serious wounds were made by something sharp. Deep knife wounds along his arms and a bad stab in his right thigh that might have grazed the bone. Thank God he had listened to her and had worn the vest.

She noticed something else that troubled her deeply. His energy, normally such a strong, vibrant and bright presence, was mottled with dark lines, like fractures. Had the Deceiver done that damage? How could it heal, or be healed? He looked like he could be breakable. The sight scared her, but she kept the emotion from her expression.

Michael helped her pull out the necessary supplies from her kit. She taped some of his deeper wounds with non-suture strips, and cleaned and dressed the more shallow wounds. Three of the cuts needed suturing. He held rock steady as she worked, and watched her face.

Finally she said, "Okay. You're done for now."

"Your turn," he told her. She eased into a chair as he ran hot water in a bowl. He washed her torso and shoulder, covered the entrance and exit wounds with thick pads of gauze and bound them in place. He muttered, "Christ, you're covered in bruises."

"The last forty-eight hours have been eventful," she said. "I just wish I had been more useful for some of it."

He snorted. "You saved my life, and you got one of the nastiest entities on the planet on the run. If you were any more useless, they could make an atom bomb out of you."

A short laugh broke out of her. It hurt, and she gripped her injured shoulder to brace it. Then she sort of pitched toward him and he leaned forward too, and somehow they ended forehead to forehead, looking deeply into each other's eyes.

The somberness of his gaze. The emotion pouring out of her. They told each other so much, and all of it in silence.

She stroked his broad, bare chest. Then she said, "I don't know what to do for your other wounds."

She didn't specify further. He seemed to know exactly what she was talking about anyway, as he nodded and straightened. "You do nothing for now. We get dressed, we pack up the car, and after you examine the drones, we leave."

After she examined them. Not after she healed them. He didn't believe that she could do anything for them.

Her face tightened, but she said, "Okay."

She didn't even try to wriggle into another T-shirt. Instead, he helped her to ease into one of his flannel shirts that could be buttoned down the front. Even though her jeans had gotten smeared with grass and dirt stains, at least she had managed not to bleed on them. Michael constructed a sling out of a kitchen towel, and slipped it over her head.

Then he limped into the bathroom. A moment later she heard the sound of running water. While she waited, she went to the sink and drank more water. Then she collected her purse, a pillow and a blanket. Packing was easy when you didn't own anything.

She put the blanket and the pillow on the table, and sat and put her head on the pillow until Michael came back out.

He wore a fresh pair of jeans and another of his flannel shirts that he left loose and unbuttoned at the waist. She caught a glimpse of the hard muscles of his bare chest and a flash of white bandage at one wrist. His limp was more pronounced, his long mobile mouth bracketed with lines of pain. She watched him stuff weapons into his long black bag.

She cleared her throat and said in a rusty-sounding voice, "I dropped your other gun outside. Round the back by the path."

"I'll get it in a minute." He looked at her. "Ready to go?"

She stood and scooped up the pillow and blanket with her good arm.

He looked at the way she clutched the bedding. A fugitive amusement ghosted across his face. "Right. Let's hope he was too rattled and busy to fuck with our car, because otherwise we're going to be on foot and then I will really be pissed."

Her eyelids dropped in a slow blink. Now there was a thought. How could they make it if they were on foot? She looked at the leg Michael favored.

"Well," he said wearily after a moment. "Let's not borrow trouble. Come on."

He carried his weapons bag and her kit outside. She followed him out to the car. With a pained grunt, he heaved the kit and the weapons bag into the back. She stuffed the pillow, blanket and her purse into the passenger seat.

When she turned to scan the clearing for Nicholas, she found the ghost standing in sunlight near two prone bodies. In full sunshine, Nicholas looked like the faintest extra shimmer of light. She was only sure it was him because she could sense his presence, warm and strong.

It was only then that she remembered she had seen his death when she had connected with his energy. Too easy tears pricked at her gaze. She had never met him when he was alive, and yet he had helped her. He was generous and brave, and it was terrible that he too was dead.

When she walked toward Nicholas and the two unconscious drones, she heard a quiet whisper of steel. She looked over her shoulder. Michael had reached into the backseat and drawn his long knife from the weapons bag.

Her stomach tightened. She turned away, and without looking back, she said, "Would you please bring my kit?"

His pause stretched her already frayed nerves. "Of course."

He walked beside her with the first aid kit in one hand, his knife in another. The growing warmth in the sunny morning messed with her already shaky equilibrium. She fought it off, staying alert by force of will. When she reached the first man, she knelt beside him and said to Nicholas, *Thank you for watching them. Thank you for everything.*

You're welcome. He knelt beside her. *Thank you for trying to do something for them.*

No need to thank me, she told him. *I have to do this.*

Flanked on either side by the men, one alive and one dead, she examined the unconscious drone. A bullet had grazed his head. As far as she could tell, that was what had knocked him out. As head wounds so often do, it had bled a lot, but it was by no means fatal.

Then she opened her other senses and examined him psychically.

The man's spirit was gone, and there was no way to recall it. She could even see how the Deceiver had killed the spirit but left the body still animate and functional. The long slashing psychic scar was readily apparent to her mind's eye.

Her breathing turned ragged, and tears pricked at the back of her eyes again. Had he committed this atrocity on Justin before he had stolen Justin's body?

How did he do that?

She looked at Nicholas, into the faintest impression of dark, intelligent eyes. At the ghost of a courageous and extraordinary man who had not deserved to die.

A chilling possibility opened in front of her. She almost hated the fact that she had the capacity to be so clinical to consider it. But on the one hand, there was one man who did not deserve to be dead. While on the other hand, according to Michael, the Deceiver created lots of drones that no longer deserved to live.

If the Deceiver could take over another's body, could someone else do it too?

It was one thing to harvest separate organs from a body once a person was declared dead. It was an entirely different thing altogether to consider harvesting the whole body.

She shook off the train of thought. At the moment, she had no answers, only questions. Sitting back on her heels, her heart aching and her mind in turmoil, she shook her head at the other two. "I can't do anything for these men."

Without bending his bad leg, Michael bent over and cupped the back of her head gently. "Now will you go to the car and wait for me?"

"Yes, all right." She took a deep breath, clasped the hand he offered and climbed to her feet.

Michael looked at Nicholas's insubstantial, shimmering form. *Thank you for coming to help her. Will you do one more thing?*

If I can, said the ghost. *What do you need?*

Just check on Astra. Make sure she's all right.

I'll do that.

Then Nicholas seemed to turn to her. She felt extra warmth on her right cheek, as if he had touched her face, and he faded from the clearing.

Her eyes welled again as she put a hand to her cheek. Then, glancing once last time at Justin's body in silent farewell, she turned to walk to the car without looking back.

While she waited for Michael, she leaned against the car by the passenger door and tilted her face up. She may not have a summer of peace in this place, but she could still let the warm, bright sun wash her clean and new.

As a doctor she'd learned to accept that sometimes, despite all her best efforts, death and tragedy happen.

But so does love, life and passion. She lost herself in memories of last night, Michael moving over her, and in her, and the words he had whispered to her.

My miracle. My home.

The next thing she knew, Michael stood in front of her.

He had retrieved the gun and held it, along with the knife, in one hand. He leaned forward and kissed her, and she lost herself in the touch of his lips.

He took her free hand. "Listen to me. We're both hurt, and Astra's strength is depleted. Thanks to you, the Deceiver has to recover too, but we don't know how much reinforcement he has, so we can't stop in one place again. I can drive for a while, but you need to concentrate on healing yourself. Nothing else matters. Heal yourself so you can take over driving, because soon I'm going to need your help. Do you understand?"

She nodded. "Yes."

"Good."

He kissed her hand. She curled her fingers along the lean edge of his cheek, hating how he looked so haggard, so worn. His physical wounds would be exhausting enough. Coupled with those worrisome fractures in his energy, he seemed drained of all vitality. He opened the passenger door for her, and after she had slid in, he walked around the car and eased into the driver's seat.

They shared a quick, tense glance. She whispered, "Come on, start."

He turned the key.

The engine purred into life with smooth perfection. It was such a mercy she could have wept. "Now we need to make tracks," he said. "We've miles to go before we sleep."

She eased the seat belt around her aching body. "'Miles to go before I sleep.' That was a Robert Frost poem, right? It was some poet anyway."

"Whoever it was," he growled. "I've got a bone to pick with him."

"At least we're alive and together," she pointed out.

He shifted the car in gear and pulled onto the gravel drive. "And at least we get another day or two. Maybe more."

"A veritable wealth of minutes."

One corner of his mouth lifted. "A staggering fortune in seconds."

Struck by a thought, she said, "Hey. You never did steal any flowers for me, you know."

"I'm with a woman who is developing a memory like a steel trap." His lips pulled into a real smile. "I'll have to get right on that."

They drove off, into the morning's falling light.

Epilogue

HE DROVE AWAY from the cabin in a white heat.

Out of his whole elite strike force, he was the only one that had escaped.

As the armored black limousine roared down the highway he made a rapid series of cell phone calls. His first call insured that Mary and Michael became fugitives from the Michigan state police. Then he called for reinforcements to meet him at a designated place. He was still raging when he hung up several minutes later.

Dead or alive, he'd told his people. Dead or alive. He would rather wait for the conflict to come to a head in another lifetime than risk them reuniting with Astra in this one.

Damn them, *damn them*, *GODDAMN HER*.

Once upon a time, long ago and far away, he had nursed such pretty hopes. With a little effort and experimentation, he believed he could alchemically change Mary's spirit. He wanted to weaken it in all the right places so he could take over her will. He had intended to turn her into a drone, so she would be as obedient as his human servants and yet still retain her healing abilities. He had wanted her as his insurance policy against accidental death or intentional harm.

Living a high-roller life meant he enjoyed some juicy perks, but there were a lot of risks too. It made sense to maintain a personal physician. What better physician than one of their own? Besides, he had also imagined such lovely hypothetical scenarios of getting at Michael through her. He might even be able to control Michael in a way that no one else ever had managed before.

So today, what did he do? He'd let that old acquisitive lust take over his judgment. He had panted after Mary like a stallion after a mare in heat, when a part of him *knew* he should have ripped apart the bird he'd had at hand.

In that one dazzling moment, when he had Michael's spirit straining toward a fractured dissolution, the victory had felt too quick, too easy over the cunning bastard who had so plagued him throughout the ages.

He hadn't wanted Michael destroyed in the work of a few moments. That seemed too much like premature ejaculation. He had wanted Michael to suffer while he turned Mary into his creature, a pet obedient to his beck and call.

But now it was abundantly clear that she had become more trouble than she could ever be worth.

Phantom pain shot through his chest. He had existed for so long without suffering more than the brief discomfort entailed in changing host bodies, or the ache he felt as those bodies wore out. The memory of the heart attack still shocked him. He pounded the steering wheel.

"This is my world," he growled.

Mine.

He had been the one to discover this world. He had been the first one of their kind to learn how to transmigrate from his original self and come here to lay claim to it. Yet the closest he had come to fulfilling his vision of conquest had happened thousands of years ago when he had killed the soul of a princely fetus.

He had entered that tiny body while it was still in the womb and drifted through the long months of gestation with dark patience. He had suffered through the primitive birth and early childhood, his old soul watching the world through young eyes as he plotted and laid his plans. His mother, the queen, had sensed the infanticide but had not understood what had really happened. She claimed lightning had struck her womb. His father, the king, had been overjoyed.

When he was twenty, he had the king assassinated and he ascended the throne, and he consolidated his power by murdering all his other rivals. Then he reinforced his borders, crushed rebellions, and he swept through the Persian Empire with the unstoppable force of a juggernaut. Asia Minor, the Levant, Syria, Egypt, India—he made them all bow down when he took his rightful title as King of Kings.

His cadre of bodyguards had been specially trained. The group had been unable to get close to him. Rather than using direct force, they had killed him by using subterfuge and trickery. They had bribed a caravan trader who persuaded his cook to serve him poisoned dates as he summered in Nebuchadnezzar's palace in Babylon.

Those early defeats always come back to Babylon. Once he had loved the city with its legendary beautiful hanging gardens. Now he loathed it. His memories were filled with betrayal and vomit, and the claustrophobic defeat from that earliest life when he huddled deep in the city's catacombs and choked on the dust of the dead.

Now that little bitch *all on her own* had forced him into another ignominious retreat. She had forced him to leap into the body of a soldier that he did not want. Sure it was strong enough, but its strength was ugly, coarse and brutish. He preferred his cruelties and his hosts to embody more elegance, and preferred to live his life with some sort of refinement. This body was little better than an ape. He looked at the meaty hands in disgust. It had hairy knuckles, for Christ's sake.

His rage needed an outlet. Pounding the wheel just fed a sense of futility. He had been working too close to his limits anyway. The battle had left him feeling too stretched thin. He had also lost twenty highly trained drones. Now he had to call in all his reserves.

Worse, much worse, Mary and Michael were still free.

He needed a quick infusion of energy, and he craved the bitter taste of violent death that was so like a dark chocolate liqueur. His gaze roamed the passing scenery with restless hunger as the black limo purred along the roads toward his rendezvous point.

At last he came upon a roadside establishment named Northside Restaurant, twelve miles northeast of Wolf Lake. He counted eight vehicles in the parking lot. The nearest buildings were two gas stations, easily fifty yards away.

This was perfect.

The limousine rolled to a smooth stop. As he stepped out of the vehicle, he checked that the drone's handgun was in place in his shoulder holster. Then he strolled into the restaurant, his energy compressing in anticipation like a snake coiling to strike.

He stood just inside the doorway and counted the humans inside. Look at them, as lovely and vulnerable as a herd of gazelles. It was too bad he didn't see anyone that would be suitable as a new host. He would have been happy to get rid of the ape suit. There were two waitresses, a short order cook (he might have to slaughter that greasy little man from a distance), a father and son, a couple of men lounging on stools at the counter, and a trio of bored teenagers.

Teenagers: young wanton, chaotic energy. Delicious.

"Mine," he whispered to them. "You are mine."

Look at them, living their lives in such ignorance. They should all bow down to him, the King of Kings.

One of the waitresses, a leggy woman in her forties with dyed blond hair, gave him a bright smile as she whisked around the end of the counter with a coffeepot. His gaze dropped to her name tag. Her name was Ruth. "Sit anywhere you like, hon," she told him. "I'll be with you in a moment."

He smiled back and shook his head. "No, hon," he said, in the drone's coarse, husky smoker's voice. "You'll be with me right now."

Her quick stride faltered and her smile faded. "Excuse me?"

After compressing his energy, he released it outward. Filled with the force of his pent-up rage, a psychic storm slammed into the restaurant. Napkins, condiments, dishes, glasses, cups and cutlery flew through the dining area, tossed airborne by the blast. The doors slammed shut. He walked to the leggy blonde, wrapped one of his disgusting hairy hands around her neck and jerked her toward him.

Her brown eyes filled with uncomprehending panic. She dropped the coffeepot. It shattered. She struggled against his hold. He put a hand at the back of her head, fastened his open mouth over hers in a travesty of a kiss and, in one long luxurious inhale, he drained her of her life's energy.

It was like sucking nectar from a flower. Her traumatized spirit, separated so abruptly from its body, hovered near the ceiling of the restaurant before it fled with a wail.

He let go of her neck. The leggy blonde body collapsed to the floor.

Smiling, he looked around. The other seven occupants were too shocked by the poltergeist activity to have realized something terrible had just happened to Ruth.

A couple of teenagers pounded at the front doors, trying to get them open. The father had shoved his son underneath a table. As various items flew through the air, the father batted them away with his hands. Hissing smoke billowed from the kitchen. The short order cook screamed as boiling liquids splashed over him. A steak knife struck one of the men at the counter. The wounded man yanked the knife from his neck. Blood jetted from the puncture. The other man slapped the counter towel over the wound in an effort to staunch the bleeding.

Yes, it was self-indulgent of him. He supposed he shouldn't succumb to temper tantrums. You could look at it as a waste of energy when he was already stretched too thin. Still he felt that, given the strength of his anger, he'd restrained himself rather admirably. Besides, Ruth's life force sang in his veins, a potent aperitif. And he had more than enough victims in the restaurant with which to replenish himself.

He had always identified with the fox in a henhouse. Like the fox, he might be able to satisfy his need with just a couple of chickens, but once he got going he preferred to slaughter the whole flock for the sheer frenzied love of murder.

After he had slaked his appetite, the silence of a tomb fell in the restaurant. He pulled out his gun and shot the bodies. Then he called one of his drones at Quantico. Soon Mary and Michael would become the FBI's prime suspects in the Michigan massacre, which would be discovered by a passing state patrol car within the next half hour.

It always paid to have corruption in high places.

Mary and Michael will return in
the next installment of

Game of Shadows

Coming to Piatkus 2014 . . .

Turn the page for a special preview of
the next Novel of the Elder Races by

THEA HARRISON

Coming soon from Piatkus

ARYAL SPUN AND floated in the wild dark night.

She didn't mind living in New York as some other Wyr did. The city was edgy and raw in a way that appealed to her. But this lonesome realm that hung high over the top of the world—this was her true home. This was where she came to think, or brood, or fling her fury into space.

She flew so high that the air felt almost too thin for even her powerful lungs. The clouds lay below her, air castles of shadowed ivory, and the stars above her whirled in their dance of constellations, their lights telling ancient tales of places from unimaginable distances. At this altitude, the stars were so brilliant she almost felt as if she could leave the shackles of gravity behind forever and fly into them.

Almost.

There was always that one moment when she reached the peak of her ability to fly, that one instant of perfection as she hung weightless in the air, no longer straining to rise but simply existing in flawless balance.

Then gravity would reign supreme and pull her back down to earth, but she always carried with her the memory of how she could touch that one perfect moment.

Tonight, she didn't fly for pleasure. She flew to brood in solitude.

She had two hates. One, she held close and nurtured with all of her passion. The other, she had to release.

Her first hate was Quentin Caeravorn.

As soon as she could figure out a way to do it without getting caught, swear to gods, she was going to kill him.

She would prefer to kill him slowly, but bottom line, at this point, she would be happy to take any opportunity she could get.

It was bad enough when Quentin's friend and former employee Pia ended up mating—and marrying—Dragos Cuelebre, Lord of the Wyr. Once Pia had been a thief who had stolen from the most powerful Wyr the world has ever seen. Now she was his wife and the mother of his son.

When Pia had moved into Cuelebre Tower, the gryphons had gone bat shit gaga over her; they all thought she pooped sparkly rainbows or something.

The Wyr in general had a more reserved—sane—response to her presence, especially since she continued to refuse to reveal her Wyr form, which Aryal thought was not only a shortsighted decision but a rather wretched one. How could anybody expect the Wyr to accept or follow her when they didn't even know what the hell she was? The very fact of her existence made Aryal's teeth ache.

Outside of the Wyr demesne, however, Pia's popularity had skyrocketed. Her daily mail had gone from a trickle of letters and cards into an avalanche that required a separate office and its own small staff. Pia even took Dragos's last name, an old-fashioned move that had Aryal rolling her eyes. Now she was Pia Cuelebre.

Last names . . . they were like word parasites. They attached to people in strange ways, moved across cultural and political lines, traveled the world and reattached to others, certainly at whim and seemingly at random.

Why didn't anybody else see how creepy last names were? They labeled a person as coming from a particular class or geographical area or linked their identity to another person, as if someone's identity had no merit on its own unless it was latched on to another. Aryal refused to pick a last name for herself, as so many of the first immortal Wyr chose to do, nor would she ever take anybody else's.

Pia was her second hate.

Earlier today, Aryal finally, grudgingly, *painfully* conceded she was going to have to let go of her snerk over Pia. That was a bitter pill for her to shove down her own throat. It was sugarcoated by the most lethal weapon in Pia's armory to date: the unbelievable sweetness in her newborn son's face.

After Pia and Dragos had gotten married, they had gone on their honeymoon, where Pia had given birth unexpectedly. Yesterday, she and Dragos cut short their trip to upstate New York to return to the city. When they arrived back at the Tower early last evening, everybody had to see, touch, hold and/or coo over the baby.

The other sentinels acted like Dragos had conquered all of Asia overnight, while Dragos radiated a ferocious pride. Almost seven feet tall in his human form, with a massive, muscular body and a brutally handsome face, he would always carry in his demeanor a sharpness like a blade. But Aryal had to admit, she had never seen him look so . . . happy.

As for her, she refused to go anywhere near Pia and the rug rat. She didn't want to have anything to do with them.

Unfortunately, that hadn't lasted long.

Less than twenty-four hours, to be exact.

Earlier today, when she had charged around the hall corner outside of Dragos's offices, she nearly mowed down Pia, who pushed some kind of ambulatory, complicated-looking cart with the sleeping baby tucked inside of it.

Pia looked tired. Her pretty, triangular face was paler than usual and her ever-present blond ponytail was slightly lopsided with wisps of hair trailing at her temples. One of her new full-time bodyguards was with her. The mouthy woman, Eva. Eva thrust herself between Pia and Aryal, her bold features and black eyes insolent with hostility. She stood as tall as Aryal, a full six feet in flat boots, dark brown skin rippling over toned muscle.

"You're a menace just walking down the hall," said Eva. "Do you know any speed other than one that might get someone hurt?"

"You and me," Aryal told her on a surge of happiness. "We're gonna go someday."

"Let's make that day today," said Eva. "We can go right down the hall to the training room. With or without weapons. You pick."

"Lower your voices," Pia said irritably. "If you wake up the baby, I'll take you both down."

Eva's expression softened as she looked at the occupant in the cart. Before she could stop herself, Aryal looked too.

And found herself snared irretrievably.

She was astonished at how tiny the baby was. His entire face, in fact most of his head, was smaller than the palm of her hand. He was wrapped tightly in a soft cloth. It looked restrictive and uncomfortable, but she knew absolutely nothing about babies, and he seemed content enough.

Aryal sidled a step closer, her head angled as she stared. Eva made a move as if she would block Aryal, but Pia put a hand on her bodyguard's arm and stopped her.

The sleeping baby carried a roar of Power in his soft, delicate body. Aryal shook her head in wonder. She hadn't sensed any of it before now. How had Pia managed to conceal that much Power when she had been pregnant?

The baby opened his eyes. He looked so alive and innocent, and as peaceful as a miniature Buddha. He had dark violet eyes like his mother's. The color was so deep and pure it seemed to hold all the wildness and mystery of the night sky.

Some vital organ in Aryal's chest constricted. Her hand crept out to him and hovered in midair as, out of the corner of her eye, she saw Pia twitch.

Comprehension clipped her like an uppercut to the chin.

Pia wouldn't trust her anywhere near the baby as long as

Aryal held on to any lingering resentment or hostility. She wouldn't teach Aryal how to hold him, and she sure as hell wouldn't ever leave him in Aryal's care. Nobody would, which was hideously unfair because Aryal would cut off her own hands before she would do anything to harm a child, no matter who its parents were.

As she struggled with the realization, the baby worked an arm loose from his straitjacket and stuck his fist in one eye. Surprise and confusion wobbled over his miniscule face. With a Herculean effort he managed to jerk his fist to his mouth. He started to suck on it noisily.

That vital organ in Aryal's chest—that was her heart, and she lost it to him forever.

"Okay," she said, her voice hoarse.

"What exactly is okay, Aryal?" asked Pia.

Aryal looked at her. Some sort of suppressed emotion danced in Pia's gaze. Triumph, maybe, or amusement. Whatever it was, Aryal didn't care.

She said without much hope, "I don't suppose you would at least consider cutting off the cheerleader ponytail."

Pia said gravely, "I will consider it. Not very seriously, but I will."

Aryal met her gaze. She asked straight out, without posturing or bullshit, "May I come visit him?"

Pia studied her for a moment. "Yes, you may."

Aryal looked down at the baby again and a corner of her mouth lifted. "Thank you."

"Don't mention it." The baby started to burble plaintively. Pia said, "I think he's already hungry again. I'd better take him back upstairs."

She pushed the contraption toward the bank of elevators that would take her up to the penthouse at the top of the Tower. Eva followed Pia, walking backward.

"Don't you fret none, chickadee," Eva said in a gentle voice to Aryal. "We still gonna go one day."

Aryal balanced back on one heel and beckoned her with both hands. Bring it, baby.

She laughed when Eva made a face before spinning to

follow Pia and the little prince onto the elevator. Then Aryal turned toward Dragos's offices and came to a standstill. She couldn't remember why she had been going to see him in the first place.

Behind her, she could hear the two other women's whispers clearly just before the elevator doors closed. Pia said, "Behold the Power of the peanut. His body mass may be small, but his influence is mighty. The last holdout in the Tower has officially fallen to him."

"If you say so."

Eva sounded skeptical, but Pia had called it. Aryal had fallen in love with that mysterious new person.

For his sake, Aryal released the last of her resentment into the night.

After all, Pia had only stolen once. While Aryal had been more stubbornly suspicious than anybody, even she had to finally admit that Pia had no real knowledge of Caeravorn's activities, so it wasn't as if Pia had actually ever been a career criminal.

Granted, Pia's theft had been a bad one, but *Dragos* had not only forgiven her, he had mated with her. And Dragos was not known for his forgiving personality.

If a dragon could do it, so could a harpy, right?

Giving up her hate on Pia for the sake of the baby was one thing, and that was hard enough.

Quentin Caeravorn was an entirely different disaster.

Aryal turned her attention back to her first hate, the one she held close to her own breast and nurtured with all of her strength.

Caeravorn *was* a career criminal. He was also a "triple threat," a rare and Powerful mixed-breed creature who was part Wyr, part Elven and part Dark Fae. Aryal didn't have the details of his family history, but one of his parents had to be full Wyr, while the other parent was a half-breed, because his Wyr side was strong enough that he could change into his animal form. That gave him all the status and legal rights of a full Wyr in the demesne.

Because he had the legal rights of a full Wyr, and he

hadn't been convicted of any crime, he had been eligible to enter the recent Sentinel Games. He had fought his way through to become one of Dragos's seven sentinels, who were the core of Dragos's governing power in the Wyr demesne.

And he had accomplished that because, in spite of almost two years of investigation and several months of concentrated digging before the Games began, Aryal couldn't pin a single goddamn thing on him.

She knew he was dirty. *She knew it.*

Her leads had turned into dead ends and her sources had dried up. She would track down somebody only to find out that they had moved out of the Wyr demesne, or maybe they had died accidentally (and didn't *that* get investigated thoroughly too). Or they weren't directly involved in any illegal activity connected to Caeravorn, they had only heard of things—hearsay and rumors that dissipated into thin air when she tried to nail them down into concrete evidence.

Caeravorn was a magician, surrounded by a labyrinth of smoke and mirrors while he stood at the center of it all, untouched.

Dirty.

He had gained access to the very heart of the Wyr demesne, and all because Aryal couldn't get him.

Her mood blackened. While she thought back to the events that had happened two months ago, in January, she flew higher then dove just to hear the wind scream in her ears. The sound matched the scream of outrage in her head.

SHE HAD WATCHED Caeravorn's fights at the Games, absorbing every detail. He was killer-fast and elegant, and highly, superbly trained. Normal civilians didn't train to fight to that extent. Why the fuck didn't anybody else have a problem with that?

A few times he had chosen to fight in his Wyr form, a huge black panther with electric blue eyes that gleamed under the white-hot lights. In his human form, he had kicked ass. As a panther, he was sinuous, muscular and moved like lightning. He had owned every inch of that fight arena and had captured the imagination of almost twenty thousand spectators.

Directly after the Games were over and Dragos had presented his new sentinels to the Wyr demesne, Caeravorn had strolled like a conquering hero into the great hall at Cuelebre Tower along with the other seven sentinels. Aside from Quentin, there were the five who had re-won their places—the harpy Aryal, the gryphons Bayne, Constantine and Graydon, and the gargoyle Grym—along with the other new sentinel, the pegasus Alexander Elysias.

It was a hell of a party, like a hundred years of New Year's Eves all rolled into a single night. There was endless liquor, and loud music from famous bands, and gourmet food and confetti, and a general stampede at all of them, but especially at the men who were all buff and reeking of testosterone and victorious swagger.

It was a night of triumph for every sentinel—for Aryal as well, and she had her fair share of propositions too—but she couldn't let go and enjoy any of it since the night had also been her failure.

She held herself aloof, bitterness a hard, heavy knot in the pit of her stomach while she watched Caeravorn laugh as someone upended a bottle of champagne over his head. He was six-foot-two, with a long, lean body and a cat's quick grace, spare graceful features and dark blond hair he had once worn longer. He had cut it very short for the Games, and the severe style lay close to the strong, clean lines of his head.

As she stood with her arms crossed, Grym came up to her side. In his human form, Grym was dark haired with even features. In his Wyr form, he was nightmarish, with huge batlike wings, a demonic face and gray skin as hard as stone.

He had his own small share of groupies, as did all of the sentinels, but Grym actually didn't like to talk much and that fact tended to put females off, at least after the first night or two. He was one of the few entities whose companionship Aryal actually found peaceful, and he had used that fact more than once to defuse her volatile temper.

She had wished more than once that there was a sexual spark between them. Unfortunately there wasn't. Years ago, they'd experimented but neither one of them had any interest in taking things past first base. They had long since settled into an unconventional yet entirely comfortable friendship.

Grym stood close enough that their shoulders brushed. "You didn't get him," he said. "Sometimes it happens. You gotta let it go."

"No, I don't," she said. She scowled at him.

Grym rubbed the back of his neck. "Aryal, with the kind of hours you've put into digging into Quentin's life, if you haven't found any hard evidence by now, it's very likely you're not going to."

She shook her head. "Doesn't mean I've got to let it go. Just means I haven't found it *yet*."

He turned to face her, his mouth pursed. "Have you ever considered that he might be innocent?"

She angled out her jaw. "He's not."

"Well, if he isn't, sooner or later he's going to trip up. In the meantime, you earned this night too," Grym told her. "Don't let him ruin it for you."

She made a face as Grym clapped her on the back and disappeared into the crowd, headed for the nearest bar. Caeravorn *was* ruining the night for her. Just the fact of his presence at the celebration made her stomach tighten. Watching him enjoy himself was about as pleasurable as taking a bath in acid.

He exuded testosterone along with all the rest, an alpha male supremely confident in his own abilities, and why wouldn't he be? He had just clawed his way to the top of the Wyr demesne and earned his place with the best of the best.

Her gaze narrowed. He was a beautiful man, she'd give him that. He owned a popular neighborhood bar named Elfie's, where he tended to wear clothes that were more upscale, but here he dressed simply, like the other sentinels, in jeans, boots and a dark blue T-shirt that turned his blue eyes brilliant.

Sex would have always come easily for him. It would come even easier for him tonight. He could have as much sex with as many people as he wanted.

One of his companions was a corporate lawyer for Cuelebre Enterprises, a Wyr lioness who was the antithesis of Aryal in almost every way. Aryal studied the other woman, assessing her as if she were an opponent. Instead of Aryal's six foot height, the lioness stood at a snuggly five-foot-six. Males were suckers for females of that size. The other woman had a sinuous, curvaceous torso, while Aryal had an athletic build, her muscles long and lean.

The lioness's limbs were tawny and sun-kissed, her piquant face cleverly made up to emphasize her tilted eyes and full mouth. She wore four-inch heels, and her waist-long hair tumbled down her back and had expensive golden highlights.

Aryal had gray eyes and angular features, and the only time she had ever worn makeup was when she had gotten drunk with her friend Niniane who had somehow managed to coax Aryal into letting her put pink lipstick on her. That experiment had lasted all of five minutes. Aryal wouldn't be caught dead in heels of any height unless they hid a spring-hinged blade, and she barely remembered to brush her thick, black, shoulder-length hair, which was why it so often ended up tangled, especially just after a flight.

The lioness stood on tiptoe and leaned against Caeravorn's arm as she said something in his ear, deliberately brushing her breast against his bicep. Then she sent a warning glance around to the others who stood nearby while she licked at the champagne that dripped off his chin, and Caeravorn grinned and cupped her ass. Clearly if that chick had anything to say about it, she would be his only partner for the night.

Aryal's lip curled. Aw, look. Two Wyr felines going into heat. There wasn't even any suspense to it.

Caeravorn turned to give the female a slow, sexy smile,

and his gaze fell on Aryal. His long blue eyes narrowed, and his expression chilled. He said something to the female as he pulled away from her. She gave him a pouting, kittenish smile and made as if to follow him, but as she tracked his trajectory, her gaze fell onto Aryal and she jerked to a halt.

Yeah, that one was irritating but she wasn't stupid.

Caeravorn shouldered past a few people and approached her, his eyes glinting. He was broad-shouldered, lean-hipped and long-legged, and he had a lithe, almost boneless stride. Aryal's gaze drifted over his hard face and equally hard body. Under the cover of her crossed arms, her talons came out, quiet and slick like well-oiled switchblades. She clicked them together as he prowled close.

So dirty.

He was an outlaw in masquerade. Her gaze fixed on the bulge in his jeans. Was he an outlaw sexually as well?

Kitty lawyer's antics must have been doing it for him, because as he came toe-to-toe with her, he smelled like healthy male, champagne and arousal. Aryal *hated* the fact that he smelled incredibly delicious.

"You are the most ungracious, obstinate creature I have ever had the misfortune to meet," he said. She cocked her head and contemplated his hard, well-cut mouth. "Give it up, sunshine. You lost."

Genuinely amused, she smiled. She leaned forward until she was literally in his face, and she whispered, "I know something you don't."

His teeth were even and white as he snapped out, "You fucking wish you did."

"No, I really do know something, Caeravorn. What are you, a hundred and sixty, a hundred and seventy years old?"

He sliced at the air with one hand. "What difference does my age make?"

"You young Wyr are all alike," she said. "Maybe your panther side will dictate a limit to your life span, or maybe your Elven and Dark Fae blood will prolong it, but either way, you don't really understand what it means to be immortal. The past is nearly as limitless as the future."

"Make your point," he growled.

Her voice grew softer, pitched for his ears alone. "I'll give this to you. You've been meticulous, you really have. You've covered your tracks well. But nobody in this world is perfect. That means that you have fucked up somehow, somewhere. That's what I know. I have all the time in the world to find it, *all the time*, and do you know what that means? That means I've already got you. It just hasn't happened yet."

She watched the rage build in his face and body language as she spoke. She might not have gotten him yet, but she got him good enough for now, as she shoved him over the brink and his temper splintered utterly. He lunged for her throat.

"You're not a harpy," he snarled. "You're a fucking pit bull with lockjaw."

Her head fell back, and she laughed as his iron-hard hands circled her neck. Fingers tightening, he cut off her air supply. She hooked an ankle behind his leg and threw her entire body weight at him, knocking him backward.

They crashed to the floor together. People shouted and scattered, while others leaped toward them. All the ruckus seemed to happen somewhere else. Right here it was just her and Caeravorn, in intimate, struggling silence.

As he hit the ground his hands loosened from her neck. When she landed on top of his muscular length, she twisted to bring up one elbow, hard, underneath his chin. The blow connected and snapped his head back. For one pulsating moment his long, powerful body lay supplicant beneath hers, his neck bared as she straddled him.

It was glorious.

Then a freight train slammed into Aryal, knocking her several feet from Caeravorn who flipped, still snarling, onto his hands and knees. With his head lowered and teeth bared, his gaze fixed on her and he prepared to spring.

Wow, he had really lost it. She must have said something. Out of the corner of her eye, she saw Bayne, Constantine and Alexander pile on top of him, their combined weight knocking him flat again.

Her freight train resolved into Dragos's new First Sentinel,

Graydon. Graydon was the largest of all the current sentinels. In his human form he stood almost six-foot-five, and he carried a good thirty pounds more than the other gryphons.

All of that weight was hard-packed muscle that currently took up residence on her chest. He pinned her arms to the floor by the wrists. Normally his rough-hewn features were set in a mild, good-natured expression, but not at the moment.

Not even bothering to struggle, she looked up at Graydon with her eyebrows raised. "What?"

His dark, slate gray eyes were furious. "People have been through hell this month. We've all gone to war, and then we beat the shit out of each other in the Games. Everybody needs a little goddamn R and R, and you can't leave well enough alone for a few fucking hours at a party?"

Angling her jaw out, she savored her next words for the rare treasures they were, as she said with perfect, pious honesty, "He started it."

piatkus